Borne Back

Borne Back

a novel

Shlomo Shyovitz

Thaler
Books

Published by
Thaler Books
thalerbooks@earthlink.net

ISBNs: 979-8-9890624-0-9 (paperback)
979-8-9890624-1-6 (eBook)

Book production by Gary A. Rosenberg (www.thebookcouple.com)

Cover photo by Shlomo Shyovitz

*For Suzanne,
a rose among thorns*

*"**The distant past** is among those areas
which knowing nothing about may enrich us."*

—from a newspaper article
by Jorge Luis Borges

*"I threw the past in the path of **the present**
to make the present stumble."*

—from a speech
by Günter Grass

*"**The future** is inexorable for all.
For some it is set like a trap."*

—from *Angle of Repose*
by Wallace Stegner

The Days

Day One *Return*

— Chapter One —

I take my seat on the right side of the plane and lower the window shade halfway in one practiced motion, knowing harsh sunlight will invade after takeoff. I open the valve over my head and inhale cool air tinged with engine fumes. The Boston skyline bobs in the trembling haze. My mother tongue rises and falls in neighboring seats. I close my eyes and feel perspiration collecting in my eyebrows.

This is how I return home: wet and wary, like a diver descending or ascending.

The airport terminal had been thick with travelers, armed police, and German shepherds sniffing luggage and feet. There was some commotion at the departure gate for my flight to Tel Aviv.

"I don't know what all the fuss is about," said a ground crew member to a nervous passenger. "It's just a stupid little war back home."

Security staff inquired politely and rummaged gingerly. One of them checked my U.S. passport and asked, "Do you also have an Israeli one, Mr. Holzman?" Embarrassed, I said I had left it at home and immediately called Lori who arrived at the gate ten minutes before boarding.

"Fly carefully," she called after me as I walked through the gate.

It just so happened that during my tour of duty some twenty years ago there wasn't a single war to fight. Don't blame me for the fortuitous timing of my birth or for the breakout and early cessation of hostilities two months before my draft date. This is no reflection on my patriotism. True, while friends only a year older were savaging the enemy and occasionally being savaged themselves, I filled sandbags and studied for high school finals. And while those sons whose mothers had conceived mere months before mine were being killed or maimed or decorated, I spent nights in our building's crowded bomb shelter, wondering if the little generals and commentators inside my transistor radio knew what they were talking about, and if Mrs. Goralnik from 3A was wearing nothing when the sirens went off and just grabbed the first stitch of clothing she could find in the dark, and was it sheer or lacy. But how was any of this my fault?

And now, another war back home.

A flight attendant hands out cups of cold water. I gulp mine and dry my face with a napkin. This is not how I imagined marking the watershed moment when my years in America equaled the twenty I had spent growing up in Israel.

Nor could the location of my birth be possibly held against me. Do I really owe allegiance to a particular set of coordinates just because it happened to be where Mother gave birth? What was she doing there anyway, six thousand miles east of the Statue of Liberty? I mean, she was lucky to have survived World War II and luckier still to have gotten an immigration visa to America. Yet she surrendered it when she agreed to follow Father to a desolate stretch of the eastern Mediterranean coast just because she loved him and because he was sure it was the only place for them. Touching as this may sound, Mother eventually came to think of it as tragic. How can that locale now have any claim on me, an innocent survivor of a difficult birth that could just as well have been suffered stateside?

And now this war.

I went to the army for the same reason I had gone to kindergarten: it was compulsory. I was a good soldier, served my homeland from behind a desk, and received my honorable discharge with a surge of pride equaled only by my relief at having survived unscathed.

Anxiety, fear, and something akin to shell shock — these I experienced just a few months ago when Josh was born. By that time the front line had moved to suburban Boston. A truce took hold only after he consented to sleep through the night, freeing me to engage in career battles and evade office ambushes.

A few weeks ago, as Grandma lay dying back home, fighting broke out, spreading unchecked some fifty miles north of her bed in the oncology ward.

"Don't you dare come," whispered Grandma on the phone. She let me do all the talking for a while, gathering enough strength to say, "I swear, Dannika, even if I never see you again, don't come now. It's not safe here." And a moment later, "Promise me you won't."

I promised. I knew my promise had the same life expectancy

as Grandma when Mother, who usually sanitized facts for my own protection, admitted, "Grandma is not like she used to be, but where you are now, what good does it do to tell you?"

Where am I now? Neither here nor there. That the ocean is far below me means I'm high above it, but how high do I have to be for a bird's-eye view?

Lori always says there are reasons why things happen. Grandma always says there are reasons why things don't happen. I suppose both have their reasons for saying what they do.

I do a quick calculation and come up with 1,040 — the number of weekly letters I sent home over the past twenty years. I always posted them on time and am glad I did. Now when I count my regrets, this is not among them.

"She doesn't have much time left," Mother said on the phone the other day. I booked a flight.

One last call from the airport. "I told her you were coming," said Mother. "She promised she'd wait for you."

— *Chapter Two* —

I arrive in Haifa fifteen hours later and, true to her word, Grandma is waiting — in the morgue, shrouded in white. The burial society is waiting too as is a chartered bus with relatives from near and far. Now that I'm here there's no reason to wait any longer. We drive to the cemetery and bury Grandma under the cypresses across from the municipal beach where she and I had spent many summer days, often sitting on a submerged rock with warm seawater up to our chins.

After throwing a handful of dirt into the open grave, I have a sudden urge to hail a cab and head right back to the airport. I feel the need to be with my own little family, living happily in a far away land removed from death and war, enjoying blissful anonymity without having to witness the death throes of a beloved past. I yearn for my remote new world where I can hook up my past to life support in a sterile and safe environment so it might survive and coalesce with fragmented wishes and selected memories, spawning a host of little pasts that will never age, only frolic and tease and laugh, always remain sweet and pure and unadulterated, always be soft and silky and all mine, to mold as I please, observe at my will, recall as I choose, play with at my leisure, and be comforted by for the rest of my days, forever and ever. Amen.

Quiet sobs blend with the hum of traffic from the coastal highway as I lean against a tree trunk and close my eyes. Only the scraping of a hoe against the graveside mound of fresh soil saves me from the embarrassment of dozing off. I'm sure I'll cry later after the jet lag wears off and the hay fever kicks in, or on the plane on the way back home, listening on my headphones to old songs that always elicit tears.

Someone I don't recognize says, "You had a long trip, but it's good you came. You won't regret it."

Grandma's friends and relatives are milling about, chatting, hugging and gossiping as they would at a family reunion. With the older generation departing at an ever-increasing rate, these gatherings have become quite frequent of late and, with little time or reason to meet under different circumstances, are almost welcome opportunities to mingle with flesh and blood in the shade of the family tree.

A light breeze from the beach leaves in its wake a salty smell laced with a whiff of an artificially flavored local ice cream called "Old Vienna," the taste of my formative years and the standard by which I still judge frozen desserts. I feel like the outsider that the founder of that company must have been when he arrived in this dusty corner of the Levant. I have no idea who most of the people around me are, and few seem to recognize me.

The deceased and dearly beloved Grandma and her siblings repose under a row of tombstones in the shade, pretending not to notice the interred interloper from Miami who came to rest among them. No one has ever discovered who Marvin Birenbaum was or how he managed to stake a claim in such hallowed ground. I always thought of his grave as the Tomb of the Unknown Sucker who had fallen for the hype of being buried in the Promised Land, unaware that it was not the tranquil place where he had longed to spend eternity.

"So now I'm the only one left," says a voice behind me. "How could this be?"

I turn to see Uncle Avrum, the youngest of Grandma's nine siblings, staring at the graves. His pre-purchased plot is here too, with a carved headstone missing only his expiration date.

We embrace in silence. I look at the man I have always associated with smoked duck and see a rosy, stubbled, but otherwise faithful likeness of Grandma's face.

Every Thursday, Uncle Avrum would come over for lunch, a good nap, and afternoon tea on the balcony. Grandma would serve her specialty of smoked duck with baked beans which, according to Uncle Avrum, was the fastest way to recapture a distant past he had feared lost since his previous visit. They would sip a few glasses of tea, letting the scalding liquid wash over sugar cubes lodged behind their teeth. Between contented slurps, Grandma and her brother would conjure forth remembrances now etched in my memory, where they reside to this day — real or imagined, recalled or dreamed, theirs and mine.

Uncle Avrum lives alone in a fifth-floor walk-up facing the bay. Back when Independence Day parades were still popular, and when it was Haifa's turn to play host, family and friends would flock to his large rooftop terrace overlooking the parade route. He enjoyed those times almost as much as the solitude of the intervening years when visitors rarely scaled the steep terrazzo stairs to his apartment. After years of Grandma's nagging, he finally got a phone, but by then people were so used to not calling him that they saw no reason to start.

We don't say much. Pointing at his headstone, he asks me what I, as a design professional, think of it and wonders aloud whether it might not be high time to chisel in the end date and be done with it. Mother saves me from having to answer by walking toward us, leaning on Aunt Mitzi's arm.

"How long can you stay, Dannika?" Mother asks.

I take her hand and notice its roadmap of blue veins, holding no clue as to where things might go from here.

"I'll have to go back soon, but not before I know you'll be all right."

"I'm fine now that you're here. I can't imagine going through this without you, but I don't want you to have to sleep in Grandma's room," she says, dabbing her eyes with a soggy handkerchief. "I still can't bring myself to go in there. Aunt Mitzi said you're welcome to use her daughter Esti's place. Why don't you tell him, Mitzi, while I sit with Uncle Avrum in the shade for a moment."

"Boy, are you in luck," says Aunt Mitzi much too cheerfully. "Esti and her husband are on sabbatical in California, so you're more than welcome to stay in their apartment. It's really nice: three bedrooms, four exposures, plenty of cross ventilation, and a view of the sea. And so much more: a microwave, toaster oven, mixer, blender, food processor, and even an electric can opener. And of course, a big refrigerator, two ovens, a washer and a dryer. They have done very well for themselves, those two. You see, we have everything in this country, absolutely everything."

I decide to take Aunt Mitzi up on her offer. Sleeping in Grandma's room would not be a good idea now, even though it was my refuge when I was growing up. Back then, Grandma would sit in her rocker and work on her needlepoint while I lounged on her bed engrossed in a novel. Once I found a piece of stale bread under her pillow. Taking it from me, Grandma explained it was a habit she had developed during the war, when every morsel not consumed had to be saved. She pushed it back under her pillow and changed the subject, giving me a piece of chocolate from deep inside her nightstand drawer.

I don't really mind Aunt Mitzi's satisfaction at being able to prove to an expat that he can be back in his homeland and still live like an American. Better, actually, because in the land of the Bible, electric gizmos operate on 220 volts, not a wimpy 110. Then again, I could be reading a bit too much into her gloating.

I have no trouble falling asleep in my cousin's spacious apartment, but the window I foolishly left open lets in hot, humid air that wakes me, drenched in sweat, at four in the morning. I go into the gleaming chrome and white kitchen and make myself a cup of coffee. I turn on the radio and find the BBC station that kept me company during many sleepless army nights. I switch to an all-night music program that assaults me with tender songs of old wars and young lives lost, then quickly turn it off.

I pour myself a second cup and step out onto the balcony. A gentle stirring in the humid air is almost cooling. Grandma has been in the ground for some fourteen hours now. Peering into the darkness that is slowly taking on the pallor of dawn, I can make out nearby apartment buildings crowned with solar panels and water tanks. Beyond them lies a dark abyss where sky and sea meet under a veil of fog, becoming one. The neighborhood looks like the margin of a flat world. A few careless steps out there, and one might tumble over the edge to oblivion and be soon forgotten.

As I discovered at the funeral, I've already been forgotten by many and am entirely unknown to others. Someone unknown cannot be forgotten. He may, however, forget, but I have steadfastly refused to do so. Trivial details of inconsequential events will suddenly surface when I close my eyes in the shower or take the first sip of my morning coffee. Like uninvited guests they linger, interfere with carefully planned routines and uncage barely tamed recollections. Often it's my own fault. During solitary rides to the supermarket, I hum old army songs and submit to the bites of memories before forcing them back into their coffins.

The world is turning lighter, and buildings, trees, and smoke stacks come into view against the murky haze overhanging the bay between the refineries and the port. It's a feeble reproduction of something achingly familiar, barely resembling the original safely locked inside me, which will never fade or lose its brilliance.

Day Two *Missed and Missing*

— *Chapter Three* —

After the 6:00 a.m. news, I switch on the coffee maker and walk to the corner grocery for a newspaper and fresh rolls. They are still warm when I get back. I place the rolls, butter, jam, and coffee on a tray, take it to the shady utility balcony and set it on the washing machine whose GE logo I notice and greet as an old friend and fellow traveler. Sitting down on a folding chair, I reach for the newspaper and a roll. Both smell of a new day. A bite of the crusty roll with apricot jam. A list of the latest casualties up north. A sip of strong coffee. A downturn on the New York Stock Exchange. Another bite. More coffee. A heat alert along the coast. A new exhibit at a Tel Aviv museum.

I am now nothing so much as a painting myself, removed from its traditional place in this gallery so long ago that no one misses it anymore. A faded rectangle on the wall is the only evidence it had once hung here. Those who notice its return remember it differently, somehow. Didn't it use to be larger, more vibrant, better framed? Should it be rehung? Left in a corner, it will soon warp and gather dust. How long will it be before it's discarded altogether?

I still don't know much about babies, but on this peaceful morning I find myself wondering if my infant son misses me. Can he even remember me, and if so, will he recognize me when I return home? When I left for the airport, Lori was putting him down for a nap. Did he think I was only leaving for a moment? Did he wait for me to reappear, or was he distracted by toys or toes, never giving his absent father a second baby thought?

The doorbell rings, and in the hallway stands a young suntanned woman wearing a skimpy dress, twirling a wayward strand of her long hair.

"Danny? Hi, I'm Tamar. We're neighbors. Mitzi asked me to look in on you and see if you needed help with food shopping, bus schedules, or whatever. She told me you live in America."

"That's right. Thanks for the offer, but I'm fine. I'm not planning to cook or travel while I'm here."

I can't tell whether she is relieved or disappointed. She leans on the door jamb and scratches one long leg with the high-heeled sandal of the other.

"I don't have to teach during the summer, so I'm home most of the time. Stop by if you need anything." Her eyes flit from mat to doorbell to mezuzah, and when she speaks again, she seems to be struggling to remember some lines or their appropriate tone or even a reason for reciting them.

"I'm taking my kids to the beach. Would you like to come?"

Not with your body parts exposed and Grandma just across the road from the beach, her shroud already damp with ground moisture.

"Maybe another time," I say encouragingly, but her pale pink lips, rouged cheeks, and gray eyes register no reaction. "I have too much to take care of right now."

For some reason I feel I should say something. "I'll come by tonight to see what's on TV. I don't even know when the evening news comes on."

"If you feel like it. It's going to be a hot day, so drink plenty of water and stay out of the sun. It's not good for your fair skin."

She walks to her door and leaves me wondering whether it was a veiled insult or a valuable piece of advice innocently given to an expat who has been away far too long.

I call Lori and barely say hi before being drowned out by a grinding noise. I tell her to stay on the line as I walk to the window. A flock of helicopters is swooping down on the military hospital compound by the bay. Mother has been telling me about the incessant stream of casualties flown in from the war zone. This reminds me of the opening credits to *M*A*S*H*, and I only wish I were viewing it on TV from a decades-old perspective.

"Sorry," I say when I pick up the phone again. "Just some noise outside. How are you and Josh doing?"

"We're fine. He'll be OK. Don't stay too long though, Danny, and don't get any ideas from watching those helicopters out there." Lori knows her helicopters. I forgot what a huge *M*A*S*H* fan she is. Come to think of it, she was the one who introduced me to the show and interpreted some of the colloquialisms back in the day when my eyes still searched for subtitles at the bottom of the screen. God, what I wouldn't give now for back-to-back episodes of *The Andy Griffith Show* and *The Beverly Hillbillies*. Lori often marvels at my love of old sitcoms. She finds it strange that I can feel nostalgic for times I haven't lived through in a country not my own. She tells me I suffer from ANS — Acquired Nostalgia Syndrome.

— *Chapter Four* —

When I arrive mid-morning, Mother's apartment is crowded with condolence callers. As tradition dictates, Mother is observing Shiva. I find her sitting on a low stool, leaning against the wall. She looks up and smiles weakly, bemused, it seems to me, at having been singled out for such misfortune, or else at having to endure this foolishness.

I sit next to her and take her hand. She puts her head on my shoulder and we look at the visitors sitting in a semi-circle around us. They are reminiscing about Grandma, with tears of sadness and laughter flowing. "Everyone loved her," whispers Mother.

I leaf through a leather-bound photo album on the coffee table in front of us. Perhaps I should snap some pictures during my visit. Composing a shot always gives me the pleasant illusion of being in control, allowing me to frame only what I choose. In my desk back home I keep a box of prints of friends and family over which I've long since lost control. They are old pictures of young people whom I may not recognize anymore, but they evoke a vivid black and white past next to which the colored present can seem dull.

The photo of a solitary tree in a wheat field at twilight still hangs over Mother's dining table. I can see it from where I sit. Its browns fade to black against a gray horizon with just a hint of orange brushing the treetop and wheat stalks. Whenever she felt low, Mother would say that she was that tree, alone in the middle of nowhere. She may be getting ready to say so again, judging by how she keeps staring at it.

Grandma's album was one of the few possessions she managed to rescue during the war and bring with her from Europe. She would always display it at family gatherings and occasionally at bedtime, when she'd open it and recreate her early life and Mother's youth in German-speaking Bukovina. In the meticulously composed sepia photographs, men, women, and children posed rigidly, seeming to defeat time with frozen postures and stoic expressions, as if careful not to draw attention to themselves. In that they failed, and the last few pages of the album remained black and empty, an accurate depiction of their fate.

I turn to a page with an oversize photo of a Ferris wheel. A caption in the corner in neat handwriting reads "Greetings from Vienna, 1910." Another picture shows Grandma at sixteen in front of an imposing hotel entrance. And here she is dancing with a mustachioed man. Whenever I asked her about him she would claim not to remember who he was.

The music, the dancing, the *One*-two-three, *One*-two-three… My God, that Strauss knew his waltzes, and Grandma danced every one of them until the orchestra quit for the night. From the table at the occasional family wedding, I used to watch her with amazement. She would be worn out after those weddings, but as soon as the music died and the hall emptied, she'd already be inquiring about who might be getting married next.

"So, what do you think of her?" says Aunt Mitzi.

I look up at her grinning face, over at Mother's teary eyes, and down at a photo of Grandma staring out a train window. The sky is overcast, and there are raindrops on the windowpane that make her appear to be crying. A high-pitched whistle. A bell. A sigh from the awakened engine. A puff of steam. A handkerchief clutched in her hand. Goodbye, Vienna. The train is moving away from me and across the table as a stranger pulls the album toward him. Who is he and what does he want with Grandma?

"Tamar, I mean," says Aunt Mitzi, her smirk cutting a scarlet furrow across her powdered face. "Some girl, huh? Raising two kids all by herself, teaching biology or English or something like that, and still managing to look like a model. And with her husband missing for more than a year already. Well, anyway, how are you enjoying the apartment? Have you tried the TV yet? You know, it has a much higher resolution than American sets. My son-in-law told me that American sitcoms actually look better here than there."

My past looks better there than here. I've always felt that memories reach full bloom only when once or twice removed, allowing me to remember what I've never known and to recall what I've never done. But here there's almost no one left. Mother, certainly. Father, maybe — alive yet absent, last spotted roaming the hemisphere from a friend's apartment in New York to a cousin's flat in London to a sister's house in Düsseldorf, patiently waiting for the glaciers to melt and for Grandma to become extinct. Now that she has, he may no longer be an endangered species and could reappear at any moment, but will he?

Mother is trying to find a comfortable position on her stool. I wonder if it's time I returned for good to compensate for the many years away from her. I immediately feel a stab of anxiety in my gut, which I usually associate with leaving, not returning.

I close my eyes and rehearse such a return: quitting my job and cutting professional ties in Boston; Lori's leaving behind everyone and everything she knows and loves; a short elation upon arrival followed by bureaucratic hassles; the insult of being considered an immigrant in my own homeland; and the sudden realization that I don't know the Hebrew equivalents for architectural terms like double-glazing, cladding, or drywall.

Pretty weak, on the whole. This play will need a lot of work and may yet close during tryouts.

Were I to return, I'd no longer be far removed from relatives and old friends. Running into them or getting together for forced camaraderie would surely alter the memories, not always based on true events, which I have painstakingly scripted overseas.

Were I to return, I'd mourn daily the changes in Haifa and the loss of the distance that has allowed me to blend fantasy and reality. No amount of morning fog or evening haze can hide the fact that my shiny city is now tarnished.

Were I to return, it would be more difficult to look away, imagine, or pretend. Truth may be the child of time but, for me, so is her half-brother Fiction, whom I have adopted and may be forced to disown if I return.

— *Chapter Five* —

I have to get away from the sweat and sympathy and step outside where the worst I might encounter are bus fumes diluted by the humidity of the early afternoon. I keep to the shady sidewalk and soon see Balfour Street sloping toward me from the foot of the mountain. In occasional nightmares I am driving up Balfour, my car clawing its way up the monstrous ascent, the overexerted engine expiring just short of where I now stand. That's also where the civil engineers who had contrived this risky route conceded defeat and switched from a foolhardy incline to sensible hairpin curves.

Once upon a time we lived on Masada Street, just off Balfour. A hundred feet or so below our apartment floor, a Swiss company was boring through solid rock to construct an underground cable car. The view across the bay was always clear. From the observation terrace on Panorama Street one could see snow-capped Mount Hermon. Close to sundown on Fridays, a bearded man would lean out of a speeding taxi and sound a trumpet, ushering in Shabbat. On Saturdays, large DeSoto cabs taking people to the beach would encounter only light traffic because few owned cars. After napping and before reminiscing over coffee and pastry at Café Ritz, the elderly would go for a stroll or sit on benches overlooking the sea, enjoying the gentle breeze that made the weather easier to bear. All in all, it was a close approximation of a Day of Rest.

And God, I'm sure, looked down and saw that it was pretty good.

*   *   *

There are many nights when, with my eyes closed, I watch shaky footage of the very locations where my walk now takes me. One clip starts with a pan shot of four apartment buildings surrounding a drab courtyard crisscrossed by well-trodden paths forming a network of neighborly connections. Bed linens and down pillows air out on window ledges. Pickling jars line kitchen windowsills.

Off-screen, key strokes from Miss Rosenzweig's piano lessons float across this outdoor room and fold into Mr. Goren's voice practice, producing the kind of cacophony that makes otherwise docile citizens stuff their ears with cotton, turn up their radios, or yell "Quiet!" A neighbor sets his watch by Mrs. Saadia's shouting which starts the moment her husband returns from work at five o'clock. A few kids play in the yard, braving a verbal lashing in High German from the diminutive Frau Bergman whenever they stray onto her property.

Smells from a dozen kitchens seek each other out and combine into powerful odors. Itzik, the oldest teenager in that theater, trains his air gun on tin tubs and basins hanging from balcony rails. Shmuli, staying with his grandparents in their top floor apartment during his parents' divorce proceedings, angrily urinates on fresh laundry drying below. On the hour, a dozen radios beep in unison and join in a solemn recitation of the news.

A nighttime shot of open windows: mothers scolding, dishes clanking, fathers bellowing, toilets flushing, children yelling, and bath water splashing. Later, all is quiet, except perhaps for a classical music program or a shortwave broadcast stuttering in a foreign tongue.

Balconies are awash in yellow light. An occasional meow, bark, or laugh punctures the silence, momentarily turning heads from cards or newspapers or books. Only then, her last pupil gone, does Miss Rosenzweig sit down at her piano to demonstrate how an étude should be played. Mr. Goren falls silent, waiting until she is finished before jumping to his feet, applauding and calling out, "Brava! Bravissima!" Miss Rosenzweig waves to him across the yard, lowers the key lid and goes to bed.

*   *   *

My old domain could be painted with just a few brush strokes and a murky palette of peeling beige stucco, rusty balcony rails, weathered shutters, shady yards, and dusty trees.

I enter cautiously, the same way our boys up north approach quiet, seemingly abandoned hamlets across a hostile border. Safe as it may look, there is no way of knowing which memories might be lurking in dark staircases or which ghosts might be hiding in the shadows, ready to pounce if I show momentary doubt or imprudent nostalgia.

Fortunately, Lori is not with me. If she were, I would be wasting precious time on convoluted explanations, perhaps missing an opportunity to neutralize this hornets' nest of memories. Had I been forced to put it all into words, it might have sounded odd even to me, calling into question the wisdom of reentering my childhood mazes. The less said in the presence of a dead past the better. One should not tarry in a morgue — just make a quick identification and get the hell out.

My territory encompassed both sides of Masada Street, a few back yards and a couple of shortcuts — the area of a regulation size soccer field. Lining the street were two schools, a playground, a synagogue, and low-rise apartment buildings with ground level shops.

Toward evening, a light sea breeze would flush the stagnant heat from the neighborhood. Having finished my homework, I would roll on my one skate as far as the water tower at the corner of Balfour, cross over to the other sidewalk and return home. Along the way, I'd look at store windows, browse in shops whose owners preferred one kid with loose change to no customers at all, and stop by the workbenches of the watchmaker and electrician working outdoors to escape the stifling heat of their shops.

* * *

On Thursday afternoons, after the four o'clock news which I had to translate into German for Grandma, we would take down two baskets from the back of the kitchen door and go Shabbat shopping. We never knew what we'd find. Although the latest war had recently ended, food deliveries were still sporadic.

At the fruit and vegetable store we purchased four cucumbers, four tomatoes, six potatoes and, on impulse, a few plums and apricots. At the grocery store we picked up two challahs, some cheese, six eggs, and a small bar of bittersweet chocolate. Two doors down, at the butcher shop, we bought a bag of chicken wings, necks, and feet. Grandma gave me a reassuring smile as she tore off a coupon from her ration book. I could see there weren't many left. Next week she would spend half a day standing in line for a new book.

The smell inside the fish store made me hold my breath. I watched the gray carps in the tank while Grandma chatted in Yiddish with Mr. Ashkouri, the Iraqi fishmonger. Every so often I had to step outside for fresh air. At long last, two thrashing fish were scooped up, wrapped in old newspapers, and dropped into Grandma's basket. We raced the fifty yards home, and I immediately turned on the bathtub faucet. Grandma dropped the squirming fish into the rising water and I watched them swim and enjoy their new surroundings. I gave them names and threw in some bath toys to help them pass the time. After brushing my teeth at bedtime, I leaned over the tub and wondered when fish slept.

When I returned from school early Friday afternoon, the bathtub was empty. I went to the icebox for a drink of juice, and there, on a large platter, were horseshoe-shaped slices of carp stuffed with gefilte fish and garnished with carrots and parsley. Grandma and I never discussed what had taken place in her kitchen that morning.

* * *

At Mr. Porat's bookshop, books could not be touched except with permission, and then only under the owner's watchful eye. Every Friday afternoon I would go there for the weekend newspapers: one Hebrew, one Yiddish, one German. I would end up browsing through foreign magazines and recently published books with uncut pages. I never tired of fingering those virgin volumes and hearing their pages rustle in meek protest.

One thing Father gave me before he left and changed my life forever was a love of books. Watching him, I learned early on to approach a book by first reading its dust jacket, carefully examining the binding and embossed spine, checking the copyright page, reading the first and last pages, and then looking pensively into space.

I once asked him which Russian novel I should tackle first. "It really doesn't matter," he replied. "Just start at the beginning and keep at it until you reach the end."

* * *

The most enticing attractions on my street were two workshops. One was a large, brightly lit space lined with huge canvases on which Mr. Marcovicz would paint color enlargements of movie posters to be displayed on billboards above theater box offices. I felt privileged to stand so close to famous movie stars. Mr. Marcovicz would also tell me about lesser luminaries in the cast and, if no deadline loomed, would delve into filmographies, coming attractions, and Hollywood trivia. This was how I became the first in my class to learn that Paul Newman was Jewish. It was the kind of insider information that made my classmate Ruthy eye me with admiration which had to last until I could come up with something even more impressive.

What I came up with next was sure to leave Ruthy speechless. Mr. Marcovicz had shared a tip that key scenes of the major motion picture *Exodus* were going to be filmed the next day three blocks from the corner of Balfour and Masada. I immediately set to work and convinced Ruthy to skip classes and join me at the police barrier surrounding the set. Huge cameras were mounted on dollies, lights on tripods augmented the bright sunshine, and old military vehicles were arrayed around the perimeter. Suddenly, from among the cast and crew milling about, a man in crisp khakis emerged, followed by microphones on long booms.

"Wait, isn't that…" whispered Ruthy.

"It sure is," I said, hardly believing our proximity to Paul Newman whose blue eyes shone in our direction. "I think he's looking at you."

Ruthy giggled and grabbed my hand.

Someone called out, "Quiet on the set!"

"Places!" called another.

"Action!" yelled a bald man with a megaphone.

And then Paul, tearing his gaze away from Ruthy and me, sprang into it. I turned to my star-struck companion and suggested an ice cream, knowing she'd be too weak-kneed to refuse.

The other workshop, a few doors down from Mr. Marcovicz, was a sprawling studio where mannequins were made. It was there that I discovered the female body's third dimension. One day, after a long gawking session, I was late getting to the movie theater and ended up in the last row for a sold-out showing of *Cleopatra*. Despite my furious squinting, I had trouble following the action or, at times, even telling Elizabeth Taylor from Richard Burton.

This was of no small concern to my family, because a pair of glasses in those days represented two weeks of Mother's wages. I tried to put everyone's mind at ease by assuring them I could do without glasses even if it meant groping my way down theater aisles and sitting in the front row. I soon came to regret my pledge when I saw the Cinemascope version of *Carthage in Flames* from two meters away, wishing that Hannibal's elephants would stampede off the screen and trample me, sparing me neck pain and the future embarrassment of wearing glasses in public.

∗   ∗   ∗

It's almost two o'clock when, suddenly thirsty, I reach a row of shops. Ragged patches of sun and shade camouflage the sidewalk. An unfamiliar man steps out of my favorite ice cream shop holding a long rod and preparing to roll down the steel shutter before going home for lunch. I ask if he would mind fixing me a quick *Eiscafé* before closing. He shakes his head and says, "Only soft drinks, sweets, and sunflower seeds."

"Just a cola, then," I say and follow him into the shop. Even the smells are unfamiliar, but then great strides have been made in the field of artificial flavors over the past two decades. At least the coke should hold no surprises. I pay and go outside to sit on an aluminum chair under a faded umbrella. The coke has the familiar, comforting taste of home. It reminds me of the Fourth of July cookout just three weeks ago in a faraway backyard.

Pigeons coo nearby and a ship in the harbor below sounds its horn to announce its arrival or departure. I finish my soda and walk on slowly toward number 27A. I pass a boarded-up store, annoyed at myself for not remembering what it used to be. Next door, an elderly man in a white smock, my old barber, is napping in one of the swivel chairs in his shop. I decide not to wake him to say hello. He probably wouldn't remember me anyway.

A pair of tall cypresses sway noiselessly, nodding as if sharing a secret. A bird calls, another answers, no doubt commenting on the stranger moving about in this, the most tranquil of hours.

What if someone saw me? If flora and fauna recognized me, what about people? They must have been peering out of shuttered windows and following my every move down the street. That's the kind of wariness I've harbored since the moment my excuses and cover-ups crumbled and my parents' divorce became public knowledge. Decades have passed, people have moved away or aged or died, eyes have dimmed and memories dulled, but to no avail. A beard and mustache now disguise my face but provide no refuge.

Did I truly think I could approach the old house, check for signs of my former life, stand in the middle of the courtyard, look at the balconies suspended over me like empty cradles, and wonder if I'd ever dare knock on the door of our old apartment and ask to have a peek?

I pass 27A without stopping but soon turn back and steal into its shady backyard. Along the fence are large boulders ensnared in a mesh of gnarled roots. Early in grade school, my friend Yossi and I went there with hammers and chisels and a box of model cars. We surveyed the largest boulder and carved into it a network of roads teeming with toy traffic. I push away some of the roots to look for telltale scars on the boulder but find none. I tell myself that roots are just roots — struck or severed, exposed or buried, deep or shallow — yet still they entangle my root-bound self.

On my way out, I run my fingers on the building's textured wall and break off a thin wafer of stucco which I put in my shirt pocket. Someday I may need proof that this place had in fact existed.

Back on the sidewalk, I quicken my step and duck into the cave-like entrance to the underground cable car station. Cool air tinged with machine odors wafts up from the platform deep below. I run down the steps into the bowels of Mount Carmel through layers of rock and time toward a demonstration out of high school physics: one cable car ascending, the other descending, in perfect synchrony, exerting equal and opposite forces and carrying me up to the peak where I may look back, down, into, and beyond.

— *Chapter Six* —

Before Lori and I got married, I used to think that American movies were inferior to European ones, and that peanut butter, while possibly an adequate bonding material for architectural models, was nothing I'd want to ingest. Over the years, however, Lori managed to dispel these and some of my other entrenched beliefs.

One conviction I'll always hold concerns vegetables. My homeland has a woefully low rainfall, making its fruits and vegetables small, dense, and flavorful, not large, waterlogged, and bland like many of their American counterparts. When Israeli cucumbers are cut into tiny cubes to maximize surface area, tossed with thin discs of scallions, diced tomatoes, chopped peppers and sliced radishes, and dressed with oil, salt, pepper, and a squirt of lemon juice, what emerges is a salad tossed in Eden. Preparing it is a prelude to time travel and eating it a means of transport to the days before people shriveled and landscapes withered.

Salads in America, although made with less assertive vegetables, do have one distinct advantage for me. The reminiscing they inspire occurs far from their indigenous locale, saving me from having to grapple with blighted time or watching out for hazardous memories.

In my cousin Esti's kitchen, I wash some vegetables in the triple sink, mesmerized by specks of sunlight bouncing off the polished steel. I slice and chop on a glass cutting board atop the veined granite counter. If Aunt Mitzi could see the orange

Formica countertops and avocado-green appliances in the kitchen of our Boston apartment, she'd find it hard not to gloat.

I can't find any oil for the salad but am too tired to go to the store. Deciding to take Tamar up on her offer, I check my appearance in the hall mirror and knock on her door. A young girl opens it.

"Hi, I'm… your new neighbor," I say. "Is your Mommy home?"

"Mommy! Our new neighbor is here," she yells without looking away.

We wait in silence. "What's your name?" I ask.

"Dorit," she answers. "What's yours?"

Just then a little boy rushes out from another room and runs toward us, kicking a black and white soccer ball.

"Catch!" he shouts from two yards away and kicks the ball straight at me. As far back as I can remember, catching balls has been an elusive dream of mine, but the boy had no way of knowing that. He is learning fast, though, watching in disbelief as the ball soars and passes unopposed between my left shoulder and the door jamb, over the banister and down the stairwell.

"This is my brother Eitan, always trying to show off."

Duly impressed, I run downstairs, find the ball and kick it straight up. Eitan catches it on my third try.

"Nice shot!" yells Dorit and claps her hands.

When I get back upstairs, Tamar is waiting at the door. "Wild kids. They have to do homework. Would you like to come in?"

"Sure, thanks. They're cute."

"Something cold to drink?" she asks, opening the refrigerator door.

"Seltzer, if you have any." She fills two glasses and we go out on the balcony.

"I just stopped by to borrow some oil," I say.

"I have enough to last for at least eight days," she says with a little smile, "but I thought you said you weren't going to cook."

"It's for the salad."

"What are you having for supper?"

"Salad."

"That's all? You want to go back home skinnier than you already are? You'll give us a bad name. No, you'll stay and have supper with us."

"Are you sure?"

"There's plenty of food, and besides, it'll be good for the kids to see a man at the table."

The sun drops out of sight, leaving a pale glow over the horizon. A few sailboats seem to be standing still. Farther out, a plume of white smoke from a freighter blushes in the fading light. It will be dark soon. Now I remember how quickly dusk turns to darkness in this country, a place that can ill afford quiet contemplation.

Tamar straightens her back and rubs her eyes as if to remove traces of a bad dream. "I'd better go and start supper."

"I'll get the salad," I say.

When I return, I help her unfold an aluminum table on the balcony. We're having grilled chicken, mashed potatoes, carrots, and salad. She calls her kids, who look puzzled when they see four chairs at the table.

"Hey, where did this salad come from?" asks Dorit.

"Danny made it," answers Tamar.

"This is good," says Dorit. "We haven't had this kind of salad since Daddy…"

Tamar's head jerks up, and she shoots a pleading glance at me.

"Daddy made the best salads," says Eitan, "but he was a hero, so he had to die. Stop it!" He turns to his sister, who is pulling on his sleeve, and slaps her hand.

"You stop!" she whispers. "You know how upset Mommy gets when we talk about it. Just stick to soccer."

"OK!" hisses Eitan and turns to me. "You know, Daddy was a great soccer player."

"And obviously a great coach too," I say to the freckled face. "I've never seen anyone kick the way you do."

Eitan grins and gulps down a glass of water.

"So, what grade are you in?" I ask Dorit.

"I'm going into fourth, and Eitan's going into second."

"Who wants dessert? Danny, some tea?" asks Tamar, suddenly animated, or putting on a good show.

"Sure, why not."

Tamar and Dorit clear the table. "We'll be right back. You men stay here and chat."

As soon as they are gone, Eitan leans over and whispers, "Mommy doesn't like it when we talk about Daddy."

"How come?" I ask.

"I think she wants to forget him. He's never coming back. Talking about him makes her sad, but sometimes I just have to, like when I told you about the salad."

"I understand. Do you miss him?"

"Sometimes. I was only five when he got killed. I remember his salads though." Eitan looks out to the sea.

Father never made salads but he gave great hugs. When he left, I was not much older than Eitan. I must have missed him too.

Dorit appears with a cake and a plate of cookies. Tamar is right behind her with two cups of tea when the yelling starts. A man shouts, a woman hollers, and children shriek. A door bangs. A glass shatters.

Alarmed, I look at Tamar, who is calmly sipping her tea. Rolling her eyes, she points to the building next door.

"Such a small country," she says. "No place to hide."

Dorit and Eitan are tightly pressing their hands over their ears. Both are sobbing. I touch Tamar's arm and point to her frightened children. Tamar puts down her cup.

"OK kids, time to go in."

They run into the living room, turn on the television to drown out the noise, and sink into the sofa. Tamar arranges the dishes in perfect stacks.

"There are lots of things I could tell you, but you're leaving soon, so what's the point?" she says without looking up.

I join Dorit and Eitan on the sofa. They are watching an old episode of *All in the Family*, having trouble reconciling the Hebrew subtitles, scrubbed of all slang, with the canned laughter on the soundtrack. It's not easy. Judging by the stilted translation alone, this could be mistaken for a Chekhovian drama.

Eitan is dozing, his head in my lap. Dorit is cuddled up against me. I don't dare move for fear of disturbing them.

I wake up under a light summer blanket. The TV is off, the kids are gone, and Tamar is sitting in a puffy armchair, reading a book.

"Hi," I say.

"You're awake!"

"What time is it?"

"Almost one in the morning."

"Why didn't you wake me up?"

"What for? You're still jetlagged. Go back to sleep."

"I'm wide awake now," I say. "I'll make us some tea."

"If you like," she says and goes back to her reading.

I fill the kettle and put it on the range. Rummaging through drawers and cabinets, I find tea bags, sugar, spoons, and an assortment of cups and mugs. I pick one up but put it back when I notice the words "Best Dad" in Hebrew. I make the tea and take two steaming cups back to the living room.

"Thanks. That's nice of you," she says.

We sip in silence.

"It's almost boring to tell," says Tamar softly. "We met in the Scouts, went hiking together, explored the country, explored each other, spent time together in the army, traveled through Europe, got married, and had Dorit the next year."

After another sip or two, she gazes into her cup as if trying to divine the past.

"We did like each other, and in public Tom would even flirt with me a little, but it didn't come naturally to him. He talked about making love on a haystack, like the pioneers supposedly did, or in the ruins of a Crusaders fort, but we never did, even when we had the chance. Tom finished law school and devoted himself to helping all kinds of poor souls. I hated being left alone for days at a time, raising the kids by myself and constantly worrying while he was out shuttling between slums and prisons."

For the first time she looks at me, and I look back into her pale eyes and wait. She finishes her tea and puts her cup down on the glass coffee table.

"I never did like this table, but Tom loved it. A little more than a year ago he left to help refugees in Africa. He never told me which country. He called one night and said he was going to clear mines the next day. That was the last I heard from him. Not even a picture postcard to the kids, which he used to send every now and then. He never told me which aid organization he was working for, so I had no way of finding out what happened. He must have stepped on a mine and gotten blown to bits. It's too soon to have him officially declared dead, but I know he's never coming back. I told the kids that he died. I thought it would just be simpler for all of us."

Her eyes pierce me like twin searchlights across a trench. I feel exposed to unfamiliar dangers, as if I've been tricked from the safety of a bunker into an open field.

"What if he does come back some day?"

She doesn't answer. Her eyes are closed. A few minutes later I get up, tiptoe out and go back to Esti's apartment.

My cousin's overindulgent bed is still no match for my jetlag. Even pondering the silky linen's thread count doesn't promote sleep. I turn this way and that, powerless to fend off the onslaught of uninvited memories. Hazy moonlight, too bright and evocative, collects at the foot of the bed.

I get up to close the shutters and notice that parts of the handrail are missing as I climb a circular tower with stairs protruding around its central void. Some steps are reduced to stubs while others have crumbled, forcing me to leap awkwardly and press against the wall to keep from falling. The tower's diameter decreases. The headroom diminishes. A hatch creaks open and words tumble out, collecting at the foot of the bed.

Day Three *Chalk Outlines*

— *Chapter Seven* —

I wake up tired. Since going back to sleep is impossible, I leave in search of strong coffee. The light fog has lifted only as far as the treetops. An Art Nouveau sign with a picture of a steaming cup of coffee beckons. I open a wrought iron gate and follow a path through an overgrown garden to a café with colorful awnings and round tables under umbrellas. I choose a table by a eucalyptus tree and order a croissant and large cappuccino which the server brings on a tray with the morning paper. Breaking off a piece of croissant and spreading it with raspberry jam, I glance at a front-page report detailing an ambush up north that left a dozen soldiers dead. The coffee is great but not strong enough, and I soon nod off, still holding the paper. The server, peeking over the masthead, offers me a refill which I eagerly accept.

After a few sips, I close my eyes and try to meditate, but can't remember the mantra I was given in a college meditation course. I try to concentrate on my breathing, but soon random thoughts invade my mind. In my compact mother tongue, translations from English are typically about two-thirds the length of the original. One Hebrew word means both "husband" and "owner." Another means both "return" and "rehearsal." Perhaps I'll make some sense of it after another cup of coffee or on my return flight, as I rehearse my reunion with Lori and Josh.

When I open my eyes, it's already eight o'clock. On this third day of mourning, Mother is probably just getting up to a cup of instant coffee and toast before sitting down on her low stool to receive condolence callers. I'm glad for her sake that Shiva is almost half over. For now, I'll surprise her with a pastry and a cup of real coffee just as soon as I tear myself away from this peaceful spot and the blissful anonymity it affords an ambivalent native.

* * *

Whenever I asked Grandma why she kept pictures of tombstones in her photo album, she would only nod and say cryptically, "You just never know." Now I do: So many cemeteries of her youth had been destroyed that photos were the only way to remember them, not unlike baby pictures which are the only documented proof that nervous grown-ups, haggard adults, and feeble elderly were once adorable infants.

For the past few years, I have been researching funerary architecture for a book I am working on. The countless ways death is rationalized, life memorialized, and survivors soothed within their means are pleasant diversions from downtown glass and steel monuments, the design preference of some practitioners of my chosen field, myself included. Funerary designers, it's true, have little claim to fame, but at least they don't have to worry about utility hookups, water closet ratios, parking requirements, or end-user complaints.

Sometimes, late at night, I turn off the TV and just stare at the screen. A tiny book fades in, spinning as it grows increasingly larger before coming to rest like a newspaper with a fateful banner headline in an old movie. I can almost touch the dust jacket and smell the ink.

Although I wrote the book in Hebrew and translated it into English, it felt right to give it a title in the dying language of ancestors now at rest, or turning, in desecrated weed-covered graves. *"Beis Oilam"* or *"The House of the Forever After"* in Yiddish.

Writing in one's mother tongue is a three-ring circus with ideas and associations engaged in counterintuitive contortions; erstwhile memories doing magic tricks; acrobatic quotations flying about unharnessed with no safety net of sources; and a restless nostalgia juggling timelines and events that, even had they never really happened, should by right have taken place sometime, somewhere.

A second or third language, on the other hand, is the one you use to interpret for your second or third wife the meaning of the screams in the nightmare from which she has just woken you. And yet, the act of translation, while cutting both the sweet and the sour of the original, can also signal dead ends, reveal unexpected views, and suggest fresh images and perspectives. If the mother tongue is a shortcut to the soul, translating it helps smooth the bumps and potholes besetting many a shortcut.

In my mind, I turn the pages to the preface starting, "The idea was conceived among the graves," mingling birth and death in one verbal urn. It came to me one afternoon when Lori and

I were having a picnic in a secluded church graveyard outside the small village of Sadbury. It was the first time I had ever gone to a cemetery for something other than a burial or a memorial service. I rather enjoyed the experience: a heretical combination of hallowed ground and traditional picnic fare. It started raining around the time we finished eating. We grabbed what we could and ran for shelter under the overhang of a nearby mausoleum. Holding Lori with one arm and shielding the potato salad with the other, I passed the time regaling her with morsels of my research. I told her of coming across an 1885 issue of a funeral directors' journal named "Sunnyside" which later merged with a competing publication, "The Casket," to form the "Sunnyside Casket." Another competitor, "Shadyside," folded soon after. The 1885 issue warned readers that funeral price cuts would be suicidal to the profession. It also offered a $1,000 prize for the best appearing two-month-old corpse. Lori and I agreed that the cost of exhuming, inspecting, and reburying a corpse would almost certainly have exceeded the prize money.

After going to bed that night, I thought in English about the day's events and dreamed in Hebrew of the small cemetery outside Hadera, surrounded by a wall of cypresses.

Grandpa was buried there when I was five. Every year thereafter, when the citrus trees were in bloom, Mother, Grandma and I visited his grave. I always looked forward to this one predictable day when there were no surprises and I knew precisely what to expect.

We woke up early, before it got too hot, and walked downtown to catch the bus to Hadera, a town 50 km down the coast from Haifa. Once there, we transferred to a local bus that took us through the center of town and toward the valley beyond. We got off where the white houses with red tile roofs ended and the orange groves began. As we walked down the dirt road to the cemetery, a light breeze ruffled the pointy tops of the cypresses, stirring up citrus odors and a fine red dust.

"How peaceful," said Mother.

"Just like back home," said Grandma, referring, of course, to her old town in Bukovina. What other home could there be?

As we neared the gate, Mother and Grandma covered their hair with sheer scarves, and I put a kippah on my head. With a sigh, they noted the years Grandpa had been gone and the new headstones in the military section.

The sounds of a hammer and chisel came from the stone-mason's hut behind the eucalyptus trees by the rusty gate. We entered and passed a large black van with a white Star of David on its side. Even though its rear door was open, I didn't dare peek in. Grandma took down a brush that hung from a nail in a tree trunk, and we walked down the main path next to ruler-straight rows of graves. A small bearded man in a black suit sitting under a shade tree stood up as we passed and silently joined us.

As if to announce our arrival, Grandma touched the headstone briefly, and the man began to chant the Kaddish in a plaintive voice. Once finished, he turned and walked back to his tree. My women leaned against the headstone and closed their eyes, leaving me to summon grief on my own, which became more difficult with each passing year. Watching their tears and perspiration flow, I felt more sorrow for the mourners than for the departed.

Grandma was the first to look up. She met my stare with a sad smile and wiped her face with a handkerchief. She brushed off sand and dry leaves from the top of the grave, and each of us placed a small stone on it. The added weight, I was quite sure, prevented the headstone from being carried away by a gust of wind toward the blue hills on the horizon. On the way back to the gate, Grandma gave the man a few coins and received a blessing in return. She hung the brush back in its place and we washed our hands before reentering the world of the living.

We would end these annual memorial days with a walk back to town, catching our breath in any rare shady spot we could find until we reached Aunt Koka's house. Its shuttered windows promised a pleasant, cool darkness. After washing down sweet preserves with cold seltzer and sharing the latest family news, we'd take the bus back to Haifa where I knew precisely what to wish for and enough not to get my hopes up.

— *Chapter Eight* —

I take an early bus to Tel Aviv to check in with my army reserve unit, as I am required to do whenever I return from abroad. It's a small office at Army Headquarters staffed by a young woman soldier who, although clearly put out, quickly completes my paperwork and returns to the magazine she keeps on her lap under the desk. On my way out, a new recruit guarding the gate, sweating profusely and apparently unfamiliar with military protocol, smiles and wishes me a good day.

What I should do now is walk around town and see what's new in local architecture and construction, but in the oppressive heat I feel lethargic and unmotivated. I can think only of a dark, cool apartment and cold seltzer with raspberry syrup. I hurry back to the crowded bus station and board the Haifa express before learning that our departure has been delayed. Street vendors seize the opportunity to sell food and drink through the open bus windows. I buy a sticky triangle of baklava and a bottle of Coke, which do little to relieve my hunger and thirst.

Minutes pass. Patience expires. Tempers flare. Finally, a dispatcher comes on board to announce that bus service has been disrupted because of an accident on the coastal highway. As an alternative, he suggests transferring to a slower local bus whose route is the old two-lane road further inland. Although it makes frequent stops in small towns and villages, a few of us decide to take his advice.

Soon we are traveling northward amid fields and orchards.

Intoxicating smells of overheated grain and fruit waft through the open windows. I close my eyes to better appreciate the bouquet and, drifting off, think of the overripe apples and peaches left rotting on the ground, and of the dead below ground, and of Grandma and her recipes that no one will be able to follow. How could they? With instructions such as "Fill with water to the mark inside the pot," or "Mix with 10 Hellers-worth of yeast," no one could possibly replicate her delicacies even if they could decipher her German Gothic script.

"Hadera!" announces the bus driver. "This bus continues to Haifa."

As I wake up, slightly disoriented, I wonder if I should stay on the bus or get off to visit Aunt Koka. Come to think of it, I didn't see her at Grandma's funeral. On impulse, I jump up just as the door closes and ask the driver to let me out.

"No refund!" he calls after me.

I get a cold drink at the kiosk, check the schedule for later buses, and find a pay phone to call Aunt Koka. The last time I saw her was twenty years ago, when I visited Grandpa's grave before leaving for America.

"Hello?" says a familiar voice. Good old Aunt Koka.

"Hi, Aunt Koka, this is Danny."

"This isn't Aunt Koka. Who's speaking?"

"Danny Holzman. How are you, Aunt Koka?"

"Hi, Danny. This is Sarah, Aunt Koka's daughter. Remember me?"

"Of course I do. You were just ten years old the last time I saw you."

Even at that young age Sarah was a beauty on whose

enchanting face I honed my portraiture skills. Sarah with a flower in her hair, with her back to the camera and her head turned, with her huge eyes filling the frame. Where are my old black and white Sarahs now?

"You sound just like your mother," I tell her. "How is she?"

"She died three years ago."

"I'm so sorry."

"How come you're calling now? I thought you were in America."

"Actually, I'm at the Hadera bus station so I thought I'd call. I always liked your mother."

"I know. She liked you too. We all did. Anyway, are you back for good or did you just come over to wish us good luck with the war?"

"Neither. I flew over for Grandma's funeral."

"I had no idea. I'm so sorry. Amazing how our family drifted apart. I haven't seen or heard from any of them since my mother died. Do you have time for a quick visit?"

"I'm on my way."

Aunt Koka, as I called her, was actually Mother's cousin. When I was growing up, she and her husband Julius were the only people I knew who owned a house. Theirs was a two-story structure with a calm symmetry and peeling stucco sufficient to impart a sense of charm and character. Its wide French doors opened to a manicured garden in the back and a screen of cypresses that hid the lumberyard, the source of the family wealth. Their shiny black Austin was parked under an elaborate canopy.

The ornate entrance and front yard were the first to go when the road to the cemetery and the valley beyond was widened and paved. Sidewalks were later added, further encroaching on the property. After the work was completed, only a narrow stoop remained by the front door, and the Austin had to be parked by the side of the house.

Uncle Julius passed away shortly after I started high school. The lumberyard was sold, relocated, and replaced with apartment buildings. The Austin, by then a rusted shell, remained parked among overgrown weeds, but the neighborhood kids put it to good use, sitting in it, trying to turn its unresponsive wheel, chasing dreams.

The interior of the house never seemed to change. If some of the furniture had been replaced, I never noticed it since the windows and shutters were tightly closed to keep the heat and harsh sunlight out.

Sarah always brightened the gloom, and I could understand how a fairy tale hero would spend years fighting dragons while waiting patiently for his beloved to grow up. Now, of course, Hadera is fresh out of dragons and I am someone else's hero.

A tall, slender woman opens the door, her hand flying up to block the glare. With her disheveled hair and squinting eyes, she appears older than her years. The dark interior exhales a stale breath. I barely say hello before Sarah grabs my hand and pulls me in, quickly closing the door.

"Can't let in the heat," she explains. "Just seeing sunlight makes me perspire."

I agree and tell her that a sunny winter day in Boston is enough to make me close the blinds. In Sarah's house, even electric light is scarce and I can barely see her face. We go into the living room and sit down on a modern but comfortable sofa.

I notice the silhouettes of a seltzer bottle and two glasses on the coffee table.

"Remember the overstuffed sofa and armchairs my parents had?" Sarah asks, following my eyes as I look around. "After my mother died, I got rid of everything and bought a few Scandinavian pieces. They have no character but are just what I need: sterile and anonymous furniture without associations. That's the only way to live when you're alone. The secret is to eliminate the familiar so as not to trip over unwanted memories."

My eyes are getting used to the dark. There are bookcases along the wall, sensibly lined with paperbacks on the top shelf, hardcovers in the middle, and the dark, foreboding volumes of Encyclopaedia Hebraica on the bottom. I can also begin to make out Sarah's face. Her eyes still dominate it, but their sparkle has dimmed.

"Would you have recognized me if you saw me in the street?" she asks with a sad smile.

"With those eyes?" I protest a bit too vehemently. "I'd have known you anywhere, at any age."

"I'm not so sure." She looks closely at her fingernails as if to decide whether they need a manicure, then lunges at one and noisily bites off a corner. "I wouldn't either, if I bothered to look in the mirror. Luckily I don't have to. No matter how I look, my patients always tell me I'm beautiful."

"Patients?"

"Oh, that's right. How could you know? I finished medical school last year and now I'm doing my residency at a nearby psychiatric hospital. Actually, it's an intimate little asylum, plain and simple. A few soldiers, a few parents of dead soldiers, and a few Arabs afraid of soldiers. Poor bastards, all of them. At least I'm alone at night. Good thing I don't get depressed easily, huh?" Her unsmiling mouth utters a chuckle. "I don't know, Danny. Maybe it's my self-discipline or my sunny disposition, what do you think? No, it's probably that people once loved me."

She looks at her hands again, and I avert my eyes until another fingernail is savagely clipped.

"It must be lonely," I say, and hope she didn't hear me.

"Well, I admit I haven't made much of an effort. Relatives used to visit one another and write letters and send postcards when they went away on vacation. We don't visit anymore, and there's no reason to call either. As for those who went abroad, well, they're lost for sure, except for you. I'm glad you came, even though I'm pretty sure we won't see each other again."

I busy myself pouring seltzer into the glasses.

"Wait. I still have some of my mother's preserves," says Sarah, hurrying to the kitchen and returning a moment later with a glass jar and two spoons. We each take a spoonful of the sweet, gooey fruit and wash it down with seltzer just as our elders used to do.

I hear myself ask, "Feel like joining me for a visit to my grandfather's grave?"

Is that the old sparkle in her eyes? "We'll do better than that," she says. "I have a motor scooter in the shack. We'll take a ride to the cemetery, then to your old house and the synagogue and the witch's hut."

"You still remember all that?"

"Of course. Those nostalgia walks we used to take are some of my fondest memories."

I quickly stand up, eager to rediscover my birthplace. Here our family was whole. Here there is still red dust in the streets and a scent of citrus in the air and even an occasional horse-drawn cart. Here I'll be accompanied by Aunt Koka's voice and Sarah's eyes. With any luck there will be no surprises.

Sarah opens the front door, seeing how eager I am to get going. A crescent moon and street lamp greet us from the dark. With the shutters closed, we haven't noticed that night had fallen.

"Well, it was a good plan, anyway," I say.

Hearing the disappointment in my voice, Sarah says, "Don't give up yet. Why don't you stay here tonight? Tomorrow we can get up early and take as long as we want to see everything. What do you say?"

I agree, which makes Sarah very happy. Suddenly energetic, she prepares a nice supper and serves it on trays in front of the TV. After the nightly news, she shows me to a neat little bedroom in the back of the house.

"This used to be my room growing up. There are still a few dolls around to keep you company and the original Hebrew translation of *Little Women*. You won't be bored."

She steps out and returns with fresh towels and a new toothbrush. "The bathroom is across the hall. Sleep well. I'm going to make sure that tomorrow is a very long day."

"Good night," I say, "I'm lucky to have such a hospitable cousin."

"I'm the lucky one," says Sarah before closing the door. "I finally managed to trap a live family member. I may not release you into the wild again."

*   *   *

"I love you, I miss you, I kiss you," says a voice in the dark. A brief search reveals a doll hiding under the pillow, smiling with her eyes closed. When I pick her up, she gives me an affectionate look and says, "You're a good girl!" I prop her up on the nightstand and switch off the lamp, throwing the room into darkness.

I worry about tampering with well-ordered memories and scaring up new untidy ones. Tomorrow I'll search for bodies long gone but may find only chalk outlines. Clues are scarce, eyewitness accounts unreliable, and second-hand memories tainted. Even previews of upcoming dreams are no help as I toss and turn and count the many stones that still need turning.

— *Chapter Nine* —

Memories don't freeze well. Once defrosted, they are no longer what they used to be, much like the fools who froze them in the first place.

I'm just such a fool or worse, having allowed my recollections to be mixed with those of others, leaving the freezer door ajar, and causing an early thaw.

* * *

Mother used to call me her little angel. The reason was plain to anyone who stopped to peek into the wooden baby carriage she wheeled around the neighborhood during my first autumn. I was fair and rosy, all milk and honey which, despite Biblical covenants, our land was not.

One unexpected thing about little angels was that they seemed to attract the Holy Land's wildlife. Mother and Father discovered this when renting a room in an old stone house whose back yard bordered a fragrant orchard. Mother would tell the women in the little playground how she once found a tiny frog resting in my crib beside my cheek, and how a snake once slithered in through a crack in the wall, curling up at the foot of her bed while she was nursing me. Lucky for us, our landlord, who had just returned home, remembered where he had left his pitchfork.

After Father took a clerical job at the paper mill on the outskirts of town, my parents were able to afford a larger place.

Our new home was a ground floor apartment in a three-story building that shared a hilltop with a water tower. Directly above us lived Mr. Willenski, a portrait photographer. Each afternoon, during the hottest time of day, he would return from his studio, climbing the hill and seeking shortcuts among the clumps of weeds and brambles. Mother's bedroom window faced north, and in the shade in front of it, Mr. Willenski would stop to catch his breath and wipe his forehead, then turn and approach the open window.

This was the hour for afternoon nursing, a routine by which Mr. Willenski seemed to time his homecoming. He would greet us quietly from the window so as not to startle me. Mother would nod ever so slightly. He would stare at her bare chest, which she was too tired or hot or indifferent to cover. She would look impassively at the thin, tired man, his flushed face glowing with perspiration, telling herself that he was probably just studying her as an artist would an object of beauty. Anyway, since he was looking in from the outside, the room was surely too dark for him to see much of anything, yet his expression revealed that what he did see he faithfully committed to his photographic memory.

Mother was never sure how long he stood there. After a while, she would drift off or avert her eyes from the bright window. Before turning to leave, he would mumble, "Madonna and Child, Madonna and Child." A few minutes later she would hear him pacing upstairs. When Father returned home later in the afternoon, his tiptoeing would wake her. She would realize with a start that she must have dozed off and would force herself to get up to prepare supper.

* * *

My first birthday was celebrated under the water tower, which consisted of a cylindrical tank atop four concrete columns that seemed too slender to support its weight. In its shadow, the tenants found refuge from the brutal sun and their stifling apartments. To the west, one could see the silvery ribbon of the Mediterranean. Mother liked to watch the sunsets from there, even though her yearning for dazzling colors was rewarded only by dull pinks in a pale, cloudless sky.

Neighbors helped arrange folding tables in the shade and secured tablecloths with clothespins. Mother laid out bowls of fruit and bottles of juice and seltzer next to Grandma's frosted sponge cakes and children's candy.

Mr. Willenski could barely contain his excitement. Scurrying about, he kept relocating his tripod and taking numerous readings with the light meter hanging from his neck. Shortly before the guests arrived, he positioned Mother, Father, and me next to the party table and disappeared under his camera's dark cloth to take the official birthday portrait.

On that tranquil Saturday, the hot air made the town shimmer and ripple below us. Smells of wild flowers came and went with the shifting breeze. Birthday balloons and bubbles of laughter floated in the orange-scented air. I fell asleep in Grandma's lap.

As the afternoon wore on, people reluctantly got up and left. At last Mr. Willenski covered his camera and folded his tripod. He kissed me and left without a word.

Mother said, "It suddenly feels so lonely."

Father took his time formulating an appropriate response. "Willenski didn't take his eyes off you," he said.

"Poor man," said Mother, suddenly remembering it was time to nurse. "He always looks so forlorn, except when he is photographing Danny or trying to make him laugh. He looks so disheveled, eating by himself, sleeping alone. We should try to find someone for him."

She waited in vain for Father's response and, when she could no longer bear the humid silence, picked me up and went into the bedroom. A late ray of sun found its way in, lighting her breasts and my head between them. Madonna and three spheres in the dying light, she thought. That sounded like delicious material for Mr. Willenski and his lenses. She imagined him behind the camera, trembling with excitement and overflowing with creativity. She would boil a few potatoes for supper. Father liked them with margarine, slices of onion, and a pinch of salt. She was thirsty. Thank God there was seltzer left over from the party.

— *Chapter Ten* —

Shortly after supper Father turned to me and said, "Let's go for a walk, Danny." Father would take his daily walk with or without me, but I knew he liked it better when I joined him. Not that he ever said anything about it, or much else, unless I asked him a specific question or begged for a war story.

Father and I conversed in Hebrew, but the common language in our household was German. Yiddish was used for gossip and Romanian for discussing issues that did not concern me, such as my future. Mother abhorred Russian, Grandma didn't speak French, and neither understood a word of English. Only Father spoke all seven with ease, even though he rarely had the opportunity to do so after the linguistic crossfire of World War II had ceased.

When it came to Father, however, Mother and Grandma used silence to speak volumes and body language to turn a phrase with uncommon eloquence.

That day we had potatoes, farmer's cheese and salad for supper. Father ate carefully, using a knife and fork, with the contentment of a landed gentleman having returned to the Manor, enjoying a sumptuous repast after the hunt.

"Only a few more weeks till first grade, huh, Danny?" Father said, breaking the silence.

"Uh-huh," I replied without much enthusiasm. Whenever school was mentioned, I thought of a children's song I learned in kindergarten about a boy taking stock of his young life before his first day of school. The carefree days of childhood are about to end. He says good-bye to his three best friends — a puppy, a cat, and a dove. He tries to explain to them and to himself why they cannot accompany him to school and wonders who will take care of them.

Even though I had no pets, I could understand his predicament from an old folk tale that Grandma used to read to me about Ox holding Leviathan by the tail. As long as they didn't move, the balance of the world was preserved. I was convinced that those two brutes resided in our yard. Once, when Father gave me an old steering wheel, I showed him which tree to attach it to so that I could keep an eye on the wrestling beasts while driving around my little universe. With me at school, there would be no one to supervise and no telling what might happen. The world could lose its balance on my account: much too high a price to pay for a grade school education.

"This is delicious," Father said, complimenting the kitchen at large. "May I have more?"

The kitchen didn't budge. Grandma, chatting with Mother, finally passed the potatoes to Father. I handed him the salt shaker then asked for more milk. Both Mother and Grandma sprang into action, one getting the milk from the icebox, the other a glass from the cupboard. Father didn't look up, as if balancing potato, cheese, and salad on his fork required his undivided attention.

"I'll wash the dishes, yes?" inquired Father without much hope. Grandma waved her hand dismissively, as if to say, "I don't need a stopped-up sink and greasy dishes that I'll just have to wash again."

"All right, I'll take out the trash later," Father said

magnanimously, secure in his knowledge that it was the one chore he would not be denied. Grandma put on her apron, and Mother began clearing the table. Father rolled up his newspaper, tucked it under his arm, and we went out into the clear summer night.

From the edge of town, we could identify the dim street light down by Mr. Reznik's store as easily as the Dippers and North Star. Father inhaled deeply. I did the same and smelled the sweet fragrances the heat had coaxed from field and orchard that were now settling into nostrils to spend the night. A light breeze brought greetings from far-off cowsheds. From beyond the cypresses lining the road came croaking, chirping, and buzzing, at times soothing, at times menacing. To be on the safe side, I held on tightly to Father's big hand.

We walked in silence for a few moments, and then Father began whistling softly as he often did when he had nothing to say. It was always the same piece, a one-note High Holiday blow of the ram's horn transcribed for pursed lips. I imagined the Children of Israel circling Jericho, forced to whistle this monotone for seven days due to a severe shortage of ram's horns, which was enough to make the city capitulate, its inhabitants breaching their own walls to escape the mind-numbing noise.

We stopped under the lamppost in front of Mr. Reznik's grocery store where Father lit a cigarette, something he would occasionally do after a good meal. Across from the grocery store was the bus stop and a weathered billboard layered with posters of movies, concerts, and political rallies. Diagonally across from the lamppost was the witch's hut.

Earlier that spring, while walking home from the Independence Day celebration downtown, we sat down for a brief rest on the bus stop bench. An old woman in rags came out of the hut, carrying a bowl of milk for her emaciated cats.

"Poor soul," sighed Father. "Who would think her brother was one of the founders? Some day I'll tell you about her. It's a sad story."

On the billboard behind us, a few yellowing election posters were flapping in the spring breeze, sounding like the flock of white doves released into the air after the playing of the national anthem. It was our homeland's birthday and we were supposed to rejoice. The exiles were returning, ingathering from the four corners of the earth, flying in on magic carpets or special charter flights. Be that as it may, it was a day of pride and joy in which everyone should take part, even a witch. And a witch she was. I was sure of it, whether Father knew it or not. He likely knew, but pretended not to.

After Father stomped out his cigarette, we walked on as far as the next lamppost. A shallow ditch separated the road from wheat and cotton fields and from the jackals standing some distance away, staring with glowering eyes, howling and sending shivers down my back. Father's hand never stopped being big and warm.

Light was spilling from the kitchen window when we returned home, illuminating the fig tree and the unruly shrubs whose shadows stretched across the yard. Father closed the gate behind us, walked over and sat down on the porch steps. While I searched in the dark for my red tricycle, he held his newspaper to the dim light, tried a few angles, and finally gave up.

"Ready for bed, Danny?"

"Two more minutes," I said. I found my tricycle and began

pedaling between the gate and the porch, ringing the bell on the handlebars.

"It's late," called Grandma from the kitchen window.

"Two more minutes," I said.

Riding back and forth along the path, I remembered a kindergarten story. We were learning about the Ten Commandments, and the story concerned honoring parents. It told of a young man whose mother stepped barefoot out of the house. Noticing this, the man got down on his knees, placed his hands under her feet and had her walk on them around the garden and back to the house. I looked at my hands and wondered whether they were big enough for mother to stand on, and what I would do if both Mother and Grandma came out barefoot at the same time.

"Go to bed now, Danny," said Father. "I'm going to sit out here a while longer." I kissed him goodnight and went in.

Grandma was at the kitchen table, chopping vegetables for a large pot of soup. She wiped her hands on her apron, giving a sign she was ready for our nightly routine. I sat on her lap, put my arms around her neck, kissed her on both cheeks and said "I love you" three times. After she had done the same, I was ready for our race to my room.

"How was your walk?" she asked in a whisper.

"Same as always," I whispered back, puzzled.

"What did your father say?"

"About what?"

"Just... in general. What did he talk about?"

"I don't know. He smoked a cigarette. I guess that meant he had a good meal. Oh, and he said something about the witch."

"Mitzi? She's not so bad. Nosy, yes, but basically a decent person."

"No, Grandma, the witch down the street. You know, the woman who lives with her cats in the little hut."

"Ah, yes. The woman who's supposedly related to one of the founders. The one who goes around all day mumbling to herself and sometimes sticks leaves and twigs in her hair. Do you know that when we first moved here, your father wanted to go and have a talk with her? To your mother he never says a word, but for crazy people he has time."

I was confused. Wasn't it Mother who almost never spoke to Father?

I went to the front door and looked out. Father was sitting where I had left him, gazing at the silvery haze around the moon and whistling softly.

"Why don't you ever talk to Mother?" I said.

He turned and stared at me. At last he said quietly, "What?"

"You never talk to Mother. For witches you have time, but not for Mother!"

Only when silence was restored did I realize that I had shouted at him. He said nothing but kept looking at me until I went back inside and closed the door. I noticed Grandma turn away quickly and go back into the kitchen. I stood at the kitchen door, waiting for her to commend me on my initiative.

"Go get ready for bed," she said. "I'll come tuck you in when I've put the soup on the stove."

On the way to my room I peeked into the living room. It was dark except for the glowing dial of the Phillips radio in the corner. The weekly concert of the Broadcast Authority's Symphony

Orchestra was in progress, and even though I could not tell from her silhouette, I was sure Mother's eyes were closed, the better to escape.

She tiptoed into my room after I was in bed.

"Is the concert over?" I asked.

She sat down next to me. "The good part." She took my hand and stroked each finger separately. "Don't be angry with Father. He's a good man"

"But he cares more about witches than he cares about you," I said.

"That's not true," said Mother. "It's not so simple."

She may have said something else too, but I was already drifting off to sleep.

— *Chapter Eleven* —

At breakfast, our resident chameleon set out on its morning stroll along the top of the fence outside our kitchen window. It moved slowly, contemplating every step, its eyes darting, its long tongue catching unseen insects. I slowed my chewing to match its gait and waited to see its color change from the brown of the rusty fence to the green of its ivy destination.

I had my own camouflage: words and gestures of others, faithfully mirrored, and an array of intonations and facial expressions colored by the last person I spoke with or the last thing I ate.

Grandma had the run of the kitchen and, thus, an unfair advantage. It was her unshakeable conviction that Father was to blame for everything. She never came right out and said it because it would have made Mother unhappy and, after all, Mother had not had an easy life, and let's just leave it at that.

"Father already went to work," I said after the chameleon disappeared in the greenery.

Grandma nodded, dismissing the matter with a wave of her hand.

"Yah," I said. "He always leaves so early and is never here to help, right?"

"Right."

"But he works hard at the office, right?" I said, filling the silences.

"Well, I'm sure he talks to everybody there. He's good at talking to strangers."

"And he needs so little to be happy." This was actually a direct quote from Mother. It didn't seem like such a bad thing to me, but I thought Grandma would appreciate it. She'd know what to do with it.

"If it were up to him, we wouldn't have a stick of furniture in the house. He'd be happiest in a tent with a cot, an army blanket, a book shelf, and a surface to write on."

"How do you know, Grandma?"

"After a long year in Cyprus I know too much."

I had no idea where Cyprus was and did not ask, perhaps because I was too busy sampling the fresh challah with *schmaltz* and roasted onions that Grandma had served me. It could also have been hot *mamaliga* or thick bean soup which, if not by itself enough to sway me, would help ingrain her convictions by their association with my favorite foods.

Mother shuffled sleepily into the kitchen.

"Good morning, child," said Grandma cheerfully. "I waited for you with breakfast. How did you sleep?"

"So-so." Mother's voice was still drowsy. "It's already hot and humid."

She sat down across from me and let Grandma serve her a cup of weak coffee.

"We could have been in Chicago, Mama."

Grandma's cheer was suddenly gone. "Ah, what's the use? It's too late for that."

"Shh..." said Mother. "Not in front of the boy." She looked up. "Dannika, go play outside before it gets too hot."

Truth be told, I was waiting to get out. I had to inform Ox and Leviathan I'd be going to school soon.

— *Chapter Twelve* —

At bedtime, Grandma would read to me *Winnie the Pooh* in German until one of us fell asleep:

"Wie schön eine Wolke zu sein / Zu schweben ganz allein."
(How nice to be a cloud / Floating all alone.)

Like Pooh, I too sometimes imagined that I was a cloud. Floating high above the world, I saw far beyond the hill with the water tower. The sea shimmered in the distance, the checkered fields and orchards stretched in all directions, and right below was the intersection with the witch and skeletal cats resembling a children's book illustration. Sounds never reached me up there, not even quiet bickering in the dead of night, only an occasional whisper: *all alone.*

* * *

A few days before school was to start, Grandma decided I needed a new pair of shoes. I tried to talk Mother into coming with us. Of course it was hot, I told her, but at least there would be a breeze on the bus with all the windows open, and most of the stores downtown had fans. Mother smiled and stroked my hair. No, it was much too hot for her. I was born in this oven of a country, but she hadn't had a comfortable day since leaving Bukovina. Now that was a place fit for people: a picturesque town in a valley surrounded by snowy peaks and green forests, with a blue river and a bridge and bells tolling every Sunday. How did Grandma ever get used to this heat? The woman was a marvel.

I found Grandma in her room, transferring money from her rosewood nightstand to her pocketbook. When she saw me, she opened another drawer, took out a chocolate bar and broke off a square. "Eat it slowly," she advised.

We walked to the intersection and sat down on the bench to wait for the bus. The door to the hut across the road squeaked open, and the witch emerged with her feline companions. Dressed in rags, her long gray hair hanging down like frazzled ropes, she looked around as if trying to figure out how she had gotten there. The cats were meowing pathetically, brushing against her bare legs.

I looked at Grandma.

"Poor woman," she said. "On all my enemies a fate like hers!"

A noisy bus picked us up and continued its circuitous route through outlying neighborhoods. As usual, I had to go to the bathroom as soon as we took our seats. With some effort I kept things under control until we arrived downtown. Grandma took my hand, leading me to a bush in the corner of an empty lot. While she stood guard, I did what little I could to irrigate this parched land where every drop counted.

This was how Grandma bought shoes. Having already identified the optimal style and size, she asked the store owner, "So, how much?" with a smile that might as well have been that of his own grandmother in a language that certainly was. Regardless of his answer, she then said, "And the discount?" Regardless of his answer, she then said, "Mr. So-and-So, who used to chase geese and roll in the mud and eat at our house every day, now refuses to give me a discount and claims he doesn't remember me. I don't think you're like that. We have to help each other out in this godforsaken land because no one else will. So, how much?"

With my new shoes in hand, and most of Grandma's rosewood money still in her pocketbook, we got on a bus that took us to Grandma's old house.

Only up close could one see that it was made of wooden shipping crates: large cubes, three meters on a side, used by immigrants to ship whole households from abroad. It was originally built as a storage shed by the owner of the house next door, but then, with housing in short supply, he cut out a door and a few windows, applied a diluted coat of paint, built an outhouse, and rented it to Grandma and Grandpa. After what they had been through, it seemed palatial.

If nothing else, it was ideally located: down the street from the water tower, adjacent to the hospital where I was born, and close to the field where I learned to walk. They lived there for five years until Grandpa died suddenly. Father felt sorry for Grandma and insisted she move in with us. She agreed, but it took her a long time before she could bring herself to abandon the little hut altogether. She would go there once a week, air out the place, dust a little, and leave with a few things. Now it was almost empty.

The air inside was hot and stale. We opened the windows. Grandma gave me a glass of water and began looking through cardboard boxes that she pulled out from under the bed. Faded rectangles on the walls were the only indication that pictures once hung there.

"Come here Danny, I have something to show you." She was sitting on the bed holding a stone tablet the size of a box of chocolates with an inkwell set in its center. Its surfaces were engraved with reliefs of ships and tents and guard towers but also a tractor and a plow and a child on a swing. And there were carved quotes: *"If I am not for myself, who is for me,"* and *"If not now, when?"*

Grandma moved her fingers over the petrified memories with a gentleness I always believed was reserved for me alone. "Your grandfather was an artist," she said.

"What is this thing?"

"Proof of his patience. He used to sit for hours in the shade behind the tent, carving away with a dull pocket knife."

"What tent, Grandma?"

"The one in Cyprus."

That place again. "What were you doing there?"

"After the war we were invited to go to America to live with Grandpa's brother in Chicago. We had all the necessary papers to enter the U.S. but then your parents got married and your father convinced us that Israel was the only place for Jews. Instead of sailing to New York on an ocean liner, we came here on an overcrowded freighter. The British were still in control and didn't let us in. Our ship was captured before it reached Haifa, and we were taken to the island of Cyprus for a year. This was what it looked like." She pointed to the tents and towers on the tablet.

"What's that tower?" I asked.

"Oh, that was how the guards kept watch to make sure we didn't attempt to cross the sea and enter the Promised Land."

"What did you do there for a whole year?"

"We cooked, sewed, went to adult education classes, and spent time in the infirmary. Mostly, we watched your father have the time of his life. He was busy from morning till night teaching Hebrew, giving pep talks, organizing debates and book clubs, writing for the newsletter, lecturing on Russian and Yiddish poetry, and waking us up when he returned to the tent and bumped into our cots in the dark. When the British left Palestine, we left Cyprus and came here. For a while, things were worse than before. We still lived in tents, but now we were never sure of our next meal. After a few months, Grandpa and your father found work and things began to improve. When you were born, that made everything worthwhile."

She caressed the tablet, and I ran a careful finger along its sculpted edge.

"One day this will be yours," Grandma said as she lovingly wrapped it in one of Grandpa's handkerchiefs and laid it carefully in its box.

"Don't worry," I said. "When one day comes, I'll take good care of it."

Day Four *Ghost Traffic*

— *Chapter Thirteen* —

The sound of clanking dishes wakes me from a fitful night's sleep in Sarah's old room. With snippets of vivid dreams still swirling in my head, I dress quickly and find my way to the kitchen, worried we're already behind schedule.

"Good morning," I say. "Sorry I overslept."

"There's no rush," says Sarah cheerfully. "Just relax, have a cup of coffee and look at the paper while I make us an omelet."

The strong coffee makes me wince. "Things are not looking so good up north," I say, scanning the headlines.

"Let's not worry about that right now, Danny. Today is all about the past and happy memories."

After breakfast we get on Sarah's scooter and take the shortcut to the cemetery down the road.

As we walk toward Grandpa's grave, a small bearded man in a black suit silently joins us. I give him a few coins and tell him that I will say my own Kaddish. I brush off pine needles from the grave, place a small stone on top of it, close my eyes, and recite the prayer.

After a few minutes, we walk back to Sarah's scooter. We cross an empty lot, skirt a hill and head up a quiet street away from the center of town.

"Let's stop here for a moment," I say.

At the top of the hill stands the old water tower and the apartment building where we lived when I was a baby. A few lizards are sprawled on hot rocks nearby. The sounds of children playing reach us from down the street.

Sarah sits patiently on her scooter. I can't think of a thing to say except, "Over there, on the other side of those trees, is where I learned to walk," even though she already knows that.

"I'll be right back," I say and walk toward the dense row of cypresses separating road and field.

A young woman materializes in the trembling haze, pushing a toddler in a wooden stroller. She stops and picks him up. Slowly they walk hand in hand into a field carpeted with wild flowers. After positioning his plump legs far apart for balance, she runs a few meters, turns around and calls out, "Come here, Dannika. Come here, little angel. Come to Mommy. Come on, that's my good boy..." He wobbles, takes a few steps, stumbles and falls, gets up and drops into her outstretched arms. Mother kisses and hugs me, runs a short distance ahead, turns around and again calls out to me.

Only when I push through the fragrant trees do I notice a chainlink security fence enclosing a sprawling house and a manicured lawn. A red Mercedes is parked in the carport, and young children are splashing in a free-form pool.

I quickly get back on the scooter behind Sarah, and we ride on toward the synagogue and our old house. This day will soon end. Its light will diminish, fade through a short dusk and expire in a clammy night. There's hope yet.

— *Chapter Fourteen* —

From the intersection, I could see the dirt road recede under a canopy of intertwined branches. At the far end stood a dilapidated building with some of its windows boarded up. Seven crooked steps led up to the door with a faded inscription over it: *"This is the gate unto the Lord, the righteous shall enter it."* Clearly there was a shortage of these since only a few old men entered regularly. I used to wonder whether only the righteous were allowed in, or if anyone who entered immediately became righteous.

I went to the synagogue with Grandpa whenever he and Grandma visited on Shabbat. I would look around and try to figure out how righteousness was transmitted and how contagious it might be. The stale air and musty smell made me want to flee, but when hushed chanting and chatting commenced, Grandpa would look over with his kind blue eyes, and I would stay put.

"It won't be much longer," he said one Friday night, looking up from his prayer book. "Just think of all the good food waiting for us at home."

Suddenly, to the tune of the prayer welcoming Shabbat, I imagined fish, vegetables, and assorted chicken parts parading in front of the ark's velvet curtain, each pausing briefly to take a bow under the eternal flame.

Father sat on my other side, reading the Shabbat Torah portion from a tattered Pentateuch, occasionally looking up at the ceiling, nodding cryptically and sighing.

"What?" I whispered.

"I was just thinking of your Aunt Hilda and Uncle Bruno."

I quickly returned to the food processional because I couldn't bear to see the tears welling in his eyes as he remembered his sister and brother-in-law.

Uncle Bruno had had the foresight to leave Germany in time and, in hindsight, the good fortune to make his way to Palestine via Romania. There, in a little town, he was to join other would-be pioneers traveling to the hot and barren land of their non-German-speaking forefathers. Luckily, he met German-speaking Aunt Hilda and married her a week later. They went on to Palestine, but after encountering the hardships of pioneering, they boarded a train for Jerusalem and settled there into the *gemütlich* life of a bus driver and a hausfrau. Berlin became a fond memory. Bruno had longed to return there until he learned, after the war, that his entire family had been rounded up by fellow Berliners, shipped off to the camps and gone up in smoke. Some years later, however, when Bruno and Hilda had concluded that Israel would never be Germany, they returned to his fatherland to live a quiet, anonymous life far from the beastly heat of the biblical homeland and the fiery nature of its inhabitants.

After the service was over, we went out into the silent night. We walked slowly toward the intersection, crossed the puddle of light under the street lamp and were soon home. Mother and Grandma had lit the candles and set a lovely Shabbat table with challahs, wine, and wild flowers from a nearby field. The day of rest was upon us.

Grandpa collapsed while Grandma was serving dessert. As if

he had secretly trained for such an emergency, Father grabbed my hand and quickly led me out, saying only, "I'll get the doctor."

We ran over to the Rezniks, the only neighbors who had a telephone. Father called the doctor and asked the Rezniks if I could stay with them until after... well, until later. He put his big warm hand on my shoulder, told me everything would be all right and left.

The Rezniks had no children and only one bedroom, so I spent the night wedged between them in their soft double bed. Mrs. Reznik was soft too. She kept snuggling up to me, patting my head, saying soothing words and holding me with a plump arm against her soft bosom, which engulfed me whenever she reached over to shake her husband out of his snoring.

Although Mrs. Reznik gave me a Shabbat morning kiss and did all she could to spoil me with pastries and a grownup chess set, I was worried about Grandpa and kept wondering what was going on at home and why no one had come to get me.

Father stopped by briefly that afternoon. He hugged me and told me about the time he went off to war and never saw his parents again. He then went into the kitchen and spoke in hushed tones with the Rezniks. I heard him say that the burial society wouldn't pick up the body until after Shabbat and that the funeral would be held the next afternoon. I didn't know what a funeral was and decided to ask Father about it, but first I had to fret about spending another night in the Reznik's bed.

Mr. Reznik closed his store early on Sunday and came home to look for his kippah. Not finding it, he took a clean handkerchief, tied knots in its corners, tried it on, took it off and put it in his pocket.

"I'll be back after… well, later," he said to his wife on the way out.

Father came to pick me up that evening. "What a little angel you have," Mrs. Reznik told him. "He could use some sleep though, I think."

"Grandpa went away," said Father before we reached our house. I didn't know what that meant, but I didn't ask and he didn't elaborate.

The house was full of people. For some reason, Mother and Grandma were sitting on low stools. Their eyes were red, and they started crying when I went over to hug them. Father tucked me in and sat next to me on the bed, holding my hand and speaking softly.

"At some point during the war, my unit entered a small village. The Germans were only a few kilometers away. We were retreating rapidly. We would spend the night in a village or town, move out in the morning, and by noon it would already be occupied by the enemy. It was getting dark and we were ordered to make camp for the night. While the cook was preparing supper in the mobile kitchen, I wrote a postcard to Aunt Hilda. I said that I was fine, that we were in retreat, and that I could not be sure when, or if, she would receive my card. I wrote her Jerusalem address on it, walked down to the village square and dropped it in a mailbox. Sometime after midnight we were given the order to evacuate. As quietly as possible, we collected our gear and left the village, heading for Stalingrad. At dawn we could hear cannon fire from somewhere behind us, but we were already well beyond range. When we were finally reunited years later, Aunt Hilda showed me that postcard, as crisp as on the day

I mailed it. Those Germans took mail delivery seriously, even in the heat of battle."

After a pause, Father said, "Grandpa won't be coming back, Danny, but we'll always remember him. And if you ever forget, I'll remind you."

"I won't forget. Is he far away?"

"Very far."

"Will he at least send us a postcard?"

Father shook his head. I closed my eyes, and he sat with me until I fell asleep.

— *Chapter Fifteen* —

Sarah chains her motor scooter to a bench near the bus stop, and we sit down to share a bottle of water. A yellowing poster on the billboard rustles in the afternoon breeze. A young woman walks by, holding her toddler's hand. Two old men turn the corner and walk slowly up the road toward the synagogue. A tractor coughs persistently in a nearby field.

"I keep thinking of what has changed and what hasn't. It's as if someone is testing me on the difference. Here's the grocery store, over there the witch's hut, behind us the synagogue. The place is full of ghosts. Am I the only one who sees them?"

If you jumped off a slow-moving train and hopped on again, you wouldn't end up in the same car. Chances are you'd find yourself in the rear with the luggage, crates, and cages, and who knows what might crawl out of those.

I feel Sarah's hand on my shoulder, which, for some reason, annoys me.

She starts to say something but falls silent.

"You've never been away," I say. "You can't see the big picture because there isn't enough room here to step back." Poor Sarah doesn't deserve this lecture, but I can't help myself. "I envy your lack of perspective. Two-dimensional facades are so much simpler. Misleading, yes, but uncomplicated and without converging lines or a particular viewpoint."

Sarah is not offended. "If it'll make you feel any better, Danny, I do see some of the changes. I see new streetlights, a phone booth, and fewer potholes. The witch's door is padlocked and the windows boarded up. All in all, the ghost traffic is pretty light today."

"Father promised to tell me about her, but he never did."

"Let's leave the scooter here and go have a look at your old house."

My house, my country — if they are mine, why are there strangers squatting in them?

As we near the house, sounds get louder: a ball bounces... ice cubes rattle in a glass... soda fizzes... a beer can hisses... grease sizzles... "Honey, I'm ready for the buns now!"

My old house is unrecognizable. It is freshly painted, topped with a gabled roof and adorned with neat flowerbeds. Men in Bermuda shorts, women in cutoffs, and children in Red Sox T-shirts are gathered around a barbecue grill under my tree.

"Hi there!" says a middle-aged man with a Boston accent. "I'm Sam. You look alarmed. I hope we didn't startle you."

"Sorry for staring like this," I say. "I grew up in this house. We just came by for a quick look."

"I'll be right back," says the man as he runs over to the grill to flip the burgers and hot dogs.

"Listen, why don't you join us?" he says. "We'd love to have you."

I look at Sarah. "Fine with me," she says.

"Great," says the man as he opens the gate. They moved to Israel about a year ago. They just love Hadera. The warm weather with no rain all summer long is so nice. And the people are great. There's no way you can be lonely here. This is truly a homeland. Whatever made me leave and go to Boston of all places? Hadera must have been a wonderful place to grow up in. What was life like around here back then? Must have been rather isolated, but there was always the telephone, right? It's so picturesque here in a casual sort of way. If only someone did away with that boarded-up shack down the street. A real eyesore and creepy too. God only knows what must be crawling around in there. Someone should write a letter to the sanitation department. And then there's the red dust. Gets into everything. But after they get central air, the windows can stay closed all the time. This way they won't have to listen to all those godawful noises at night, you know, the chirping and croaking and buzzing. Even trimming the shrubs hasn't helped. Where are those critters hiding, anyway? As a native I must know. Cutting down some of the trees will certainly help and will make the house so much brighter and cheerier. Gee, for a sun-drenched country there sure is a lot of shade here. Shopping is not so great. There's nothing within walking distance. Not that they aren't used to driving everywhere, but there's this padlocked shop near the bus stop that they wish someone would turn into a grocery store. Well, anyway, food's ready, people!

We have our burgers with imported Heinz ketchup and relish, French's mustard, and cans of Coke and Sprite. Sam offers to take a picture of us in front of the house, and Sarah enthusiastically approves, even managing to coax a smile from me for the occasion. His wife Joan gives us a tour of the house, and my heart sinks when I see what they've done to it. I glide from room to room on polished parquet floors. I notice the gleaming kitchen and sparkling bathrooms, the recessed lighting, the crown moldings, and the double-glazed windows. An oversize TV and stereo fill a corner of the living room. Shelves are filled with porcelain, crystal, and family photos in silver frames. A cat naps in a wicker basket. Most unsettling is the sense of contentment and wall-to-wall peace which no photo could ever capture.

I thank our hosts and walk away without looking back. Sarah puts a comforting hand on my shoulder and, as if following a map of my childhood landmarks, leads the way to my old kindergarten.

At this late afternoon hour, the gate is locked and the grounds deserted. The newly renovated building is not as friendly or inviting as it once was. There are no songs spilling out onto the playground or excited children chasing each other around the sandbox. Only silence. Still, I snap a picture of it to go in my childhood album, next to the old black and white photo of its former self.

Across the road, my elementary school and the hill beyond jog more memories and evoke a past brimming with possibilities.

— *Chapter Sixteen* —

The first thing Miss Yulia Wassertreger did when she arrived on our shores was change her name. If gnarled roots reaching down thousands of years could sprout the tender sapling of a new country, she reasoned, then her old family name could be changed to something young and fresh, as sparkling as the countless drops springing forth and irrigating the fields at the edge of town.

While the historian in her wondered about the water carriers whose surname she inherited, she disliked its association with serfdom. She wanted a name to go with her newfound freedom and independence. She considered water and waterways and other liquid motifs, solid elements like earth and rock, and the more ephemeral light and seasons. She finally settled on *Aviv*, Hebrew for spring, the season of fertility and new beginnings.

That was how Yulia Aviv introduced herself to her first-grade class. We fell in love with her right away. What wasn't there to love about her? She was pretty and cheerful and looked at us with kind eyes and reassuring smiles. Her Hebrew was somewhat biblical and her accent Germanic, making it fun to mimic, but she didn't seem to mind. She made the school year fly by, and before long it was almost Passover — the holiday of spring and of Yulia.

For my parents, tradition wasn't a cause for soul-searching or for questioning a teacher's curriculum, even if it diverged dramatically from the norm. While the other classes made Seder plates and matzo covers and indulged sandbox reenactments of the delivery from Egypt, Miss Aviv brought a crate of eggs to our classroom, handed two or three to each child, and instructed us to paint them as creatively as possible.

"This is a very old tradition, children," she explained. "Tomorrow we'll be going on an egg hunt. Early in the morning, I'll hide the eggs on the hill, then you'll go looking for them. When you find them, you will put them in your special bag and take them home." No one could quarrel with that, the price of eggs being what it was.

The nearby hill was a bump in the land topped with eucalyptus trees and underbrush. Shortly before recess, Miss Aviv handed out paper bags and led us to the foot of the hill where she blew a tiny whistle.

"When you hear this sound, come back right away. Now go, and good luck!"

Yelling as loudly as we could, we ran in all directions and were soon separated. I looked under bushes and behind rocks but found nothing. The shrieks of glee faded and my paper bag remained empty.

"Hello, little boy," said a raspy voice.

Startled, I turned and saw an old woman in black rags holding a wicker basket. I had never seen the witch up close, and it took me a moment to recognize her. She attempted a smile, but even in the midday heat her black teeth made me shiver.

"Are you looking for these?" she asked, putting the basket on the ground.

I peeked in and saw a dozen painted eggs neatly arranged on a bed of straw. When I looked up, she was gone.

Miss Aviv's whistle pierced the April air. I grabbed the basket and ran to join the others. A few children were proudly holding an egg or two, but most stood around empty-handed. Miss Aviv stared at my bounty in disbelief and suggested that I share it with the less fortunate. I gave away half my unearned treasure with a heavy heart, and we returned to our classroom.

I felt much better when I gave Grandma the eggs after school.

"Free eggs!" she said. "I didn't expect such a colorful surprise."

* * *

The first-grade graduation outfits were all white: shirts, shorts, and hats adorned with flowers. While Grandma was ironing my shirt, Mother surprised me by suggesting we go out to pick wild flowers. We walked down the road past the last house to a meadow with buttercups, marigolds, and daffodils. I picked two handfuls and was ready to turn back when Mother said, "Let's keep walking, Danny. It's still early." And so we headed down a rust-colored lane along a row of cypresses whose dagger-shaped shadows taunted puddles blushed with sunset.

"Your father was a very handsome man," Mother said.

"Isn't he still?" I asked.

"Yes, of course he is. But you should have seen him after the war." She paused and fell silent, gazing into the distance. I wanted to hear more but thought we needed to hurry home before the flowers wilted.

"He came to our town after the war to stay with cousins because he had nowhere else to go. How great he looked in his uniform! It was the only outfit he owned, but that didn't matter. I fell in love with him the moment I saw him."

"So why don't you talk to each other anymore?" I asked.

Mother weighed her answer for a long time. "On an evening like this you can almost like this country."

"Grandpa and Father were friends, right?"

"Right." Her gaze returned from the purple distance. "Grandma was another story."

"Is Mr. Willenski still alive?"

"The photographer? Of course, Danny. He's only forty-five or so. What made you think of him?"

"I just remembered the family picture he once took of us. Father and Grandma were standing next to each other, but they were still smiling. How come?"

"Oh, Danny, you *have* to smile at cameras."

Father, Mother, and Grandma came to the ceremony the following day, and we all smiled at the very same time. The school year was over. I placed all my notebooks and art projects in the brown box Father had given me and wrote on it in slightly shaky block letters, "My First Grade."

I must have slept soundly that night because I didn't hear Father tiptoe out of the house and move to Tel Aviv, 50 km south of my bed. Somehow Mother and Grandma must have explained it to me the next morning, promising that Father would come to visit. Somehow I must have understood what they said or at least their unspoken plea that I not ask any questions.

In early autumn, two strong men loaded all our belongings onto a small truck and moved us to Haifa, 50 km north of our kitchen table. I didn't ask any questions because it was drizzling and Mother and Grandma were nervous and upset. And besides, I had a pretty good idea of what must have happened: when I wasn't looking, Ox let go of Leviathan's tail and the world lost its balance.

Still, I was excited when the big city came into view, and a billboard welcomed us with a warning that the use of car horns was forbidden. A strange pressure in my stomach didn't start until we entered the tiny apartment that was our new home. That evening, we ate supper in the cramped kitchen, and I brushed my teeth in the tiny bathroom. Surrounded by boxes, we lay in our beds in the living room listening to unfamiliar city noises lurking outside the window.

"Don't worry, I'm here," I heard myself say in the dark, getting two sighs in response.

— *Chapter Seventeen* —

By the time I get back to Haifa, it's close to midnight. Sarah had insisted I eat something before leaving, calling it our last supper.

"After all," she said, "as an architect you should know that two dimensions shouldn't mingle with a third unless chaperoned by a fourth, and time is not on our side."

Sitting behind Sarah on her scooter, with the wind blowing through her hair, I thought she was too young to let it go gray. Although I was exhausted when she dropped me off at the bus station, I knew enough not to make these my parting words. "Thanks for everything," I said. We hugged in silence, and I boarded the bus, taking a seat on the left side to be closer to the invisible sea.

Haifa is shut down for the night. I walk the dark streets to Esti's apartment, enjoying the peace and the fact that I have no associations with this neighborhood. I feel anonymous here, the way I do in Boston. Resident and alien in both, content enough in either, truly at home in neither. I pay no attention to a sudden stirring in the shadows. I have no time for someone else's ghosts.

A young woman in army fatigues is curled up on the dimly-lit landing, her head resting on a rucksack, hugging a black assault rifle as if it were a teddy bear. This girl could be my daughter. She wakes up with a beatific smile and explains that she doesn't have a key and is waiting for her mother to return home. I offer to get her a cold drink, but she just thanks me and goes back to sleep.

I open the apartment door and find a note from Tamar on the floor: *"Where are you?!"* I go back into the hall and knock lightly on her door.

A moment later she opens it a crack and calls over her shoulder, "It's one of the neighbors. I'll be right back." She is wearing a Disney T-shirt with Pluto's head resting comfortably between her breasts. She takes hold of my hand and smiles nervously.

"Whew! I guess this is how it feels to get caught in a lie," she whispers. Pluto, wide-awake now, wiggles his nose and sniffs her left nipple. "My husband's in there. Thank God the kids are asleep. I'll talk to you in the morning."

I clear my throat, but Tamar interrupts. "Please don't say anything now. Good night."

Day Five Lonely Miss Haifa

— *Chapter Eighteen* —

The phone is ringing. Gray light is seeping in through the shutters. The ringing had better stop before it wakes up Dorit and Eitan next door, lest they come out of their rooms bleary-eyed and run into their dead father. I really must get more sleep before calling Lori.

The phone keeps ringing, and I finally get up to answer it.

"Danny, thank God! What took you so long?" says Lori.

"I was asleep. Why are you calling?"

"I was worried. Are you all right?

"I'm OK."

"Listen, is there a Pensione Meggido near your cousin's apartment?"

"Why do you ask?"

"Just tell me!" Lori raises her voice. "I'm sorry, Danny. It's important."

"It's a couple of blocks from here." I remember passing it last night. "What's going on?"

I hear her catch her breath. "What floor are you on?"

"Third. What's wrong?"

"First promise me you won't go near the windows or open the door for anyone."

"Uh-huh."

"I'll take that as a promise. It's strange that I'm calling from halfway around the world to tell you what's happening around the corner from you. They've just interrupted the TV program with a live report from Haifa. A gang of terrorists came up from the sea, climbed the mountain and took over this little hotel. Some shooting has been reported, but according to a police source speaking on condition of anonymity, the property is currently vacant and under renovation."

Lori sounds like a field reporter hiding her anxiety behind facts and figures. All I can think of are buckets of paint and rolls of wallpaper the guerrillas might use as camouflage in order to gain some advantage in the ensuing room to room combat.

"Wait," says Lori, "I'm putting the phone up to the TV so we can both hear it."

"The situation is tense but calm," says the newscaster. "Police and border patrol forces have surrounded the hotel and are confident that all the guerrillas will be captured. This just in: sources have expressed concern that some of the terrorists may have escaped under cover of darkness and, as daylight breaks, may be roaming the adjacent neighborhoods in search of hiding places. Radio broadcasts and police cruisers equipped with loudspeakers are warning residents to stay inside and keep away from back yards and wooded areas."

Poor Lori, unable to do anything except warn her husband and hope he doesn't do anything foolish, like drinking his morning coffee on the balcony overlooking the back yard. One stray bullet ricocheting off the GE washer is all it would take to start a war, the Big One, between Lori and Mother. As in most wars, the pretext would be territory: should I be interred in the bosom of my homeland and buried under two meters of homeland soil, as Mother would phrase it in an unexpected outburst of patriotism, or under six feet of Diaspora dirt in the far reaches of the Suburban Boston Pale?

"Don't worry," I try to soothe her. "Things always sound worse from far away. I'm sure this report is mostly a teaser for the morning shows. Now I'm not saying they made it up, but I wouldn't worry too much. Go to sleep, and I'll call you tomorrow morning your time. It's not like I'm up north or anything."

A long pause. "Are you all right?" I ask.

"I'm fine. Be careful, Danny. Bye"

I go to the kitchen and put the kettle on. I peek out through a crack in the shutters. The pink horizon is turning blue. A bus stops in the street below to pick up a few riders. I make myself a cup of instant coffee and turn on the radio. It's clear that Lori's Boston sources are reliable. In a calm voice, the announcer warns all residents of this part of town to stay indoors until further notice and to refrain from opening doors or windows. I turn off the lights, make sure all the shutters are closed and wash the dishes. Over the running water I hear a door squeak, then rapid footsteps. Arms lock around me from behind, and I am pushed against the sink.

"Shh... don't say a word. God I'm glad to see you," whispers Tamar, hugging me fiercely. I just stand there motionless, focusing on thin lines of daylight between the shutter slats until my heart resumes its normal rhythm. I turn and lean back against the counter. Tamar is draped in a long, white T-shirt, ghostly in the half-light.

"How did you get in?" I ask.

"Through the door inside the hall closet. This apartment and mine used to be one. When it was subdivided, they left a connecting door between the closets. Your cousin and I decided to keep it unlocked and to use it only in case of an emergency. I figured that what I just heard on the radio constitutes an emergency."

"What about the kids?"

"They're still asleep. There won't be camp today. I left them a note to come here when they wake up."

"And your husband?"

"He left shortly after you got back last night."

I make more coffee, and we have it with toast and jam at the kitchen table. Sunlight creeps in through the shutters and paints wavy stripes over Tamar's body.

"This is so nice," she says.

"Nice?"

"I mean, such a relaxed morning. I don't have to rush like crazy to get the kids ready. You know, I can't remember the last time someone made me a cup of coffee in the morning." She leans back and closes her eyes contentedly. Slowly she slides forward on the slick plastic chair, and the sunny ribbons adjust themselves to her topography.

"I hardly recognized him," she says, apparently feeling safe enough behind the bars of light to broach the subject. "So skinny. And that crazy beard. I wonder what made him hide his handsome face." Tears fill her eyes. She collects them in a paper napkin and crushes it in her fist. She stands up, takes a deep breath as if preparing to say more but only shakes her head. She picks up the empty cups and walks over to the sink, rinses them and keeps watching the gushing water.

After a minute I walk over and shut the faucet.

"It's OK. You don't have to tell me any more. Really. Like you said, I'll only be here a few more days. Why confide in a stranger? Let's have more coffee and listen to the news."

I fill the kettle and put it back on the range. Tamar speaks haltingly, choosing her words with care. One by one they leave her lips, like paratroopers dropping from a plane. Like them, once out, they cannot return, bound either to land safely or crash.

"It took years after my parents' divorce before my mother started seeing other men. One day in sixth grade, as I was coming in from recess, I heard giggling and whispering and saw everyone staring at me. Then I noticed neatly chalked words on the blackboard." Her voice is cracking. It's not going to be a soft landing.

"It said, 'Tamar's mother is a whore. She got bored with her husband and now goes out with anyone she can find. She sits in their cars at night, hugging and kissing. Everyone can watch for free.'"

Tamar looks at me with teary eyes, trying to gauge my reaction. Would it comfort her if I told her this is a variation on a painful episode from my own childhood, or should I let her speak since she seems eager to continue?

"I wanted to walk up and erase those horrible lies but realized that I'd be standing alone in front of the entire class, so I sat down and buried my face in my hands. Someone touched my shoulder, and without looking up, I made a fist and swung my arm as hard as I could. When I sat up, I saw my teacher, Mrs. Grossman, holding a handkerchief to her bloody nose. I said, 'Oh, I'm so sorry. I didn't mean to,' and through my tears, I could see she understood."

I pour more coffee and wait.

"I was always worrying about what my classmates would think. I had almost reached the point where I could go to the movies by myself or with my mother without feeling that everyone was staring at me, wondering where my father was. Of course I still preferred to enter the theater in the dark, after the movie had started. You must really think I'm crazy, don't you? I bet you're an only child, brought up by two adoring parents, spoiled rotten, encouraged to do whatever you wanted, even if it meant going to America and leaving your elderly parents behind. Am I right?"

A police siren goes off nearby, saving me from having to correct her misconceptions. Tamar shudders and crosses her arms as if hugging herself. I too have the urge to embrace this lonely Miss Haifa, but stop myself when I remember that her kids might appear at any moment.

"One evening, about a year ago, Tom put the kids to bed and came into the living room. We watched the news, and he said he had to leave. He had made the decision to follow his calling and go to Africa to help the poor and starving. He was sick and tired of fighting for justice and parking spaces. He was frustrated by the political agendas of archaeological digs and by the incessant milking of sacred cows. And besides, he couldn't stand everyone always sticking their noses into everyone else's business around here. He kissed me on the cheek and went to bed."

"What did you do?" I ask.

"I flung open the living room window. I don't know if I intended to jump or just clear my head in the cool night air, but a wave of heat and humidity rolled in with a putrid smell from the refineries. I quickly closed the window, changed the air conditioner to the coldest setting, and spent the night on the sofa under a down comforter. By morning I was ready with my ultimatum. This is what I told him: 'When I was little, my father left my mother and me. Now you're leaving me and our children. The only way I'll go along with it is if you let me handle it. As soon as you leave, I'll tell people that you followed your idealism and went to Africa to help mankind. After a while I'll say that you went missing. From time to time, I'll put on a sad face and look worried. All you have to do is never come back.'"

She shakes her head as if she can hardly believe it herself.

"Tom told me he would go along with my script. He kept his word and disappeared without a trace. Sometime later I told the kids their father died a hero. It sounds cruel, but I know what it's like to grow up without a father around here. It's a lot easier on you if you lose him to death than to divorce."

I turn on the radio. It's playing an old Jacques Brel song. Now there's a guy who could have done something with Tamar's story.

"Mommy?" Dorit's voice sounds muffled behind the closet door.

"In here, sweetie. We're in the kitchen."

"Why didn't you wake us up for camp?"

"There's no camp today. The army is out there trying to catch some bad guys." Tamar is interrupted by an announcement on the radio advising us to stay indoors. "Go back to sleep. I'll be there in a little while to make you breakfast. Love you."

Tamar's long fingers move about restlessly, caressing the sugar bowl, curling around her coffee mug, grasping the edge of the table. They briefly touch my hand but retreat as she stands up.

"Stop by later," she says and heads for the closet.

"I will," I call after her. The door clicks shut, and it occurs to me that I've never uttered the words "I love you" in Hebrew.

— *Chapter Nineteen* —

Lieutenant Mia first addressed me at approximately 1300 hours on a winter day that was late shedding its morning fog. It rolled slowly down the mountain and collected in the valley below, shrouding the squalor of the town and obscuring the road to Nazareth. Bell towers and minarets reached out of the mist like a disembodied show of hands.

Our fortress, although the color of the parched terrain around it, did not blend well into its surroundings, disrupting the gentle curve of the hilltop and blocking the legions of dusty pines struggling for a foothold on its slopes.

I had just finished lunch and walked over to my favorite reading spot, a strip of coarse grass surrounding the flagpole. I leaned against a whitewashed boulder and opened my book, a forgettable Canadian novel I thought I might translate into Hebrew to escape the tedium of military routine. While reading, I made notations in the margins regarding anatomical terms used in the graphic accounts of lovemaking among Finnish immigrants in northern Ontario. Mia walked over and sat down a short distance away, closed her eyes and tilted her face toward the pale sun. A thin volume of poetry rested in her lap.

"What are you reading?" she asked quietly without opening her eyes, as if talking in her sleep.

Because I had traveled abroad as a teenager, I prided myself on a trace of an American accent, a broad perspective, and liberal views. And yet, I held it to be self-evident that all kibbutz girls were created equal, or at least ended up that way by the time they were drafted: arrogant, loathing all but kibbutz men, and sporting firm bodies and stubbly legs. Mia was soft-spoken, slender, and smooth. She was an officer from a small kibbutz on the coast, improbably addressing a skinny and bespectacled corporal from the city. It had only been a week or two since I had gotten permission to grow a beard, and the mature Abe Lincoln look I was after was still a confusion of teenage fuzz. Whatever reasons she might have had for striking up a conversation, my rank and looks were definitely not among them.

I had never spoken to a woman officer before, but then, realizing her eyes were still closed, I looked at her and saw a pretty girl my own age. I cleared my throat and told her about some of the tamer aspects of the novel, dwelling on the transplanted Scandinavians' passion for herring rather than on their proclivity for frolicking naked under a pile of furs. Mia moved her head slightly to face the sun but said nothing. Encouraged, I proceeded to tell her that, its slim premise not withstanding, it was the only English book I found on the base. *Julius Caesar* was fine, I said, but my matriculation exams were behind me, and now I wanted something lighter.

"How long have you been on base?" she asked.

"Only few weeks. Why?"

"Pity. My discharge date is next month." She paused. "I don't know anyone else who reads English novels just for fun. Can we chat again after lunch tomorrow?"

I agreed, and we met the next day and almost every day after that. We were even assigned night duty together, at first by accident and then by design. We would spend the time between rounds in the shabby duty officer's room, under a harsh fluorescent light. Across the desk from each other we would share the plate of scrambled eggs, vegetables and olives the cook prepared for us. We would sip reheated breakfast coffee in tin cups and listen to a transistor radio with so much static it made us feel far away and alone. At times, on off-duty nights, we would go out on the slope facing Nazareth. Sitting on an army blanket, sharing a mess kit cup of sweet Carmel wine, I would lean against a pine trunk, she would lean against me, and we would silently gaze at the silvery scene below.

Mia's last day of service was fast approaching. She said she had no plans for the future but never tired of hearing why I had always wanted to be an architect, how I was applying to American colleges, and what New England winters were like.

"There's just not enough time," she said one day after lunch. I didn't know what she meant but found myself nodding in agreement.

Our relationship remained platonic, whether because time was running out or because we knew our paths would soon diverge. When we interlocked hesitant fingers it was, I now believe, to construct a fence between us — protection from the occasional hints that our paths might merge if only we allowed our fingers greater freedom.

Everyone thought it strange that Mia requested to be on duty her last night on base. There were tears in her eyes when she asked me to be her duty sergeant that night. I told her I'd be at her command until dismissed.

I got a four-hour pass so I could hitchhike home and get food from Grandma. Before I left, she went to her rosewood nightstand and took out a small jar of instant coffee that an American cousin had thoughtfully sent after our latest war. She placed it in my hand and looked tenderly into my eyes, as if entrusting me with a family heirloom for protection on a dangerous journey.

"Don't worry," I said, hugging her on my way out.

Cloudy days end without the finality of a dying sun. They are born of and reclaimed by darkness without so much as a trace of color. To me, those are good days. That evening featured a travel-poster sunset, which didn't raise my spirits.

I took the first shift of guards to their posts and returned to the office, finding Mia behind the metal desk with tears in her eyes. I gave her a comforting hug. She just stood there in her olive-green overcoat, a petite army issue girl. I peeled off her damp coat and discovered she was wearing a non-regulation cream colored blouse, well coordinated with her military skirt. I spread a tablecloth on the desk and pulled out a chair for her before lighting a candle. From a dented file cabinet in the back of the room I produced a bowl of sweet and sour meatballs and placed some on each plate.

"This is lovely," she whispered.

We ate in silence. Mia seemed lost again. To cheer her up I told her about Grandma's recipe notebook which she had carried with her during the war and later aboard refugee ships and in detention camps. It was a good story. Mia listened attentively, but I could tell her mind was elsewhere.

I served the cold chicken with cucumber salad.

"I'm so sorry," she said.

She took a small bite of cucumber, put her fork down, and wiped her mouth. "I'm more scared than I thought I'd be. I've never done it, and I hate to be so unsure of myself."

"I understand. Everything is so simple in the army. There are rules, regulations, and manuals. And, just to be sure, someone's always around to bark orders. Now you're going to be on your own, so it's only natural to be a bit worried. Still, the kibbutz should provide structure and..."

"No, no," she interrupted. "That's not what I meant." She hesitated a moment, then managed a smile. "So what's for dessert?"

"Plums in syrup and Viennese crescents." When I returned to the table, carefully balancing two bowls, Mia suddenly turned and hugged my waist, sending a shower of crimson drops onto the white tablecloth.

"Would you please kiss me?" she asked timidly, the way someone might ask to borrow a large sum of cash from a stranger.

I bent down and placed my mouth on hers. Her lips parted without warning and, falling in, I encountered a cold tongue. Even with my limited experience in matters of the heart, I could tell how nervous she was. I retreated, kissed her forehead, and sat down.

"When I said before that I was scared, I didn't mean about civilian life. I've never been in love, but now I think I might be, and it scares me." She stood up resolutely and looked straight at me. "I'd like us to make love. Sorry for being so direct, but we have no time to waste."

I reached out and wove my fingers through hers, but that didn't stop her.

"Hold me," she said and pulled me toward the door.

With arms around each other's waist we walked to the clerk's office. Mia gave instructions to call her in case of a problem and steered me toward the women's quarters.

We entered through a back door, moving quickly and silently until we got to her room. Once inside, she bolted the door, drew the curtains, and turned on the light. Mia had transformed the spartan cell into a cozy bedchamber. An imitation Persian rug covered the floor, and framed posters added color to the room. The narrow iron bed with fresh linens and frilly pillows had been turned down. On a scarred ammunition crate stood a bottle of chocolate liqueur and two glasses. Mia lit a new candle and put her arms around me.

"I'm sorry for being so inexperienced," she said, looking down at the spot where our bodies touched. "Will you help me?"

We sat down on the rug, and I poured some liqueur into the glasses. I raised mine and she followed suit, taking a tiny sip with a sigh of relief. I kissed her gently, she kissed me back assertively, and soon we were entwined in a passionate if somewhat acrobatic embrace.

The transition from platonic to amorous bypassed any reservations we might have had. At times she opened her eyes to assess the situation. She so wanted to do the right thing. Flattered as she made me feel, the fact remained that this was new and unfamiliar territory for me as well. What next, I wondered as I felt her trembling hands reach for my buttons.

She opened my shirt pocket before realizing she was off course. Changing direction, she reached under my shirt, not so much caressing me as counting my ribs. Her civilian blouse posed no obstacle, but her military skirt put up considerable resistance.

"Just tear the damn thing off," she muttered. "I won't be wearing it again."

It was the first and last time I vandalized army property. Something in the tearing and ripping injected fresh heat into our simmering encounter. She grabbed my left ear and in a beguiling whisper said, "Pick me up and take me to bed, soldier, and that's an order!" I carried her over and lowered her onto the bed, stupefied at the uncensored scene unfolding before me. The candle flame flickered and shadows danced wildly as I descended into her open arms. I could hear her rapid breathing, the groan of the unpracticed bedsprings, the discharge of a submachine gun.

We froze. Someone outside the window called Mia's name. "Coming," she replied in a loud but unsteady voice. We dressed quickly and ran outside to check the guard posts. At one of them we found a badly shaken soldier who had accidentally discharged his rifle, forever scarring an aging eucalyptus and cutting short a valiant attempt at lovemaking.

Back in Mia's room we sat on the rug, sipped the remaining liqueur and looked into each other's eyes, vainly seeking to rekindle the mood. We smiled and interlocked our fingers.

Mia's alarm clock woke us early next morning. Sunlight was filtering in through the curtains. Her head was in my lap, mine on the edge of her bed. The candle had long since drowned its wick. We combed each other's hair and went out to dismiss the guards. At the flagpole she said, "I'll see you later," and peeled off toward the officers' dining room. I continued to the soldiers' mess for a breakfast of hard-boiled eggs and weak coffee.

After lunch, I went to the flagpole with my book and sat down on the patch of coarse grass. The flag above fluttered in the breeze like an angel's wing, or a vulture's. I read and made notations in the margins. No one interrupted me.

— *Chapter Twenty* —

Someday Josh and I will step off the bus and ascend the steep road to my old army base. It will be hot and quiet with a breath of distant smoke and a call to prayer carried on the breeze. I will recall how the sun broke through the clouds shortly after Mia left, its light collecting in the barren courtyard. We will gaze at the outwardly sinister building where I spent two years of my life. The guard at the gate will patiently listen to my explanation of nostalgia and the need to tame restless memories. He will check with the duty officer then politely decline to let us in. On our way down the hill, Josh will slip his hand into mine as if to say, at least you've got me. The fortress behind us will keep shrinking and Mia will keep fading, but never completely.

* * *

It's early afternoon, and this is what I know now:

About the Pensione: It's surrounded by soldiers and police. Neighbors are cooperating by hiding behind curtains and shutters. The terrorists might well be relaxing in the air-conditioned guestrooms. The situation remains fluid.

About Mother: She sounds almost upbeat when she calls to tell me the stream of visitors has slowed to a trickle. Only Uncle Avrum lingers, as if hoping a smoked duck will fly in for lunch. I promise to come and visit as soon as we get the all clear.

About the apartment: My cousin's appliances are doing fine, pleasing in both form and function, their usefulness beyond reproach. Aunt Mitzi will be thrilled to hear how fond I've become of them.

About my past: It no longer has my undivided attention. The present keeps intruding.

About Tom: All is hearsay.

About Tamar: As unsettling as I find her wishful rewrites of her past, I somehow understand her motives when she sits across the table from me. I can't help but empathize when I see her grab the salt shaker to steady her hands.

The closet door squeaks open, and Eitan rushes in with a sandwich on a colorful paper plate.

"It's from Mommy. She says you'll like it. Guess what. I thought I heard Daddy's voice last night. I'm almost sure of it, but Mommy says it was just a dream. Mommy says you should drink a lot of water and stay out of the sun. Oh, and you should come for supper tonight." He runs back into the closet and slams the door behind him.

The gentle breeze from the sea blows across the coastal highway and through the cemetery, climbs a gorge and takes Pensione Meggido from the rear. It caresses sweaty troops and guerillas alike and steals into Esti's apartment down the street with scents of wild flowers and salty air, perhaps a warning disguised as a bouquet of Haifa past.

* * *

I should have guessed that what is probably the only La-Z-Boy recliner in the Middle East would be found in my cousin's apartment. Aunt Mitzi never mentioned it, probably because it's not the motorized model with automatic massage and built-in speakers. Sadly, this overstuffed throne of crushed velour has been relegated to a dark corner like an old pet that has outlived its cuteness but not its sentimental value. With a sudden surge of homesickness, I sink into its decadent softness, pull the lever, and assume a dozing position.

The sound of a loud explosion catapults me from the recliner's warm embrace. I reach the window in time to see two solar panels soar above Pensione Meggido like silver wings flapping in the late afternoon sun. For a moment, they hover high above, their shattered glass surfaces reflecting what looks like a coded message, then glide down and disappear in the gorge. Smoke from a second explosion billows up, spreading in all directions.

Tamar emerges from the closet and rushes over to hug me. I reach for the transistor radio and fumble with the dial, but she grabs my arms, locking them behind her back. When she releases me, I turn on the radio in time for a live report from around the corner. Our forces have stormed Pensione Meggido, killing, wounding, or capturing all of the guerillas. No losses on our side.

The phone rings, but I decide not to answer it. It's probably Lori, and I'd rather speak with her in private. After three rings, Tamar looks up quizzically.

After the fourth she asks, "Aren't you going to answer it?"

After the fifth I say, "Not right now."

Another ring, and an answering machine I didn't know existed blares out a greeting. Lori's voice fills the room.

"Just heard the news. So relieved it's over. I'd still be careful though. What if one of them managed to get away? They showed an aerial photo of the hotel, and you could see a wadi behind the building. Looks like the perfect escape route to me. Anyway, enough long-distance advice."

Tamar is slumped in the recliner, holding on to both armrests as if pleading for an embrace.

"Josh, say hi to Daddy," says Lori with the tone and pitch reserved for the baby in her life.

"Ooh-ooh!" says Josh, adding a gurgling sound and signing off with a hiccup.

"See? He misses you so much," says Lori and adds in a whisper, as if trying to spare the feelings of an accidental listener, "And so do I. Call me later."

The answering machine clicks off.

"Why didn't you tell me you were married?"

"I was going to."

"That should have been the first thing you told me."

She rushes into the closet, and I drop into the warm contours she left in the recliner.

— *Chapter Twenty-One* —

"Sorry, I didn't mean to wake you," says the voice on the phone.

"What time is it?"

"Ten o'clock. I thought you'd still be up."

"That's OK. Who is this?"

"Tom. Tamar's husband. I don't know if she told you about me."

"A little. Sounds complicated."

"Tamar mentioned you the other day. Something about your being an architect in America. I'd like to talk to you, if you can spare some time before you leave."

"Sure," I say. "Maybe tomorrow?"

"No, it can't wait. It's still pretty early and you've already had some sleep. Can you meet me tonight?"

"OK, why don't you come over now?"

"Impossible. How about neutral territory? Do you remember Mother's Park?"

"Of course."

"Good. We'll meet there at eleven." He sounds like Ozhik, my commanding officer: calm, authoritative, never doubting that his wishes, let alone commands, would be promptly carried out. Tom's words are not a plea but the summons to a nighttime operation.

"Stand with your back to the sculpture of the mother and baby and follow the path in the one o'clock direction until you get to the duck-shaped fountain. Turn left 90 degrees and take the steps down to the lower playground. I'll be the one on the middle swing. Any questions."

"No. I'll be there."

Tom has the last word. "Danny, this is top secret." He hangs up.

The thing about Ozhik was that he, like Tom, left you feeling important, singled out, and eager to complete the mission.

In the bathroom I find a note taped to the mirror:

> *Sorry I behaved inappropriately. We came by to invite you for supper, but your snoring was so loud we were afraid to wake you. I put your meal in the fridge. Enjoy!*
>
> *Tamar*

Suddenly ravenous, I wolf down Tamar's cold supper and hurry down to catch the bus to Mother's Park. Mozart's requiem spills out from a nearby window onto the dimly lit sidewalk. A dark figure wearing a checkered kaffiyeh approaches, carrying a heavy load. With a little sigh, the man puts down a plastic basket of fruits and vegetables and studies the bus schedule.

"Ten minutes," he says, wiping his forehead with a corner of his kaffiyeh.

"Thank you," I say.

The bus arrives on time, and five minutes later I get off at the entrance to the park. The street is choked with traffic, the sidewalks with tourists. Car horns follow me into the park, but not the city lights. The path soon widens into a small plaza. In the moonlight I make out the statue Tom mentioned. Big Band tunes from a nearby hotel float on the warm air. It's five minutes to eleven. I walk into the thickening darkness, turn left at the fountain, and find the steps to the playground. Here I stop, hesitant to descend into the black void. A siren wailing outside the park and a rhythmic squeaking from below increase my anxiety. I cough, and the squeaking stops.

"Danny?" I recognize Tom's voice.

"Where are you?"

"Down here. There are no kids around so take any swing you like."

Slowly I feel my way to the bottom. A disembodied hand grips mine.

"So glad you made it," says Tom.

We sit down on a bench deep within the womb of Mother's Park. The silence and my inability to see his face make me uneasy. Tom shuffles his feet on the ground. It's a welcome distraction and I do the same. A cap is popped from a bottle.

"What have you got there?" I ask.

"Perfume," says Tom, inhaling deeply three or four times and letting out a contented "Ahh..."

"Where did you get it?"

"The duty-free shop at the Johannesburg airport. Tamar wore it all the time. As soon as I saw it, I knew I had to have it. It was the best companion on my trip"

I am tempted to ask him to remove the cap again but fear the request might betray something I'd rather keep to myself.

"I appreciate your coming on such short notice," says Tom. "I asked you to meet me because I don't have much longer to live."

He pauses as if to ponder the words he has uttered, possibly for the first time. "I think of Tamar and me as two cogwheels, rotating in tandem but in opposite directions, our energy squandered in heat and friction."

I hear liquid being poured. "Have some coffee," says Tom, gulping. "I brought a thermos." I sip quietly from the cup he hands me.

Tom takes another gulp of coffee.

"When I was a teenager, my father was diagnosed with cancer. Somehow we got used to his emaciated figure shuffling around the apartment. His condition gradually deteriorated until he became totally helpless. My mother had to quit her job to become his full-time caregiver. Their bedroom looked like a hospital room. The last thing I remember was seeing his skeletal body before the burial society took him away. His eyes were closed, his forehead was smooth and peaceful, but his beak-like mouth was open in a frozen chirp. The worst part was the guilt we felt over our relief that he had finally passed away."

Tom sighs and continues.

"About a year ago my doctor told me I had an inoperable tumor. He suggested I think about how to tell my family so we could prepare for the short time I had left. After leaving the doctor's office, I went straight to Café Ritz and ordered Viennese coffee with whipped cream and two slices of Bavarian chocolate cake. This wasn't enough to satisfy me, so I ordered apple strudel and another coffee. With sugar and caffeine coursing through my veins, I came up with a plan."

He pauses for another gulp then refills my cup.

"I decided I wouldn't tell anyone about my diagnosis and

spare my family the prolonged suffering we endured while my father was dying. I told Tamar I was bored and disgusted with life in this country and would go to Africa to help the poor and the starving. Once I got there, I checked into a remote resort of tents and thatched-roofed huts and started to feel better. For a long time my cancer didn't slow me down, but when my symptoms got worse I decided it was time to go home."

Tom stretches his legs and pours the rest of the coffee into our cups.

"The beard I had grown made me unrecognizable. Even old friends didn't give me a second look. The other night I stopped by to see Tamar. She let me in and we started talking. There was a knock at the door, and she went out into the hall for a few minutes. Because she had told me the kids were asleep, I looked in on them one last time."

Tom falls silent for a moment.

"You know Danny, we never did get divorced. When I saw Tamar again, I thought about asking her to take me back for the little time I had left. I had thought about this many times during my travels, although I knew it would probably be too late to revise her script."

I hear the thermos knocking against the bench and reach into the darkness to steady Tom's trembling hand.

"The thing is, I never thought about what I'd do if I needed help. I read about this small hospice at a convent outside Tiberias overlooking the Sea of Galilee. It sounded perfect: compassionate care, fresh food grown by the nuns, and amazing views. I spoke with them, and they approved me for admission. Now all I need is someone to drive me there. You hardly know me, but would you be willing to do it?"

"Of course," I say without hesitation, hugging his shoulders.

Tom falls asleep at some point. I nod off too.

When dawn breaks, Tom is stretched out across the bench, one leg over the back, the other on the ground, his head in my lap. There is a chill in the air. Our clothes are damp with dew. An unseen bird breaks into song.

We emerge bleary-eyed from Mother's Park and go looking for coffee. Crates of warm rolls and bundles of fresh newspapers are stacked in front of shuttered cafés and grocery stores, but nothing is open yet.

We hug and agree that I'll pick him up at his hotel three days from now and drive him to the hospice.

Day Six *First Resorts*

— *Chapter Twenty-Two* —

The sky is slashed red and scarred purple. The humid air thumps against my chest as I stand on the balcony watching rotor blades part the morning clouds. Soon the helicopters disappear on their way north. The gash in the clouds heals quickly and silence is restored.

A moving truck pulls up in front of the apartment building across the street. Three burly men jump out and begin unloading. The father accompanies the movers as they carry boxes upstairs. The mother keeps an eye on their son, happily riding his tricycle on the sidewalk. I go back to bed.

* * *

Each sunny day is sunny in its own way; rainy days are all alike. When a mist wafts across balconies and through back yards, or when a downpour overruns a city, hurtling through its streets with a veil of spray and train of fog, that city is always Haifa on the day we moved there: wet asphalt and muddy yards; rejuvenated greenery and moisturized dust; and a soft grayness gathering in its folds rich and poor, young and old, married and divorced, all equally swathed and hidden.

The transition from small town to big city was mostly a visual experience and a slightly nauseating one. I felt as if I were on a carousel horse galloping furiously, with Hadera and Haifa circling ever faster around me, blurring into streaks of colors and lights. I held on to my horse's ears for dear life, hoping he would slow down before I got sick, and wondering where I'd find myself when the whirling finally stopped.

And so, unnoticed, Haifa's population increased by three. In my mind, our tiny second-floor apartment was like a dollhouse with oversized furniture. Besides the kitchen and bathroom, there was the living room that doubled as a bedroom for Mother and me. It opened onto a narrow balcony enclosed with plywood, which became Grandma's so-called "half room."

We were still getting used to our new surroundings when I woke one night to a frightful scream. At the sound of another shriek, Mother and I jumped up from our beds to check on Grandma. A wind gust had forced open the window next to her bed, allowing the top of a frenzied cypress to barge in and give Grandma an unexpected whipping. Mother closed the window. I hugged Grandma, and we all sat on her bed laughing until Mother went in to make tea.

A few days later, two painters arrived, carrying a ladder, brushes, and buckets of paint. They moved the furniture to the center of the living room, covered it with a drop cloth and got to work.

Grandma never hesitated to buck a trend, especially an expensive one, but this time she made an exception by going with the latest look: two adjacent walls in one color, the other two in a contrasting color, and a white ceiling.

I positioned myself in the corner and observed the men at work. They had already painted two walls a pale yellow and were getting the light gray paint ready for the other two when the painter by the window whistled softly and gestured to his partner to join him. They leaned out the window and heaved a sigh.

"Have you ever done this?" one of them asked me, clenching and unclenching his fists as if kneading mounds of dough. Unable to contain my curiosity, I joined them at the window. From our vantage point, the painters were leering at a zaftig neighbor hanging laundry over the balcony rail. The flimsy housedress she wore could not corral her ample breasts. As she leaned over, her grand bosom made a bid for freedom, a glorious struggle much appreciated by the men.

"Huh, huh?" grunted one, jabbing my ribs.

"Leave the poor boy alone. He's still young," said the other, winking at me. "He'll have his hands full soon enough." They laughed heartily as I retreated to the kitchen.

Long after our renovated apartment had shed its fresh paint smell, I kept hoping to catch another glimpse of those bounteous breasts, but to no avail. When I did see her again, our neighbor was dressed for the cooler, rainy weather. Around the same time, Grandma unpacked the down comforters and pronounced the official start of winter. Wrapped snugly for the night, I still had trouble falling asleep on my narrow bed, kept awake by whispers in the kitchen and water in the downspouts.

* * *

This was my conundrum: I had to explain love to someone five decades older than me without understanding it myself. And not just anyone, but Grandma. And not just love, but carnal love, all the while reading the Hebrew subtitles of the French movie, paraphrasing the dialogue in German, providing the gist of the plot, attempting to convey the humor in the situation, and keeping my language appropriate.

It was a stressful job, made harder by Grandma's frequent queries:

"What did she say?" (Nonchalantly, "Underwear")

"What did he say?" (Carefully, "That he had seen his mother... do something once")

"What, Dannika, *what?!*" ("I didn't get that," which gave me the 15-second respite I needed to catch up with the plot myself).

Our fellow moviegoers added to the stress by shushing and hissing at us with increasing venom, lacking any appreciation for the display of our inter-generational love.

Mother was not as adept at simultaneous translation and plot encapsulation. When we went to the movies, Grandma would soon get annoyed by Mother's lagging commentary and switched seats to be next to me, provoking a vociferous protest from the people behind us. At those times, I would sink into my seat and be thankful that movies were shown in the dark.

But the most stressful part of any movie was emerging from the theater into the world outside — a menacing, voyeuristic world buzzing with unspoken questions: "Keeping Granny and Mommy company? Where's Daddy?"

— *Chapter Twenty-Three* —

Father would visit once a week. On those days, I finished my homework early and sat on the kitchen balcony until I saw him come up the path. We often went to the movies which we both loved, whatever the genre or language. Located as we were at the crossroads of East and West, we had our choice of American, British, French, Italian, Greek, Turkish, Egyptian, and Indian films. Afterwards we would go to a small restaurant with a limited menu. It was Father's favorite because it reminded him of the old days. The offerings included hardboiled eggs with onions; pickled herring with onions; chicken soup with carrots and onions; and a salad of finely chopped tomatoes, cucumbers and onions. Father's stories supplied the props — field kitchens, tents, tanks, and troop trains — to make those meals memorable culinary events. I enjoyed his tales of danger, deprivation, and redemption even though they dealt with ancient times of at least a dozen years earlier.

One day, having exhausted menu options and war stories, Father decided it was time I had a closer look into his past and took me to the Communist club on Nordau Street. It was a converted second floor apartment, identified by a large mailbox and a plaque reading "Red Warriors' Club." Father's brand of Communism was of the idealistic, wishful type, which dwelled on what might have been but never was. The corruption of ideals, the rape of the land, the purges and mass killings were all checked at the door. Over glasses of boiling tea from the electric samovar, Father introduced me to Russian history and traced his own military exploits on faded campaign maps.

The Communist platform, as far as I could tell, consisted of a few simple planks: the smell of Soviet periodicals; the rousing Red Army Choir songs; the Russian lustily spoken by potbellied veterans; and Sergei Eisenstein's early film classics. On that platform I constructed my theory that history may have as much to do with a father's stories, propaganda films, and foot stomping tunes as with incontrovertible evidence.

Today, on my way to the pharmacy to pick up Mother's prescription, I stop briefly in front of the old house on Nordau Street for a minute of silence in honor of the veterans who used to come here long ago for tea and camaraderie. The former club is now an upscale shop dealing in gold and silver religious objects. On this very spot, Father and I once ran into a former comrade of his.

Boomy wore a khaki jacket with tarnished brass buttons and a broad smile full of gold and silver teeth. Upstairs, waiting for my tea to cool, I asked Father if the name Boomy had anything to do with the booms of wartime explosions. Father nodded. I was hoping for a good story. Instead, Father told me about the anguish of war heroes in times of peace which, for Boomy, meant pining for a glorious past in a dreary present while wishing for a short and painless future.

Boomy and his wife, Flora, had arrived penniless from Russia after the war and were forced to accept public housing in a sprawling tent city near the Haifa beach. Every dozen tents shared an outhouse and an outdoor shower. Heat, humidity, and blinding sunlight were plentiful and free. Boomy suffered silently in the heat but worried what life in that place was doing to Flora.

He somehow managed to find an old bathtub for his beloved, although he couldn't figure out where to find water to fill it. This didn't seem to bother his wife.

In late summer afternoons, Flora would put on her mink coat and recline in the bathtub outside her tent. Rusty and dented in places, its lion's feet treading sand, it was nonetheless the only tub in the tent city. Some day, she used to say, they'd have running water to fill it. Boomy would nod, and the medals on his threadbare jacket would swing to and fro, reflecting specks from the setting sun and marking the time to darkness.

When women would gather to admire Flora's coat, Boomy would turn his back on the waterless bathing ritual and wish someone would join him for a glass of tea. He would sit perfectly still some distance away, watching the sun go down. His medals, dangling at the end of frayed ribbons, were the only sign of life not yet extinguished.

At the Red Warriors' Club one afternoon, Boomy told us how a thunderclap woke Flora one night, but he had heard nothing, since explosions were just lullabies to his battle-hardened ears. He slept through the torrential rain rarely seen in summer. When he got up the next morning, he found Flora sitting on the rim of her bathtub now filled with water, running her fingers across its shimmering surface and humming an old tune. He told her how happy he was that her dream had finally come true, but she said she couldn't risk ruining her mink coat and asked him to help her drain the tub before her friends arrived.

"We should visit Boomy sometime," Father would say to me. By the time I reminded him that we never had, the Red Warriors' Club had closed its doors, and the tent city had been replaced with dense apartment blocks. Back then, most people didn't own a phone and could not be located, certainly not those known only by their wartime nicknames.

* * *

Father didn't have a nickname. His comrades in the Red Army, which he had voluntarily joined to fight the German invaders, called him by his surname which to them meant Jewish, bookish, and bespectacled.

Father didn't have, nor did he aspire to, a brilliant military career, but he was proud of his facility with languages which enabled his side to communicate with both allies and enemies.

And now Father didn't have Mother, only memories of the 24-year-old girl he had married after the war and with whom he had tried to build a life in the face of domestic skirmishes for which his linguistic skills were no match.

After their divorce, Father rented a sparsely furnished room on a quiet street in Tel Aviv. With only a narrow bed, a small desk, a bookcase, and two chairs, one of them doubling as a nightstand, he had plenty of room left for memories and dreams.

I wonder how long Father enjoyed his anonymity in the big city. No doubt he read a lot in his secluded room, maintained his correspondence, and tended to his stamp collection. He was about the age I am now, so I'm sure he spent a good part of his time remembering old girlfriends, wondering where they were, and imagining himself in their company. Looking at the narrow bed in that small chamber which sunlight never reached, he may have chuckled at the thought.

Not that tiny spaces are necessarily a bad thing. He probably remembered the tents of his teens in Romania, when he took his youth group on rafting trips down the Prut River or on hikes in the Carpathian Mountains. He still had a few photos from those years which he displayed in the corner of his desk.

One summer day after third grade, Mother put me on the bus to Tel Aviv and wished me a good time with Father. He had suggested I come so he could show me his new city, but it was so hot and humid I was glad to forego sightseeing in favor of a quiet visit in his cool room. Father showed me brochures from the city tourist bureau with maps and photos of local landmarks. When he kept glancing at his watch, I could tell something else was on his mind.

Before long, a woman I had never seen before came by for a visit. In that awkward scene, Father had the main speaking part. He introduced her as Vera, a friend. He shared things about me that I was mostly familiar with and things about her that I immediately forgot. Vera and I smiled timidly as we watched Father prepare the refreshments. He moved about clumsily, spilled some of the water he had boiled for tea, and almost forgot to serve the cookies, giving us an excuse not to converse.

Vera kept looking over at Father, but he kept his eyes on his teacup. After a while, she turned and asked me about school and my favorite subjects. I answered in a tone that discouraged further conversation. Not much else was said.

"Till soon, then" said Vera, standing up and touching Father's arm, a gesture he did not reciprocate. Suddenly I remembered my manners and called out, "Nice to meet you," as the door closed behind her.

Father ruffled my hair and sat down at his desk. I sat down

beside him as he laid out old photos of himself as a teenager. In one of them, Father was standing on a felled tree trunk in a dense forest with two girls sitting on either side, looking up at him adoringly. In another, Father and a girl his own age were sitting in front of a small tent, holding hands.

"We were very close back then," said Father in a whisper, as if thinking out loud without meaning to share. "She stopped me on the street not long ago, but I didn't recognize her until she pulled a copy of this picture from her wallet. We had tea at a sidewalk café and reminisced for a long time. After a while, it felt as if we were competing to see who remembered more. I soon realized that what we still shared of our past were random fragments which no longer fit together."

"So why did you and Mother get divorced?" I asked quietly, as if not wanting to hear the answer.

Father sighed deeply. Following his gaze, my eyes landed on my parents' wedding picture, a small print propped up against some Tolstoy or other.

"In a few years you'll be ready for *War and Peace*," he said.

We walked the few blocks to the sea and watched the sunset. Later, sitting by the open window, we had sandwiches for supper while Father told me another of his stories about Foxy, a reddish horse and wartime companion who had gotten him out of many a tight spot. Even when I began to suspect that Foxy was imaginary, I still considered him as real as Boomy and Father. To this day, I sometimes see him in trot-on cameos on the banks of the Volga, on the steppes of Kazakhstan, or under the Brandenburg Gate.

That night I slept in Father's bed. He stayed up late working at his desk and was asleep in his chair when daylight woke me.

— *Chapter Twenty-Four* —

Mother had two strikes against her when learning to type to enhance her chances of finding a clerical job. Hebrew was her fourth and weakest language, and the Royale typewriter she practiced on was a daunting apparatus. It sounded like a machine gun and tended to break fingernails, especially the long ones Mother grew and polished to further enhance her prospects. I offered to help and, being good with my hands, was assigned the task of changing the inked ribbons.

As her typing progressed and her skills improved, Mother's confidence increased, her public smiles brightened, and her new shoes had markedly higher heels. Around that time, she frequently mentioned the name Rudy. I soon learned he was a childhood friend of Mother's whom she happened to run into. Discovering he too was divorced, she allowed things to take an uncharted course.

When Rudy came by unannounced one evening, Mother decided to forgo her nightly typing practice. Grandma and I confined ourselves to the kitchen and gave the young couple the run of the living room. I did my homework, and Grandma had a glass of tea. We kept looking at each other and at the closed living room door. We heard soft music followed by a peal of laughter that stopped Grandma in mid-sip. Soon a familiar tango announced itself with an assertive opening flourish.

Grandma took that as her cue to quickly prepare a tray of tea and cake. I opened the living room door and she marched in, placed the tray on the table and, as long as she was already there, sat down to watch the dancing. Rudy, an optician, possessed the requisite peripheral vision to lead Mother across the small room in a bold yet mannered tango without bumping into Grandma or the furniture.

I watched from the door as Rudy and Mother executed the tango crisply and fluidly. When the dance was over, Grandma and I applauded enthusiastically. Rudy turned off the radio, and we all sat down for refreshments.

I had never seen Mother as charming and talkative as she was that evening, nor had I ever heard anyone lavish compliments more generously than Rudy. Charm and compliments were exponentially reinforcing. Grandma beamed, I think I smiled, and when Rudy invited Mother to a party on Saturday night, we all accepted with a sigh of relief. Grandma and I retired to the kitchen where I soon nodded off at the table.

Mother and Rudy remained an item for a number of months. She didn't talk about it, but her smiles said it all. Once I boldly asked her if she loved him. She coyly changed the subject, which I took as a yes. Not having heard Rudy's name mentioned in a few weeks, I asked her if she was still seeing him. This time she did not change the subject.

As a third grader, I was still a bit confused and wondered how Mother really felt about him. For some reason, I also felt relieved, thinking, "This place is too small for that much happiness anyway."

Although Mother's smile diminished for a time, her skills improved and her fingernails remained intact. She soon got a good job with benefits and interesting coworkers which made it easier to forget Rudy, but, for a while, she would change stations whenever a tango was played on the radio.

— *Chapter Twenty-Five* —

Herman, Mother's cousin, wore his shoes on the wrong feet and didn't mind when children called him Charlie Chaplin. What was important, I once heard him say, was that the constant pressure on his toes kept him alert even on hot afternoons in his stuffy office. It also made him long for his nightly footbath at home. What else did he have to look forward to at the end of the day in his tiny apartment overlooking a cement factory?

The serpentine street leading up the hill to his apartment block was covered with white dust from the tall smoke stacks looming like cathedral spires over the working-class neighborhood. By the time he reached his apartment, Herman looked like a ghost. After brushing himself off and leaving his shoes by the door, he reclined in front of the closed window and massaged his sore feet. Looking out, he always saw the same dreamlike wintry scene, even in the cruelest summer heat. He searched the top of the smoke stacks for a hint of breeze, but their discharge hovered there motionless in the gathering dusk.

That spring Grandma declared open season on matzos. Apparently forgetting that, unlike the forty years in the desert, Passover lasted only one week, she bought enough of the crispy perforated armor to shield us from hunger until fall. In our humid land, matzos quickly turned soggy, obliging us to chew, crunch, and grind our way through that abundant surplus before the dairy deluge of Shavuot was upon us.

One evening, in the middle of our gnawing and pulverizing,

Herman appeared with a radical proposition. That summer Mother should get away for a week to a resort, be among people, and have a good time. All by herself. Who knows, maybe she'd even meet a nice man. In my bed across the room, pretending to be asleep, I heard Grandma say, "Absolutely," as she stood up abruptly and went to the kitchen.

"I can't go without her," whispered Mother to her cousin.

"But you must," insisted Herman. "You won't be doing anyone any favors by staying single the rest of your life. A resort is the best place to meet men, and you'll do better by yourself."

Absolutely, I agreed silently.

When it came to resorts, good times, and matters of the heart, be they related to love or cholesterol, Herman was the family's widely recognized authority. Not only was he the only one of Mother's generation to have remained a bachelor and become a vegetarian but, being highly placed in the Labor Federation, had free access to the many resorts open only to union members, thus circumventing long waiting lists.

"So, what do you suggest?" asked Mother, looking nervously toward the kitchen door.

"I'll reserve a room for you — just you — for sometime in August. Go and have fun!"

"I'll do it," she said with a pained expression and went to help Grandma with the refreshments.

And so it was that Mother, Grandma, and I spent an enjoyable week that summer at the famous *Convalescent Home of the Labor Federation's Sick Fund*. We shared Mother's room, had our own table in the dining room, went together to the auditorium for the nightly movie or concert, and retired when it was my bedtime.

We met some wonderful and interesting people, especially by the pool and during afternoon coffee on the terrace. Mother made friends with several women and resolved to talk to male guests the following summer.

A year later, Cousin Herman made a new reservation for Mother, again tried to convince her to go by herself, and again was rebuffed. After that, he stopped offering advice but continued to reserve a room for her every summer.

* * *

Standing on the utility balcony in the cool dampness of the late-night hour, fragrances ripen and fill my nostrils along with the steam from my tea. I wish I had a chocolate-frosted Entermann's donut to go with it. I lean against Esti's GE washer the way cowboys in the Old West leaned against their horses on cold nights.

Grandma is resting in her grave. Mother is sleeping alone in her bed. Father is crisscrossing the globe.

I take a quiet sip so as not to disturb the stillness of the night. The hum of the sea below is faint but soothing. After seeing Mother's photo albums, I easily conjure up my younger self, receding into the distance but still recognizable. My future self is drawing nearer from an equal but opposite distance. Harder to perceive is my present self, a blurry figure on shaky ground.

Day Seven *Doubles*

— *Chapter Twenty-Six* —

Today is the last day of Shiva. I told Mother I'd come over to mark the occasion with her.

I nod off on the bus, miss my stop and get off at the end of the line in front of the old train station by the port. As a child, I came here occasionally during school vacations, sat on one of the long wooden benches, watched nervous people mill about, and listened to the garbled announcements of departures and arrivals. I got as close to the trains as the conductors would allow and wished I could board one without knowing where it was going. True, Tel Aviv and Jerusalem were the only possible destinations, and neither was terribly far, but what better escape?

Since my last visit, bus stops have been relocated and route numbers changed which tells me I've been away too long. My bus arrives, and I take a seat by the rear door to avoid close contact on this sticky day. The door closes and the bus starts to move up the mountain.

I look out the window, searching for old sights and noticing new ones: a favorite park, now a parking garage; the cozy café where, with different girlfriends, I listened to ship horns usher in different New Years, now a bank branch; the newsstand where I bought science magazines and westerns, gone.

At one of the stops, an elderly woman enters through the rear door, pushing two heavy baskets of colorful produce. While her fare is dutifully passed from hand to hand to the driver, she looks around with resigned exhaustion. I give her my seat and move farther back.

In one of the seats, a boy of about fourteen looks out the window with exaggerated curiosity. I chuckle because I used to do just that to avoid giving up my seat. As I stare at the back of his neck, he turns around and looks straight at me. I recognize myself at his age: dark brown hair combed sideways, big eyes, and a longish nose.

My young double turns away and directs his attention to the back of the seat in front of him. He is wearing my high school uniform with its light gray shirt and dark gray trousers. On his knees rests a brown imitation leather school bag, like the one my parents gave me when I started high school. His long fingers caress the lock and handle. They don't rest for a minute. Just like mine.

We are climbing a steep street. The turns get sharper, and fumes from the overexerted engine fill the back of the bus. In a few minutes, I'll be sitting in Mother's cool apartment, sipping seltzer with raspberry syrup.

Mother's street at last. I'll be getting off in a moment. I start moving toward the door. One last look at the boy. He stands up abruptly, pulls the cord, and makes his way to the door.

We get off and turn in the same direction. He walks a short distance ahead of me, the heavy school bag in his right hand, his right shoulder visibly lower than the left. Just like mine. He whistles softly as he walks, and in the light breeze against my perspiring face I can almost feel the caress of a favorite tune from my youth.

We get closer to Mother's apartment house. I follow him into the dimly lit staircase. Fourteen stairs, left turn, and there is the boy, in front of Mother's door, raising his hand to ring the bell. I move mine in the same direction, our hands touch, and a soft chime is heard from inside. Quick steps, then Mother's voice, "Is that you, Dannika?"

"Yes," we answer.

The door opens. I step inside and hug her.

"I'm glad it's you," she says.

I help Mother sit down on her low stool, and we chat about the passage of time.

"From Here to Eternity," she says, putting the title of one of her favorite novels to good use.

I help her up, and we go outside for some fresh air. She puts her arm in mine as we walk leisurely down the street to the ornate gate of the Baha'i Gardens. Mother points to the shrine's golden dome as she did when she took me to see it for the first time, when she was much younger than I am now.

On the way back, Mother says, "Let's stop and get a loaf of bread from Reznik's. What am I saying? Reznik's? That was thirty-five years ago in Hadera. I meant Rosser's, of course."

"Reznik's rye was always my favorite," I say, "but Rosser's is good too."

Sunlight and a gentle breeze stream into the apartment, as if to flush out the sadness of the past seven days.

"It's a hot day, Danny," says Mother, seeing me wipe my forehead. "Why don't you take a nice cool shower while I rest. We'll have lunch later."

The showerhead is not as generous as it once was, with only a weak stream flowing through the calcified pipes of the old building. Still, I feel refreshed.

Whenever I came home on a pass, I would first shed my uniform and step into the shower. I would stand there motionless for a long time, submitting to the whipping streams of hot water. After the bathroom grew thick with steam, I would emerge, pink and wet, ready for Grandma to feed me. Somehow she had altered my genetic code by weaving a pungent scallion through my double helix, so nothing has ever satisfied my cravings more than a slice of rye, a few scallions, olives, and a cup of coffee. Nothing has ever comforted me more, especially when eating them on an empty soul.

In the kitchen, I follow my childhood routine and cut off the end piece of the fresh rye, spread it with butter, and bite into it with a contented sigh.

I prepare a meal from the food friends and relatives brought during Shiva. I garnish the platter with olives and scallions and take it to the dining table which Mother has set with her best china and silver the way grandma used to.

"You remembered the olives and scallions," says Mother.

"How could I not? American scallions don't even come close."

"Good, so you'll come back for the scallions," she says. "With Grandma gone, you're going to need new reasons to visit."

Feeling pleasantly fatigued, I don't take the bait.

"Any word from Father?" I ask. Mother doesn't take the bait either.

— *Chapter Twenty-Seven* —

After lunch, Mother sits down to write thank you notes to friends and relatives. I clean up and fold the tablecloth. Uncertain where it belongs, I place it on top of the piano next to the silver candlesticks and the ceramic bowl with small change.

The piano Mother grew up with was a Scheidmayer baby grand, an early war casualty that likely ended up as firewood. She would often reminisce about it and hum a few of her favorite tunes when putting me to bed. On the twentieth anniversary of the end of World War II, Grandma surprised Mother with a new Yamaha upright. Everyone hugged and cried. Mother sat down and played a flawless *Für Elise*, closed the key lid, and never touched the piano again.

I leaf through the weekend paper, munch on some nuts, and feel as if I'm in an airport transit lounge. The bookcases around the room bear no trace of my past. Things that made up my former world — books, notebooks, report cards, class pictures, unsent love letters — are nowhere in sight.

Can one have a personal history without records, documents and artifacts? Can vague memories alone suffice? Right now, if I had to submit evidence of times, places and events in my life, I'd have to shake my head and ask feebly what the absence of such evidence proves.

The tablecloth doesn't really belong on the piano, so I put it in one of the cabinets under the bookcases where I find Grandma's old set of Passover dishes on the top shelf. Between the soup bowls and the dinner plates are two well-worn books. Not all evidence, it seems, has been purged. One volume is a bound collection of Buck Jones westerns from my Wild West period. Those pamphlets were quite old even when I bought them, and their brittle pages were the perfect medium for the gritty stories between their tattered covers.

The other volume has a yellow binding held together by a bronze clasp. It is embossed with a single word, "Memories." I gingerly open it to make sure none escape. Its pages bear inscriptions by my sixth-grade classmates, many of whom I barely remember:

"Dan… Danny… Daniel… All mean a loyal friend who is always willing to help with homework and to share answers in math."

"My house is one kilometer away from yours. Your heart is one millimeter away from mine." In those days, kids were neither stingy with their emotions nor sparing in decorating their entries with stickers of winged cherubs.

"Better to dwell in a humble tent in one's homeland than in a palace in a foreign land."

"Life is war. The world is a battlefield. Fight bravely!" This was accompanied by a picture of Piglet and Pooh, the latter with a thought bubble reading, *"My friend isn't Kosher."*

"You need a broom to clean your house and a flag to prove it's your country!" Under a folded corner of the page was the shadow of a word not totally erased: *"Kiss."*

The girl with the most beautiful handwriting in my class wrote, *"Childhood days pass like shadows and are wrapped in fog, but memories of friends will go on twinkling in the darkest clouds."* Evidence that, in the Middle East, one is never too young to appreciate shadows, fog, and clouds.

On the bottom shelf is Grandma's large wooden box containing old photos that never made it into the family album. The many prints with their ragged edges and curled corners reveal not one familiar face.

Did Grandma even need them, given that she often said memories don't require pictures to survive and multiply? Whether needed or not, Grandma took great pleasure in them: combing through the pile, running her fingertips along the edges of time, and finding material evidence of ephemeral memories, even those not her own.

Whenever I asked Grandma about the pictures, she'd say, "Another time, Danny. There's too much to tell." Nothing more was said, possibly because new photos kept accumulating as family members passed away. There was always more to tell, but never enough time to tell it.

I take this opportunity to ask Mother about it. She says Grandma was the self-appointed keeper of extended family photos that would otherwise have been discarded. No matter how distant the deceased relatives, Grandma would volunteer to store all of their photos before their survivors disposed of them. Occasionally, Grandma would go through them and return them to the box in random order, as if to challenge future organizers. Except for a rare scribble on a photo's back, there now seemed little chance of identifying names, dates, or locations.

"Only Grandma knew people in those pictures, but even she didn't remember them all," says Mother.

Now the box is in Mother's care and some day in mine. And some day in Josh's, who may just chuck the lot to avoid getting ensnared in time-consuming nostalgia not his own. For me, discarding the box would be out of the question, but how will I ever organize the photos or identify the people in them? The archivist in me abhors unsorted piles and already itches to arrange and affix the prints onto black album pages, not knowing if I'd be doing them justice.

Mother hands me a shoebox tied with frayed string.

"Grandma left this for you."

I start to undo the knot.

"No, Danny, please don't open it here. Wait till later."

"OK, but why?"

She shrugs and looks into my eyes, biting her lower lip. The box is very light and contains, I assume, an old sigh that Mother would rather not hear just now.

As soon as Mother leaves the room, I sit down on the sofa, open the box, and find an envelope addressed to Mother bearing a Romanian stamp. It contains a sealed envelope with my name on it.

> *My dearest Dannika,*
>
> *I should never have gone back to Romania. From the time you were little, you told me that one day we would go together to visit my childhood home. I told you so much about it over the years that you must have felt it was almost yours as well.*
>
> *As much as I wish you were here with me, it's better you're not. What I found doesn't match what I remember and what you imagine.*
>
> *After you went away to college, got a job and got married, it was clear to me that we'd never take our trip, so I felt I had to go while I still could. I asked your mother*

to join me, but she was afraid it would be too painful. Looking back is not for everyone. All you see are things receding, like looking out the back of a train. It can make you dizzy. It can make you sick.

When I couldn't get anyone to join me, I went by myself. It was a big mistake. Everything looks small, run down, and sad. The color is gone. It's all gray now. The food has no taste, the music no melody, the forest no fragrance. It's like a black and white travel brochure. Even my memories are spoiled.

I almost hope you won't see me again. We'll both be happier if you remember me the way I was, unspoiled.

With all my love,
Grandma

I reread Grandma's letter and place it on my knees, careful not to let my tears stain it. I fold it and carefully place it in the shoebox on top of a few first-grade notebooks, a Mother's Day card, a lacquered kidney bean brooch, and the last photo taken of Grandma and me, hugging by the swings of our tiny neighborhood park. Smiling, of course. A documented memory.

— *Chapter Twenty-Eight* —

I hear Mother puttering in the kitchen. I tell her I need to lie down and close my eyes for a few minutes.

"Of course," she says. "You must listen to your body. Rest well."

Heading toward the sofa, I impulsively open the door to Grandma's room. A sad twilight hangs in the window. Vague longings and a breath of lavender envelop me. On the nightstand are Grandma's reading glasses, their temples open as though she's just taken them off. A tattered prayer book rests atop a James Bond novel. It's the first English book I ever read. I stretch out on her bed and thumb through the book, the one in which Bond gets married. I recall how shocked I was to learn that his new bride was killed in the end. In fact, I refused to accept it until the publisher answered my written inquiry with a terse, "Yes, it seems she was indeed killed, thus freeing Bond to pursue further exploits without the burden of matrimony."

As I wake up from my short nap, I find myself staring at a framed needlepoint Grandma made when I was in grade school. It was so much a part of the décor I grew up with that I hardly gave it a thought, much less studied it in detail. Now I do.

It depicts a busy downtown street choked with traffic; sidewalks crowded with late afternoon shoppers; a small outdoor café with colorful umbrellas; chimneys haloed with white smoke; and a balloon attached to a flower pot in a dormer window. For the first time, I notice a boy leaning out the window, looking at the street below.

Is he alone in the apartment, I wonder, passing the time until his mother returns? Is he searching the crowd for his father? Is he estimating the distance to the sidewalk to see if it's safe to jump, or high enough? Where is this city, anyway? Is the boy happy, sad, bored? Has he done his homework? Is he hungry? Are there any cookies in the kitchen to tide him over until supper?

I close my eyes again but soon get a sense that something isn't right. I become aware of faint screams and siren wails. It must be a fender bender around the corner from Mother's, but the noise keeps growing louder and now seems to be coming from Grandma's needlepoint. I stand up and take a halting step toward it.

The sirens don't let up. I look at the dormer but there's no one at the window. The boy is lying on the pavement below, passers-by gathering around him, paramedics jumping from an ambulance. Inches away from the needlepoint, wincing at the deafening noise, I take another step, then another, and run toward the boy on the sidewalk. The noise is unbearable. I cup my ears as I run. Tears blur my vision. The paramedics reach for the boy. The crowd falls silent. I stumble and fall, feel strong arms grabbing me from behind, and hear myself pleading that they leave me and save the boy instead. A gray, cozy fog rolls in and wraps itself around me like Grandma's comforting embrace.

* * *

When I get up from my nap, Mother says, "Before you go, Danny, I need you to look in the attic to see if there's anything you want to take back with you. I'm not going to look. It's too risky. Here's a box. Whatever you don't keep, I'm throwing away." She must notice my disbelief at hearing this because Mother used to keep almost everything and prided herself on knowing exactly where it was.

"Maybe you'll understand some day. It's a curse in a way, but as time passes I seem to remember more about each item. I have to get rid of painful things before they contaminate the rest, like those moldy books in the bookcase."

What's a box of memories worth to me? Ten shekels for a shipping box, ninety for postage and insurance, and thirty for the taxi to the post office. Whatever it is, it's a small price to pay for priceless childhood treasures.

Too many of them have already gone missing — my childhood books, stuffed animals, science award citation, first published article, and sergeant stripes — casualties of mold and lack of space. I will not risk losing more or suffering phantom possession pain.

I step on the ladder, open the attic door, and grab everything within reach. I fill the box with what I want to keep but mostly with what I'm afraid to lose: a dented aluminum milk jug circa 1949 which the milkman filled each morning; a baby's silverware set dating to when I was Josh's age; a ceramic cookie jar repaired with glue that petrified into amber globules; several men's and women's watches; a dozen pens with hotel logos; several chipped porcelain plates with Alpine landscapes; tarnished family jewelry; and other emotionally charged curios.

I couldn't part with any of them, even though I know Lori will say, "What are we supposed to do with all this?"

* * *

I feel an urge to do something kind for Tamar and, after leaving Mother's apartment, stop at the florist. Tamar is surprised to see me and gratefully accepts the flowers. She invites me in and goes to look for a vase, returning with the flowers and two glasses of Coke.

"I wonder what Tom is up to these days," she says.

It occurs to me that Tom hasn't requested that I keep his medical condition a secret. Should I reveal that Tom, having played dead for a year, is now preparing for his final exit? Will Tom be angry if I tell her? Will I regret it if I don't?

Inexplicably I blurt out "My parents got divorced when I was seven."

Her stare softens, and I hurriedly continue as if to complete a hateful school assignment.

"Seven years later, when they remarried each other, I felt like a new person. Seven years after that, I left for America and they separated.

Tamar leans across the coffee table and pats my hand. I take hers and hold it for a long time.

* * *

As if jet lag weren't enough to rob me of sleep, I happen upon an irresistible *Macbeth* on BBC Radio. The poor king, even more restless than I am, thinks he hears a voice saying, "Sleep no more!" It's no help to either of us that he itemizes sleep's benefits: "Balm of hurt minds; great nature's second course; chief nourisher in life's feast."

As I drift off, his wife declares, "The sleeping and the dead are but as pictures."

Framed by the cherry headboard and footboard of my cousin's bed, I am closely observed by the dead whose eyes keep following my every toss and turn.

"Remember not to forget," Grandma used to say. "And don't forget to remember."

As I drift off, all I remember is holding Tamar's hand, already a fleeting memory.

Day Eight *Last Wedding*

— *Chapter Twenty-Nine* —

Tom couldn't have picked a better hiding place than the Summit Hotel, protruding from Mount Carmel's ridge like a lone tooth from a baby's gum. With its exorbitant room rates and the best views in town, the only natives seen there are those who come to greet wealthy relatives from abroad or those wanting to prove they can afford anything foreigners can.

We meet in the lobby at 7:00 a.m. Tom insists we sit down to breakfast.

"It's going to be a long day, so let's fill up," he says, holding on to my arm and guiding me to the buffet. Putting a bran muffin and several melon slices on his plate, he seems to enjoy watching me load mine with smoked fish, assorted salads and cheeses, olives, strawberries and an omelet. Tom smiles and downs a handful of pills with freshly squeezed orange juice.

"Don't rush, you can always go back for more," he says.

I feel at ease with this gaunt man and look forward to spending the day with him. Tom nibbles on his muffin and takes a few sips of coffee. I return to the buffet for pastries and fruit.

Tom waits patiently while I finish my breakfast. He asks casually about Tamar and the kids and quizzes me about the location of a certain cabinet in her apartment.

"I've only been there a couple of times," I say. "How would I know?"

While he settles his bill at the front desk, I carry his suitcases to my rental car.

"Let's stop at Tamar's on the way," he says casually as he gets in. "I need to pick up a few more things." Noticing my puzzled look, he says, "Don't worry. I had the clerk call her number just now. There was no answer."

We climb the stairs to my cousin's apartment, and Tom disappears into the closet. My instructions are to wait at the top of the stairs and intercept Tamar if she comes back. Ten minutes go by. I try to estimate how long it will take to drive to Tiberias, get Tom settled in the hospice, and drive back.

Hearing the click of high heels on the terrazzo stairs below, I lean over the banister and see Tamar, holding a grocery bag, halfway up the first flight. I run to the closet and whisper urgently, "Hurry. She's on her way up."

"I need five more minutes," says Tom calmly. "Do what you can to keep her busy."

"All right, but go out the front door, not the closet, and wait for me in the car." I rush back to the landing and almost collide with Tamar.

"You're up early," she says, "and already out of breath. What's going on?"

"Oh, just my daily pushups. Come in, I'll make us some coffee."

"That's nice, thanks. I bought pastries. You must be famished after your workout."

"Yeah, I could really use some breakfast." I make the coffee while Tamar sets the small table in the breakfast nook with cheerful ceramic dishes. I manage a few bites and a sip of coffee. Tamar chews prettily, searching the crumbs on her plate for something to say.

"What's it like to be married to an American?"

"As a man, an architect, or an expat?" I ask with mock-seriousness.

Tamar stops chewing.

"I'm kidding," I say. "I know what you mean. What you want to know is, can I possibly have anything in common with a foreigner who doesn't speak Hebrew, doesn't know our culture or the songs and slang you and I grew up with? Well, we both love hummus. That's about it, but still I fell in love with her."

"I envy her," says Tamar wistfully.

"I realize that marrying someone like you would have provided time-saving emotional shortcuts."

"Yes, but at the cost of missing red lights and exit signs," she says, wiping her lips on her napkin and looking at the lipstick traces as if studying a road map.

This sounds right, but I'll have to ponder it later. I clear the table and look out at the car. Tom's elbow protrudes from the passenger window.

"I have some errands to run," I say.

"Bye," she says and takes the shortcut to her apartment. I wait another minute or two, lock up, and go downstairs to the car.

— *Chapter Thirty* —

"Ready?" I ask.

"Sure, let's go," says Tom, but after two blocks he orders me to stop, opens his door and vomits. Quite normal. I know from experience that this is part of going to a scary place. I hand him a bottle of water and a pack of tissues. A moment later Tom seems more comfortable and makes a weary forward motion with his hand. As we drive off, he picks up a shoebox from the floor and puts it on his lap.

"What's that?" I ask.

"I'll tell you after we leave the city."

I try a couple of shortcuts to avoid the congested downtown, but traffic patterns have been altered, and some streets are closed for repairs. Just like that, they went and changed my city again, and I'm the last to find out. We cross the arched stone bridge which to me always signified leaving town and get on the highway heading east.

The cement factory's twin smoke stacks have been joined by a third, and the trio now spew white clouds into the pale sky. Much too pale for my taste. No longer bound by city speed limits, I accelerate and head for the Jezreel Valley.

We drive in silence until Tom points and says, "Stop under the eucalyptus tree up ahead." I stop the car by the roadside. Tom opens his box with great care. He takes out a stack of photos and hands them to me. All are badly composed, showing half faces, rooms at weird angles, and overexposed pictures of Tamar and the kids.

"These are the rejects that didn't make it into the family album," he says. "Still, they are fragments of our lives which I had to have. Tamar won't miss them. And these..." he rummages in the box and takes out a few yellowing sheets of paper, "are my elementary and high school report cards. You can bet no one will miss these or my letters to Tamar either." He thumbs through them and says, "They always manage to find pictures and documents from the early years of famous people to include in their biographies. How do they know they will be famous some day and should save every scrap of paper?"

I, for one, would very much like to read his letters to Tamar, but I can't tell him that. He shows me the rest of his mementos: a Swiss Army knife; his first driver's license; his wedding photo in an exquisite silver frame.

"This is the only item of any real value. The frame, I mean. Anyway, this will all be returned to her soon enough." He puts everything back in the box, wedges it between his feet, and looks straight ahead. I drive on and Tom dozes off.

Forty-five minutes later, Mount Tabor comes into view, rising from the valley floor like a voluptuous breast with a monastery for a nipple. To our left is a bus stop and a sign pointing toward a nearby kibbutz. I bring the car to a rough stop by the side of the road. Tom looks up, groggy from his nap.

"What's going on?" he asks.

All I can do is lean forward and rest my head on the steering wheel, setting off the horn. I lean back into the seat and close my eyes.

"Are you feeling ill?" asks Tom. "I have some Dramamine in my bag, if you need it."

It's time to explain. "When I was ten, I promised myself never to go near this place again and never to talk about it to anyone except a girl named Eli, if we ever met again. I've always thought of it as 'That Damn Place.' I really thought I'd gotten over it or I would have taken a different route."

Tom takes charge. "OK, Danny, listen up. Get out of the car, walk around a bit and take a few deep breaths. Kick a couple of rocks. It's going to be all right. We can always find a dirt road and forget this damn place. Don't worry, you don't have to go near it. Now get out!"

It feels good to follow orders. I get out of the car and walk some distance down the gravelly shoulder. I inhale the warm midday air laced with smells of plowed soil and distant smoke and wonder how my most despised spot on earth can be perfumed with longings. I step into a clump of bushes and urinate toward that damn place with a rage that can't be relieved.

Back at the car, I kick a rear tire before getting in. Tom stares at my white-knuckled fingers on the steering wheel. "OK, let's go find us a dirt road," he says. We find one a short distance away and follow it east to the foot of a jagged hill. There the road turns sharply northward and disappears among tangles of weeds and thorns. I stop the car, and Tom rubs his hands together as if enjoying the challenge. With the contented sigh of a field commander extracting his bulk from the front seat of a camouflaged Jeep, he gets out of the car and climbs the slope to reconnoiter. He returns a few minutes later, flushed with excitement.

"I saw your damn place from up there, and it looks like a

little bucolic kibbutz, but what do I know? I've been ambushed in more peaceful places. Our objective is to avoid it at all costs, right? So, let's cut through the fields and get back on the highway farther down. With any luck we'll arrive at my own damn place in time for lunch."

"What are you saying?"

"It sounds better than hospice."

"You do realize this is where the road ends?"

"Minor inconvenience," says Tom. "I didn't see anything to be worried about. Let's get going."

It's good to see him energized, and I defer to his judgment. I turn on the ignition. Tom sticks his hand out the window and makes a forward motion to an imaginary motorized column. We lunge forward. The thorn bushes offer only weak resistance and are immediately overrun. Occasional boulders are more of an obstacle, and I maneuver carefully to avoid them. A flat tire here would be a disaster.

A deep gulley opens up in front of us. Suddenly we are airborne. Tom sucks in his breath, and I slam on the brakes. Its underbelly scraping the edge of the cliff, the car teeters to an exquisite equilibrium, its front half suspended over the precipice.

"Don't move!" orders Tom in a whisper. He reaches for the backrest lever and slowly leans back as far as he can. I do the same. He slithers into the back seat. I do the same. We look at each other, nod imperceptibly and, moving in tandem, gently open the rear doors and step out slowly. We exhale and walk over to sit in the shade of a dusty fig tree.

"My fault," says Tom. "It looked pretty simple from up there, but obviously I missed something."

"Don't worry. We're safe, but we need to keep moving. It's almost one o'clock. Maybe I'll swallow my pride and walk over to that damn place for help."

"Don't you dare!" says Tom. "We're not going anywhere near that hornet's nest. Why don't we walk back to the highway and try to get help there?"

"Good idea," I say drowsily. The fact is, I'm very comfortable right now. In the shade, caressed by a light breeze, I could easily doze off. I lean against the tree trunk and close my eyes.

The sergeant has just ordered a fifteen-minute rest break and I intend to use every second. Someone yells "Figs!" and a stampede ensues. Through half-closed lids, I see the entire platoon descend like locusts on a nearby tree and pick it clean. While still in the tree, they begin devouring the fruit and don't stop until they keel over, holding their stomachs. Luckily, I have gotten a good five-minute nap and am the only one left standing to summon help and organize transport to the nearest hospital.

— *Chapter Thirty-One* —

When I wake up, Tom is chewing a blade of grass, a young Arab boy is playing a reed flute, and two-dozen skinny goats are facing us in a semicircle, as if awaiting orders. Tom speaks to the shepherd in rapid Arabic. The boy answers, pointing north, then makes a circling gesture toward the east. *"Shukran"* says Tom, as the boy walks off followed by the goats.

"Nice kid," says Tom when all is quiet again. "Turns out this terrain is trickier than I thought. He told me his village is behind a fold in that hill, which looks perfectly flat from here. He's going home to get help. He said we're lucky the men came back from the fields early because of a wedding tonight."

"Where did you learn Arabic?" I ask.

"High school," he says. "And military intelligence."

An hour goes by. We keep moving clockwise with the shade around the tree. Soon we hear fragments of voices, their echoes bouncing off the hills. The boy reappears, leading six swarthy young men, two mules, a bull and a camel. Sitting on top of the camel's hump is an older man in traditional garb, fingering a string of prayer beads and gazing into the distance.

"Ahalan!" I greet them with one of the few Arabic words I know.

"Ahalan wasahalan!" they return the greeting, and we all shake hands. One of them hands out cans of cold Coke, and we all sit down on the ground, cross-legged in a circle around the shepherd. The man on the camel empties his can in one

long draft, crushes it in his hand and throws it into the gully. Tom says something, someone responds, and soon I'm in the middle of a loud and lively conversation, not a word of which I understand.

One of the men comes over and sits down beside me. He is clean-shaven with a short haircut and wears a Columbia T-shirt.

"So, what do you think of our country so far?" His English is flawless, with only a hint of an accent.

"Why are you speaking to me in English?" I ask in Hebrew, a little annoyed.

"I thought you were a tourist. Please don't be offended." He extends his hand. "Tariq, Israeli born, Columbia, 1980."

I take his hand. "Danny, Israeli born, Harvard, 1977."

We shake hands for a long time and continue in English, the neutral and unencumbered language of a faraway country we both can love and lay claim to without emotional or historical baggage. I greatly enjoy the chance to sit under a fig tree in our land, breathe its sweet air, and talk about our years in the States. Tariq opens the last can of soda, pulling the tab and sending its contents hissing. He offers to share it with me, and I gratefully accept.

"This is a special day for me," says Tariq. "I'm getting married tonight to an American woman, believe it or not. Well, born in America, anyway. Leila's family is originally from a village not far from here. Both our villages are getting together for the celebration, but we can still help with your car."

"We really appreciate it."

He turns and looks at his fellow villagers, engrossed in a story that Tom is sharing in a hushed voice. Tariq winks at me and waits until they erupt in boisterous laughter. He calls over to them, *"Yalla, ya shabab!"* They quickly rise and get to work. The man on the camel reaches behind his saddle and throws down two coiled ropes. The men tie the ropes to the rear axle of our car and loop them through wooden yokes on the animals' shoulders. The camel driver draws a revolver from under his white robe and fires into the air. The animals stir, the men slap their flanks, and the ropes are pulled taut. A blood-curdling screech is heard as the car scrapes against the rocks, its front wheels returning to solid ground. The men cheer and whistle, and the camel driver discharges parting shots to celebrate a job well done.

We gather and shake hands again. Tom and I thank them profusely with words and gestures. I find a crumpled business card in my wallet and give it to Tariq, asking him to call me when he's back in the States. He grabs my other hand.

"You must come to my wedding!" he exclaims. He raises my hand above our heads and shouts to the others who cheer their approval. "The two of you can spend the night in my old room at my parents' house. You'll come, right?"

"I'm in no rush," whispers Tom in my ear.

"Thanks, of course we'll come," I say.

"It's a great honor to have you as my guests," says Tariq. "Follow us to the village. It's not far from here."

We get into the car and follow the short caravan. They lead us over a flat, rock-free stretch of land, then along a well-trodden path that hugs the contours of the foothills. As we ascend the barren slope, I am briefly distracted by the lush green of that damn place below and quickly tighten my grip on the steering wheel to negotiate a sharp turn into a canyon opening up without warning. It looks like a deep wound in the arid slope, oozing greenery and red blooms.

I park the car in the shady spot Tariq points to, and we follow him to a café overlooking a small square. Tom and I sit down at a table on the trellised patio while Tariq speaks to someone inside.

"My friend Salim will look after you," he tells us when he comes out. "I must go now and take care of a few things for tonight, but I'll see you before sunset." Tariq leaves us and vanishes in a narrow alley.

A mustachioed man in black trousers, white shirt, and black and white sneakers approaches, holding a small copper tray.

"Coffee," he says, putting down tiny cups of a thick brew, glasses of ice water, and a plate of pastries.

"*Shukran,*" says Tom. While we sip noisily, Salim returns with a wooden backgammon box and leaves it on the chair next to us. Tom has dozed off again.

Seeing a pay phone near the patio reminds me I must call Mother. After all, she is the reason for my visit, not Tamar nor Tom nor the excellent coffee I just enjoyed. I tell her I feel guilty for not staying with her during my visit. She again reassures me she didn't want me sleeping in Grandma's room, and besides, she says, she has plenty to do now that Shiva is over.

We pause briefly, listening to each other's breathing, and it occurs to me that I'm not quite yet ready to go home. I had planned to stay for ten days but now feel guilty about leaving.

"I'm going to stay a few extra days," I suddenly hear myself tell Mother.

"Wonderful news, but what will Lori think?"

"She'll be fine. A few more days won't make any difference."

"It'll make a big difference to me," says Mother, "but you should do what you think is right."

I say goodbye and place a collect call to Lori. She and Josh have just returned from a run to the pharmacy for Pampers and Infants' Tylenol.

"Unfinished business?" she says when I tell her about delaying my return flight. "You can tell me more about it when Josh is not so cranky. I've got to put him to bed. We'll be OK without you for a few more days. You don't go back there that often, so make the most of it. Have to run now. Love you."

I walk to the center of the square and, looking around, feel as if I'm on the stage of an intimate amphitheater. Cascading terraces and hillside houses surround me on three sides. Are eyes peering out through shuttered windows, following this nomad in the most tranquil of hours? The only sound I hear is of water lapping the sides of a stone fountain. I sit on the rim and let the cool mist settle on my face and arms.

Back on the patio, Tom looks refreshed. I suggest he call the hospice to tell them he'll arrive a day late.

"Thanks for thinking of it," he says, "but I wish we could delay it by more than just a day. This is fun." I hand him a token for the pay phone, and he reluctantly walks over to make the call.

Tariq returns to take us to his parents' house. He is wearing a black suit and patent leather shoes reflecting the rays of the setting sun. I ask Salim how much we owe him.

"Nothing," he says. "Just help our dreams come true."

Tariq says, "If you don't dream, you can't have nightmares." Later he adds, "My grandfather used to say that history should only be written in sand."

"Very wise, but sadly, around here it seems to be carved in stone."

We fall silent. After a moment I say, "This is much too serious for such a happy occasion." Tariq looks relieved.

On long tables in the yard, dozens of women are arranging huge amounts of food on large platters. Tariq introduces us to his mother and his niece Yasmeen, who is rolling dark green watermelons across the yard to several of Tariq's friends.

"It's going to be crazy around here for a while," says Tariq. "I'd better take you to my room."

Just then, everyone in the yard rushes toward the gate through which Leila is entering on a white horse, followed by a throng of dancers, drummers, and ululating women. She is helped down and led to one of two gilded chairs on a decorated platform.

"These are just the preliminaries," says Tariq. "I'll see you later this evening down in the square for the real thing. Yasmeen, please show them to my old room." He makes his way to the platform and takes his seat next to his bride. The ululation abates and the horse is led away. Tom and I settle into Tariq's sparsely furnished room. Shadows of clouds float across the curtained window. Tom looks exhausted. "Wake me up for the wedding," he says before lying down. I lean out the window and see the sun descending over the Carmel range in the distance. The sight triggers a familiar pressure in my stomach, and I quickly close the shutters.

It is dark when I wake up. Tom is snoring lightly. A cool breeze flows through the room carrying scents of lemon and spices struggling to assert themselves against the odors of livestock. The breeze shifts and sounds of an oud, a flute, and tableh rise from the square below.

I tuck in my shirt, comb my hair, and wake Tom who quickly rouses.

"I'm ready for a good wedding," he says.

The crowd in the square is so thick, the music so vibrant, the food so abundant, that no one seems to notice the two strangers walking dazed through this riot of colors and smells. We are handed tall glasses of a fruit cocktail and sturdy paper plates. Only then do I realize how hungry I am and pile my plate high. Tom circles a small table laden with mounds of fruit and arranges a small selection on his plate. He seems happy, and I can sense a smile on my own face as well. I don't let it fade even when Tom says matter-of-factly, "You know Danny, this is my last wedding, so let's have fun."

Taking Tom by the arm, I lead him around the square to enjoy the musicians and dancers and to sample more food. Little Yasmeen emerges from the crush of revelers and looks up at us with bright eyes and a hint of a smile. Tom and I wave to her and turn to look for Tariq and Leila to wish them a happy, healthy, and prosperous life. By the time I see them, they are surrounded by well-wishers.

I take a plateful of nuts and direct Tom to the cool rim of the fountain. Yasmeen reappears, smiling more broadly than before, and hands each of us a small plate of plump dates. I reciprocate with a handful of nuts.

"I see Yasmeen found you," says Tariq, emerging from the crowd. "Got room for me?"

We move over, and he sits down with a contented sigh. He hands us paper cups and fills them with juice from the bottle he's holding.

We raise our cups. "Cheers," I say

"I'm worn out," says Tariq. "I haven't danced the *debkah* in years." He takes another sip. "Ahh, this is good. Almost makes me stop missing the gallon jugs of cheap rosé from the liquor store near campus. I guess it says something that over there it takes a gallon of wine to drown out memories of home."

"If just one gallon does it for you, consider yourself lucky," says Tom.

"I don't know about you, but everything around here seems smaller each time I return."

"I know what you mean," I say. "Tell Leila we wish you both a wonderful life. We'll get together back in the States."

We shake hands and hug. Tariq walks away and Yasmeen turns to follow him.

"Shalom," she says.

"Salaam," I say.

Back in Tariq's room, Tom gets into bed and is soon asleep. I open the window and look at lights blinking in the distance. There is a single light at the top of Mount Tabor, which might be that of a lonely monk in his lonely cell trying to solve the mystery of loneliness in this lonely valley.

I close the window, worried the chilly night air might harm Tom. A blurred reflection of my face appears in the glass, looking at me warily from the dark.

Day Nine That Damn Place

— *Chapter Thirty-Two* —

Hunger gets me out of bed soon after dawn. I step outside and take a deep breath. An early rain has moistened the hard ground and awakened its hidden scents, extracting a promise of fertility from the barren soil.

Last night is a wonderful but already distant memory. The neat yard shows no sign of yesterday's festivities. Even the white horse's hoofprints are gone.

Tariq's mother is in the yard baking pitas in a mud oven. She's happy to have someone to talk to and does so in rapid Arabic. I smile and nod and am soon rewarded with a fresh pita and a cup of strong coffee. Tom shuffles into the yard and gratefully accepts the cup she hands him. While they chat, I write a short note to Tariq and give it to his mother. Tom and I thank her and walk to the car.

"She told me she knows Tariq and Leila will soon move back to America," says Tom. "She won't try to talk them out of it or make them feel guilty, but she's already mourning them."

We find a dirt road leading out of the village and a few

minutes later get on the highway. At six o'clock I turn on the car radio for the morning news: the latest tally of casualties; tremors through the financial markets; a rape in suburban Tel Aviv; and the birth of a baby tiger at the Jerusalem Zoo.

Left unspoken is Tom's approaching death. I know this won't be an easy day for him, so I switch to a station playing soothing classical music. We arrive at the hospice half an hour later. A friendly nun welcomes us, completes Tom's admission papers, and takes us on a tour. In the courtyard, we come to a circle of tall cypresses surrounding a fountain and two benches.

Sister turns to Tom and says, "Our guests often tell us they find peace here. I hope you will too."

Tom nods. We go up to his room and I help him unpack.

"Now all I have to do is wait to die," he says with a crooked smile. "I hope I see you again." He walks over to the window. "Before you go, I want you to know how much I appreciate everything you've done."

"I'm glad I could do it."

We shake hands then hug. I hurry out, get behind the wheel, and look up. Tom is at the window. I wave. He waves back. I drive off slowly and look up a final time. Tom is no longer at the window.

∗   ∗   ∗

One day I'll drive Mother and her two suitcases to a nursing home where she'll end her days receiving round the clock medical care while being deprived of everything she ever enjoyed and mourning people she will never see again. She'll spend her waking hours remembering the apartment she won't return to and the many places she loved and lost over her long life. On my way out, I'll turn and look up. Mother will be at the window, watching me get in the car. I will wave. She'll wave back. I'll switch on the ignition and look up a final time. Mother will no longer be at the window.

— *Chapter Thirty-Three* —

On the way back to Haifa from Tom's damn place, I stop at the gas station near mine. I feel the familiar pressure in my stomach when I realize it is at the intersection of the highway and the access road to the kibbutz. After filling up, I step into the coffee shop and take a table by the window overlooking the gate I last walked through thirty years ago. The nearby bump in the field is still there.

Back then it looked to me like a ramp for loading livestock: a thick concrete wall about a meter high, with compacted dirt sloping up to it on the other side. It was the highest point in the surrounding landscape. Although the gate was always open, I felt free and in some control of my life only when I walked through it and up the ramp.

Friday afternoons in the kibbutz were quiet and scary. After completing their assigned chores for the week, the adults made their way to the communal showers, emerging a short time later in white shirts, blue pants, and scrubbed sandals with barely a trace of mud.

It was about that time that I made my way to the ramp and stood at its peak, watching my shadow lengthen toward the main road and the solitary eucalyptus near the bus stop. Behind me, to the west band barely visible below the setting sun, was the city the buses came from.

My eyes stayed focused on the bend where an approaching bus could first be spotted. Once I saw it, I had just enough time to race to the bus stop and reach it the moment the door opened and Grandma, Mother, or Father — never more than one on a given Friday — got off carrying a small overnight bag.

It was a scary time because there was always the chance no one would come, and I'd watch the bus continue without stopping.

There was another reason I felt anxious during that weekly ritual at the ramp. With lizards lounging on hot rocks as my only companions, I had time to think and would always reach the same conclusion: for some excellent reason, and probably for my own good, I had been deposited in that place like a precious jewel in a strongbox — safe, secure, and out of sight.

*   *   *

I don't remember how the impending change in my life was explained to me, only that I never was able to understand why it was happening.

Grandma woke me early on a September morning so I would have time to get ready for our trip. Mother wanted to take me but couldn't get time off from work. Neither could Father.

I remember walking with Grandma down a steep street to the bus terminal. It was early morning, and a red sun was rising behind the fog. Grandma was carrying a suitcase and I was holding a shoebox crisscrossed with rubber bands.

We neared a row of buses whose tail pipes were belching clouds of exhaust fumes, making them look like a fire-spewing dragon. Overcome by the foul smell, I ran to a narrow gap between two buildings and vomited. This became my going-away ritual, as much a part of the trips as buying the tickets and boarding the old bus to Tiberias.

With the vomiting over, I smiled at Grandma and shook the shoebox on my lap to make sure my treasures were still inside. After an hour or so, Mount Tabor came into view. A few minutes later we disembarked at the turn to the kibbutz and walked toward the gate.

In the children's house, Grandma helped me unpack and arrange my clothes. I climbed on a chair and hid my shoebox behind the extra blanket on the top shelf. A few native housemates, born and raised on the kibbutz, came by and loudly bemoaned the plight of grandmothers forced to take care of the spoiled brats of spoiled parents who saddle the agricultural backbone of the nation with their offspring. At that moment, I was thankful Grandma didn't understand much Hebrew.

Grandma left the same afternoon. After seeing her off at the bus stop, I returned to the empty children's house, opened the shoebox, and took out a handful of biscuits and a few squares of chocolate. I walked aimlessly and found myself in a field bordered by cypresses. There in the glowing sunset stood a rusty airplane. A small plaque explained that it had been shot down during the War of Independence. I looked around and, deciding there was little chance I would be seen, climbed into the cockpit. I settled into the pilot's seat and munched on biscuits and chocolate, separately then together, experimenting with ways to fill the emptiness in the pit of my stomach.

It must have worked because, on the way back to the children's house, I hummed a cheerful song about a boy hiking through a field, which lifted my spirits even more.

* * *

I didn't talk much at that place but wrote home daily, taking pleasure in finding new ways to make words mingle. This I had been doing at home, speaking Hebrew with Father and German with Mother and Grandma: languages, and people, that didn't go well together. Trying to mediate between them and rationalize it to myself taught me that writing was the best way to share, manipulate, or withhold words, and the only way to find peace.

* * *

Every day, at approximately four in the afternoon, I could feel myself getting sad. I knew mother was returning from work in the city the buses came from. I would think of her seated at the Formica kitchen table while Grandma made coffee and toast. I couldn't help but wonder why I wasn't there with them to enjoy the coffee, although mint tea would have been fine too.

Around four thirty, when the natives left to go to their parents' rooms for family time before supper, a strange pressure would develop in my stomach. We "outside children," as they called us, were supposed to go to our host families, but I preferred to stay behind in the children's house. It was deathly quiet, with comforting smells of pencil shavings and white glue wafting from the classroom. I enjoyed watching the slanting rays of the afternoon sun creep across the room and seeing an occasional fly buzz through, stirring a fine golden dust in its wake.

Sometimes, I would practice the recorder or write a little. Often, I would reread old letters from home. Father's were long with small handwriting covering the entire page. He wrote eloquently and numbered the paragraphs for ease of reference. I enjoyed reading his letters as much as he enjoyed writing them. Mother's were short and full of spelling errors. Grandma's were in German but written in Hebrew capitals so I could read them.

Sitting on my bed, one of four in the room, each in its own corner, I could look out the window at fields and orchards in the setting sun. At twilight, I rearranged my slippers at the foot of the bed so they would just peek out from under the bedspread, side by side in perfect symmetry.

The eastern sky was turning deep blue. The foothills were in shadows. The Arab village on the slope across the highway retreated into the wadi. The only signs of life were pillars of white smoke. If someone from the village had looked toward the children's house, they would have seen no sign of life whatsoever.

* * *

There was another outsider in the fourth grade. On our first day, the natives told us that he and I had better become friends because none of them would ever have anything to do with us. Ezra and I heeded their advice, helped by the fact that we were of similar height and build and shared an interest in overcoming loneliness.

Ezra's mother came to visit often. She was a friendly, petite woman whose shiny black hair framed her delicate face. I soon learned that Ezra's father, "her husband," as Ezra referred to him, had decided his wife and this country were a few sizes too small for him, and so he went back home to Europe. Ezra said he hated him but was sure he'd return as soon as he began to miss his family. When that happened, my only friend would be rescued from this horrid place and go home to live happily ever after.

Ezi, as I called him, and I had the children's house to ourselves. We would look through each other's family photos, comparing relatives and memorizing memories, waiting for the distant bell to summon us to the dining hall.

After supper, the natives' parents walked them back to the children's house and supervised tooth brushing and changing into pajamas. I brushed my teeth and changed into my soft pajamas from home. Except for pajamas, I no longer wore my own clothes because Freeda, the kind housemother, had convinced my parents to pay an extra fee entitling me to the same clothes as the other children. She thought it would help me become part of the group. It didn't, but now, like everyone else, I sported starched and wrinkled clothes whose original colors had long since faded. The one thing I insisted on keeping was my leather belt. One day I noticed that the buckle tongue was missing. I searched for it in vain and mourned the loss of yet another link to my former life.

*　*　*

Except for the occasional native prank, I could look forward to eight or nine hours alone in my bed under the cozy comforter Mother had bought me, resting my head on the pillow Grandma had embroidered with my name and a chubby duck of many colors.

One Friday night, Ezi shook me out of a deep sleep. "Wake up, Danny, wake up! The natives are taking us on an adventure they say we'll never forget!"

I rolled over and wondered how to tell Ezi I was in no mood for an adventure. Not only didn't I hold out much hope for better relations with the natives, but I definitely wasn't ready to leave my warm bed. Because I had no visitor that Shabbat, I had planned to stay in bed all night and much of the following day. Ezi was in a great mood because of his mother's visit and the natives' unexpected overture, but he made it clear he wouldn't go without me.

I couldn't let him down. I got dressed without enthusiasm, and we joined the others outside. "Where are we going?" I asked.

"We're going to witness an event rarely seen," declared a longhaired native whom I had secretly named Esau. "Hey, guys, do you think Danny and Ezi are ready for this?"

An enthusiastic cheer rose from the ranks. We walked single file to the back of the guesthouse where Esau signaled us to crouch behind some bushes. He crawled up to one of the windows and peeked in, waving his hands behind his back as if to say, "Wait till you see this!" We waited. A few moments later he turned and motioned to us frantically. We jumped up and ran to the window. "Shh..." warned Esau needlessly, for we had all lost our tongues by then.

What we saw was Ezi's mother in a sheer negligee, sitting in front of a small mirror propped up on the table. As she leaned forward to examine her face, one of her breasts broke free. Leisurely, she pushed it back under the transparent fabric. The natives swallowed hard. Ezi suddenly gasped and grabbed my hand. His mother was removing her hair — a shiny black wig, perfectly coiffed. She wiped her bald scalp with a handkerchief and turned off the light. This was too much, even for the natives.

"Let's go," whispered Esau and turned to Ezi. "Sorry, I thought she would just undress." Ezi clamped my hand so hard I almost cried out. We ran back to the children's house and never spoke of it again.

* * *

When Grandma came to visit, she talked about our family's past and present, its good times and bad, and wars of all types: world, regional, and domestic. She said the domestic ones held the most important lessons and should never be forgotten. For some reason, I pictured a memorial pot simmering on an eternal flame, a kind of Shabbat stew feeding a broken family of four.

Grandma and I would spend the night in one of the rooms set aside for guests and newlyweds in a one-story concrete building that resembled an army barracks. The room was sparsely furnished with an iron bed, a thin mattress, a rolled-up olive-green army blanket, a small table and two chairs. As soon as we entered, Grandma went to work to make our overnight stay warm and cozy. She made the bed with fresh linens from home, covered the table with her crocheted tablecloth, and laid out the food and grape juice she had brought in her overnight bag. When it got dark, Grandma lit two Shabbat candles, cupped her hands over her face and whispered the blessing. I made Kiddush and sliced the challah to go with our cold supper. Afterwards Grandma read me a few of the bedtime stories I never tired of hearing. I fell asleep holding her hand the way I used to when I was still young, before last September.

— *Chapter Thirty-Four* —

Ofira, my fourth-grade teacher at the kibbutz, was a thin, serious young woman who didn't seem to like her students and employed quiet sarcasm and impatient looks to make sure they knew it. When she meted out collective punishment, her favorite kind, I almost felt sorry for the natives but soon remembered that they had one another and thrived on hating outsiders, leaving Ofira and me on the same side — the losing one.

Because both Ofira and I were newcomers to that place, I saw us as potential allies. Once or twice, she complimented me on my handwriting, giving me a sense of pride when I most needed it. We were learning about seasons and time when, pointing to a clock, she turned to me and asked what time it was. "Time for a change," I blurted out. While a few natives giggled, Ofira smiled, and I was startled to realize how pretty she was.

To elicit more smiles from Ofira, I memorized poems we had not yet studied, handed in assignments early, and expanded answers beyond the subject at hand. Once, after drawing an enlarged cross-section of an apple and identifying its parts with arrows and block-lettered captions, I added a footnote addressing color and crispness, the tanginess of a Granny Smith vs. the sweetness of a Red Delicious, and the merits of eating them peeled or unpeeled. With no room left on the page, I didn't mention the solitude of the packing shed at dusk, when the odor of rotting rejects permeated the air with unbearable sweetness.

I also omitted any mention of the fine tissue paper in which apples for export were wrapped. It reminded me of letters from home. To save on postage, they were written on onionskin airmail paper, making me feel even more removed from the city the buses came from.

One evening, Ofira caught up with me as I was leaving the dining hall.

"I was very pleased with your report on apples. You express yourself quite well. Why don't you come by my room sometime, and we can talk more about writing? I also have some books you might like."

I thanked her and promised I would. I really wanted to, but going through with it was another matter. Being an outsider was bad enough, but could I afford to make it worse by socializing with Ofira, the natives' sworn enemy?

I remembered what Esau had said to me at dinner, licking mashed potatoes off his knife and speaking slowly so I wouldn't miss a word. "You know that you're unwanted city garbage, don't you? Why did they have to dump you here and pollute this place? Say, did you figure out the math problems for tomorrow?" This from the one native who actually spoke to me.

After thinking it over for several days, I decided I couldn't refuse Ofira's invitation. The following Saturday afternoon I set out for her room, taking a circuitous route. If anyone saw me, I planned to say I was just taking a walk or was heading to my host family, both acceptable alibis for an outsider. Ofira's room was in a small whitewashed house screened by shrubs and leafy trees. The entry porch was crowded with potted plants and two faded canvas chairs. The door was ajar, but I saw nothing in the dark interior.

"Hello," I called out. In the quiet of the lazy hour, I could hear only a high-pitched metallic squeak, rising and falling with mounting urgency.

I took a tentative step inside. The rhythmic squeaking got louder, giving me goosebumps.

"Hello," I whispered. My eyes were slowly adjusting to the dark. Soon I saw faint ribbons of daylight squeezing through the shutters and coiling around two naked bodies engaged in what looked like a wrestling match. Judging by the labored breathing and moaning, not much fun was being had.

When calm was restored, a man's voice said, "Offi, we have a visitor." Ofira turned to me and said with unexpected tenderness, "I'm so glad you came, Danny. We have a lot to talk about. Why don't you take an apple from the basket by the door and sit on the porch for a few minutes? I won't be long."

I sat down in the canvas chair and took a savage bite of the apple. Pale shadows were creeping toward me, marking the lengthening hour. I finally got up and walked to the door. The rhythmic squeaking had resumed with renewed vigor. I turned sharply and hurled the apple core at the tree across the walkway. I would have hit it too, had it not been for my tears.

* * *

One evening I was late arriving in the dining hall. By the time I was ready for my orange, there was no one else at the table. I tried to score the peel, but the knife was too dull. Impatiently, I held it like a chisel over the stubborn fruit and hit it with another orange. The blade punctured the peel. I put it up to my mouth and tried to suck the juice. Even the native citrus was against me! I was about to concede defeat when I saw Ofira approaching.

"Let me help you," she said. A moment later, with her delicate fingers dripping juice, she presented me with a naked, submissive orange. I hesitated a moment, whereupon she thrust her forefinger deep into the core of the fruit, wiggled it a bit, and separated it into sections which she arranged symmetrically on a plate. With a little smile, she watched as I violated her design and ate one section after another.

"It looks like a good one," said Ofira, wiping her hands on a napkin. Actually, it was rather sour, but I couldn't tell her that. "I've just spoken with Freeda, and she said you could come to my room after supper, if you still want to. I'll take you back to the children's house later."

"Thank you," I said, forcing myself to finish the orange.

Ofira and I walked to her quarters in silence. Once inside, she turned on two lamps with colorful shades and lit a thick candle that smelled like raspberry syrup.

"Your husband isn't home?" I asked.

She looked surprised. "I'm not married, Danny."

"But I thought..."

She smiled, turned on a small radio on the end table, and found a classical music station.

"What do you like to listen to?" she asked.

I had to think for a moment, which was longer than she was willing to wait.

"I love Mahler most of all," she said. "When I listen to his music, I feel as if I am sitting in the middle of a field on a gray day. Slowly, fog creeps in and surrounds me until the music ends."

I was now ready to answer Ofira's question. "I like to listen to the radio in the dark. After supper, when Mother and Grandma are in the kitchen cleaning up, I turn on the radio in the living room, turn off all the lights, and lie on the rug with my eyes closed. It's better than a movie. Sometimes I wish I could read with my eyes closed. Waltzes are my favorite music. Grandma told me she had waltzed when she visited Vienna as a teenager. When I see her carry blocks of ice for the icebox or boil laundry on the balcony, I can't imagine it, but in the dark, I can. Sometimes, I listen to plays on a program called *The Curtain Rises*. Have you heard of it? That's where I first learned about Sherlock Holmes and Miss Marple."

"I know what it means to be lonely, Danny," said Ofira.

"How do you know I'm lonely?" I asked, surprised by the anger in my voice.

"Don't be offended. I've been watching you, reading what you write and trying to guess what you don't. I've been in this place as long as you have, and I'm as lonely today as on the day I arrived." She walked over to the tiny kitchenette and returned with a packet of sugar wafers and a jar of dried fruit. First the loneliness business and now the wafers. She had me all figured out.

"You wrote in one of your compositions that sunsets are sad, and also early mornings in the empty classroom, and evenings in the social hall, and the sound of a distant airplane, and the smoke from the village across the highway. You should know that even though most people hate to be lonely, it can sometimes lead to great things."

She took down a slender volume from a bookshelf and thumbed through it. I saw her face light up as she found the page she was looking for. She cleared her throat and began reciting a poem, carefully enunciating the words.

It wasn't hard to figure out that the poem described a hike in the mountains, but I suspected there was more to it than that. Ofira looked over and, seeing the expression on my face, explained.

"What the poet is saying here is that since her last hike in the mountains, time has diminished the light and the glow she remembers. Even so, she recalls old images and seems to hear old echoes."

I nodded slowly. Ofira paused long enough to let a cloud cross her face. She recited another poem she said was related to the first.

"The echoes have died, the poet says here, and nothing remains of her precious past. Her heart is now sad and cold. How can she face a frightening present and a scary future without comforting memories?"

The last question actually made sense to me. Besides seashells and bottle caps, I also had a pretty good collection of memories that someday might be useful.

Ofira fell silent. She seemed overcome by the poems or perhaps worried about their effect on me.

"Rachel, 1890 to 1931," she said as if reading a headstone. "My favorite poet. She came here from Russia at age nineteen, intending to paint and play the piano. She ended up teaching little children but contracted tuberculosis and spent the rest of her days alone in a garret in Tel Aviv. Only then did she start writing short, simple poems about herself, her pain, her loneliness, her doomed love, her certain death. Loneliness fueled her creativity and urge to publish. Ink was her cure for loneliness."

Ofira was clutching the book, suddenly distant. I couldn't think of a thing to say.

"Only that which I have lost is mine forevermore," she whispered, quoting a line from the poem.

After a moment she looked up. "I'm lonely too, Danny. You should know there's nothing wrong with that. As your teacher, perhaps I shouldn't be saying this, but I'll be leaving in a few months. I don't belong here any more than you do. All I want is a little privacy, a place to think quietly. I even want to eat supper by myself, if you can believe it."

"You're leaving?" I asked.

"I want a child of my own, a little boy or girl in a cozy room next to mine, not in a children's house."

"You're leaving me?"

"I have to, Danny, but I'll speak with your parents. You need to leave too and return home."

I thought about it for a long time. When I looked up, Ofira's eyes were closed. I tiptoed out, walked back to the children's house and put myself to bed.

Running my fingers over the embroidered duck on my pillowcase, I hoped Mother and Father would agree with Ofira and take me home. What if they didn't? What would I do without Ofira?

— *Chapter Thirty-Five* —

Whatever they said about Elisheva — that she was haughty, cool, aloof — they had to admit that she was pretty and that her handwriting was truly beautiful. Better than mine, in fact. Even though she was a native, I had warm feelings toward her because she was rumored to be allergic to all boys, not just outsiders like Ezi and me. I thought it might be true because her hands would sweat profusely when one was near. While not a problem when pulling weeds or picking citrus in export season, soggy palms hindered neat and clean writing, and Elisheva was nothing if not a fastidious doer of homework. Her solution was to make an occasional wry comment on the irony of suffering from moist palms in a parched land and to keep a small hand towel on her desk at all times.

Eli, as she liked to be called, was blond and freckled and an all around wet person who started her day by running to the laundry room to smuggle her soggy sheets and pajamas into the hamper before anyone noticed. She took showers both morning and evening, a source of grave concern to the adults who adhered to strict water rationing in this agricultural community. At her desk, she rested her hands on the small towel, sliding it down as she wrote, once in a while unfolding it, drying her hands thoroughly, carefully folding it up again and resuming her calligraphy.

Eli never joined in the circus where Ezi and I were the gladiators, the natives were the lions, and Esau was the emperor pointing his thumbs up or down. Mostly down. I tried to tell Ezi that Eli was different, maybe even a potential ally, but he wouldn't listen. He distrusted girls. For all he cared, I could have her. But what would I do with her? I occasionally thought of it under my comforter before falling asleep, though not as frequently as of the hairdresser in her negligee.

One winter morning I went to the classroom earlier than usual. Eli was alone, writing at her desk. Without looking up, she reached for the towel and placed it on her notebook. I was pleased to have this effect on her and sat down at my desk to write home.

A moment later she was behind me, her chin almost touching my shoulder as she scrutinized my writing.

"Ofira was right," she said. "You do have nice handwriting. You hold your pen funny, though. Your finger bends in when you write. Mine bends out."

In. Out. Was that a reason to address an outsider in public and risk ridicule by one's classmates? At any moment, one of the boys might swagger into the classroom and drop into his chair, making it clear he'd much rather be skewering snakes or exploring farm machinery.

I put my pen down. Eli realized the precariousness of her position. Before returning to her seat she whispered, "Let's compare handwriting sometime."

I remembered a children's theater production we attended in a nearby town. The heroine, leaning from a balcony, dropped a handkerchief to her lover who was serenading her below. I now envisioned Eli up there, dropping a damp hand towel into the eager lap of an outsider who was writing her a poem, holding a pen between his thumb and inward-bent forefinger.

Eli had obviously chosen me, and the first thing a chosen one had to do was submit a writing sample. I decided to send Eli a note about the comparison she had suggested and express my gratitude for her courage in treating me like a normal kid. Maybe I would even compliment her on her pretty face, her freckles, and her meticulous personal hygiene. In the end I just wrote,

> *Dear Eli,*
> *Thanks for speaking to me. I'd like to talk more, and not just about handwriting. How about tonight after dinner? I'll wait for you in the packing shed. It'll be almost dark by then, so no one will see us.*
> *Danny*

I noticed that Eli had left the classroom, so I folded the note and put it under the towel on her desk. After reading it, Eli gave me a little wave and mouthed something I couldn't understand.

I ate little for lunch, skipped dinner altogether, and left the children's house in the last light. The packing shed was empty. A nearby lamppost gave off a feeble glow. I heard a truck on the highway. The moon rose over Mount Tabor. Crickets chirped. Eli would soon arrive.

I paced around the shed and tried to mask the nocturnal noises with heavy footfalls. I sat down on a crate and faced the direction Eli would come from. It's getting late, I thought. The moon had cleared the treetops, painting the shed pale silver. I took out a small bag of biscuits and chocolate squares, counted them and ate one of each. A Jeep drove by. A jackal howled in the distance. I ate more biscuits and chocolate. It was getting chilly.

Eli wasn't coming. I brushed off the crumbs and walked back to the children's house.

As I got into bed, I found a piece of paper under my comforter. I tiptoed to the bathroom and read Eli's elegantly written note.

> *Dear Danny,*
> *Thank you for inviting me to the shed. You couldn't have known I'm afraid of the dark, and I had no chance to tell you. Let's meet tomorrow at Founders' House. Nobody ever goes there, so we won't be disturbed. Let's meet at 4:00 o'clock. I love our secret messages.*
> *Sincerely,*
> *Eli*

I went back to bed, hid Eli's note inside the pillowcase and pulled the comforter over my head. Unlike Eli, I loved the dark.

Located at the bottom of a dip in the terrain, Founders' House was surrounded by thick vegetation and all but hidden from view, either because of security considerations or respect for the landscape. It was built of irregular blocks of volcanic rock that blended with the rich dark soil around it.

This two-story building was like no other, and the only one I ever drew when fantasizing about the house I'd one day build for myself. It had a pitched roof, a chimney, and large windows framed with light-colored stone.

An elderly woman, one of the first native-born, looked after the place. There was little for her to do except dust because weeks or months could pass without any visitors. Once I went there with Father. The exhibits, mostly old photographs, maps, and letters, showed the early settlers living in tents until the climate and the pesky mosquitoes forced them to build a communal house with living quarters on the second floor and livestock sheds on the first. After the settlement expanded, the building was renovated and named Founders' House.

Shortly after my arrival at the kibbutz, we celebrated the anniversary of its founding. Dressed in white shirts and blue shorts, we joined the adults assembled in front of Founders' House for a solemn ceremony with speeches, tributes, lip service, and off-key renditions of old pioneer songs by the youth choir. The oldest surviving settler, propped up in a straw-lined wheelbarrow, made barely audible remarks. In his gnarled hands he held a sapling, and when he handed it to a toddler in a symbolic gesture, there was no telling where the roots ended and his veins began. After singing the national anthem, we sat in a semi-circle and hummed old songs that had been drummed into us for weeks. The few remaining founders were escorted to their table and enjoyed cake and juice. I couldn't help but feel sad as I watched the strangers they had become being led away to their quarters like outside children after an awkward visit with their host families.

— *Chapter Thirty-Six* —

After the school day had ended, I left to meet Eli. The afternoon sun added a glow to the petrified lava walls of Founders' House. As I entered, the caretaker looked up, surprised.

"Hello, little boy. My second visitor today! Imagine, two visitors at the very same time. This is truly a record. At this rate we'll need a bigger lobby."

"This place is very interesting," I mumbled.

"Good for you! By the way, we have a special exhibit on the snakes of the region. Maybe I can give the two of you a guided tour."

"Thanks," I said and quickly went to check the first floor. Eli wasn't there. I went upstairs and, following the sound of footsteps, found the other visitor standing behind three jars of pickled vipers.

"Well, look who's here!" said Esau, straightening up. His eyes, which had looked enormous through the preserving fluid, reverted to their usual beadiness.

"What are you doing here?" I asked the worst student in my class.

"Ofira told me to show some effort if I didn't want to repeat fourth grade, so I came here to look at these cuties. I'm glad you're here. You'll be my witness."

"What do you think of the exhibit?" I asked.

Esau glared menacingly. "Look here, I never said I wanted to talk to you. You saw me here. That's all. Anyway, I've had enough of these slimy critters." He dashed downstairs and slammed the front door behind him. I went over to the window and watched him run up the path.

"Danny," said a small voice behind me.

"Eli," I said, turning around. "When did you get here?"

"Just now. I came in the back door," she said, wiping her hands on a paper napkin she quickly hid behind her back. We stood there for a moment, quite speechless, studying the tile pattern on the floor. "I'm glad you're here," she whispered. "My parents are divorced too, so I know you'll understand me better than anyone else around here."

I did understand her. Only children are one subspecies, and children of divorced parents another, but only children of divorced parents are freaks. I told her how, back home, I kept inventing excuses to explain Father's absences to classmates and Mother's tears to myself. Even tears of happiness would cause me to turn away. It got to where I found any female tears unbearable, even in movies. That was why, when Eli looked at me with teary eyes, I quickly diverted her attention to a coiled black adder and told her about my encounter with a rattlesnake when I was three. Eli's eyes dried up.

We circled the room and stopped in front of a painting in a rough wooden frame.

"Definitely not a view from around here," I said.

"So beautiful," whispered Eli.

Neither one of us was in any hurry to move on, awed by the elegantly dressed men and women in the painting strolling along a wide tree-lined boulevard. The declining sun washed the dreamlike scene with a soft light. Streetlights bloomed in the dusk. Horse-drawn carriages left tracks in the light snow, and far away, a golden cross atop a church spire caught the last rays of the setting sun. A card pinned to the wall explained that it was painted on burlap and was the first work of art created in the valley.

I noticed a door handle protruding from the wall next to the painting.

"That's odd," I said before seeing the outline of a door in the wall. "I wonder what's on the other side."

"No idea," said Eli.

I turned the handle, and the door creaked open, releasing a musty draft. A weak light bulb illuminated a ladder to an open hatch in the ceiling.

"There must be an attic up there," I said, barely controlling my excitement. "Let's climb up and explore." Eli didn't say a word or make a move, so I grabbed her hand and led her to the ladder, closing the door behind us.

"Go ahead. I'll be right behind you," I told her.

She gave me a strange look. "I'm not going up there, Danny. It's even scarier than the packing shed at night."

I had an unfamiliar urge to place my hand on hers and was surprised she didn't recoil when I did. Stranger still, she placed her other hand on mine. There was only one thing left to do, so I placed my free hand on top of hers. Having thus sealed a secret pact of some sort, I felt free to tell Eli about attics and their secrets.

Never having had a room of my own or known much privacy at home, the attic over the hall became my refuge, but to get to it I had to ask Grandma for help. Together we would move the kitchen table under the hatch and place a stool on top of it. While Grandma steadied it, I would step up and out of one world into another.

There, I would sit and play with the small toy cars I had outgrown. Sometimes I would sort and rearrange drawings from nursery school and kindergarten and half-size notebooks from first grade. When I was satisfied that all my affairs were in order, I would rummage through marked and unmarked boxes, discovering old photographs and letters in squiggly hand writing, books in half a dozen languages, and citations and medals from Father's military service.

It was in one of those boxes that I found something I wished I hadn't. As I opened a heavy Russian volume that looked to be an illustrated account of heroic war campaigns, a photograph fell into my lap. It showed Father in uniform, standing under a wedding canopy raised by the rifles of four comrades. Beside him was a young woman, also in uniform, with a lacy white veil attached to her military cap. Father was lifting the veil, about to kiss his bride. She was not Mother.

I quickly stuck the photograph back between the pages of the book and never mentioned it to anyone. Since everyone was entitled to secrets, I was entitled to pretend I hadn't discovered this one.

We stood in the dim light, breathing in mildew. Eli's hand caressed mine in a sign language that was new to me. Very quietly she said, "Why don't you climb up and see if you can find a light."

I climbed up the ladder into the attic where faint daylight was seeping in through closed shutters. Noticing a nearby oil lamp, I struck a match and lit it.

"Plenty of light," I called down to Eli.

After Eli had climbed up, we surveyed the cavernous space filled with dark heavy furniture. Some of the pieces were covered with white sheets, others with a thick layer of dust. Along the walls stood trunks that looked like pirates' treasure chests. In one corner stood a tall bookcase with glazed doors and, next to it, a writing desk and swivel chair, the only dust-free items in the room.

Eli opened one of the trunks and pulled out an enormous pink hat that she immediately tried on. "What do you think?" she asked.

"I think the founders dressed better than they let on in those photographs with mules and bales of hay."

"I'll be right back," she said and disappeared behind an armoire. I braved the mustiness and opened another trunk. Folded on top was a dark gray pair of trousers with maroon suspenders. I slipped them on and rolled up the bottoms. Eli reappeared wearing a white dress, looking quite grown-up. She stopped short when she saw me, and just then, a moment before she broke into uncontrollable laughter, a sunbeam found both her hair and my heart.

"Are you hungry?" I asked.

"A little. Why?"

"I brought some biscuits and chocolate. City food."

"Wonderful!" exclaimed Eli. "Let's pretend we're husband and wife in Vienna. We've been married for ten years. We have a daughter, a pretty fourth grader. She's sensitive and has a great sense of humor. We love her and each other very much. So, here we are, in our salon. We've just returned from a concert and sent the housekeeper to bed. We made tea and tried to guess where she had stored the leftover strudel, all the while humming a familiar waltz. Now we're sitting in these comfortable chairs before the fireplace."

Eli leaned back in her chair. "*Liebling,* this strudel is so rich! One more bite and I'll burst."

"I'll finish your slice, Eli *Herz*," I said. "How has our sweet daughter been today?"

"Oh, the little darling is so precious! She's such a good student and so conscientious. She obviously inherited your work habits."

"Maybe, dearest, but she has your looks and handwriting."

I was warming up to my part, wondering where I had learned the lines. I walked over and put my hand on her shoulder. "You know, sweetheart, I love you even more than when we first met."

"You do love me, don't you? See, it's not so hard, is it? Why can't our parents talk like this? We're so lucky to have each other."

"Very lucky. Before we turn in, dearest, you must taste this. Take one bite from the biscuit and one from the chocolate, and chew them together."

Eli followed my instructions and made all the right sounds to express her appreciation. "I'm hungry after all. Is there more?"

When we had finished, Eli said, "My father wants to take me away for treatment."

"Wait," I said. "This isn't in the story."

"No, but it's true. My parents got divorced last year. My father lives in the city and sees me once a month, but he can't stand my bedwetting and constant washing. Don't be embarrassed, Danny. Everyone knows. I heard him tell my mother he wants to take me to America to see a specialist. No one said anything to me yet, but I'm sure it will happen soon."

"But we've just started getting to know each other."

"It breaks my heart, but I had to tell you. One day I'll be gone, and I wanted you to know why."

There were tears in Eli's eyes, but this time I made no effort to distract her. Instead, I slipped effortlessly into Mother's frame of mind and told myself this was fate. You had to have luck, and I didn't.

We sat there for a long time, holding hands. It was getting late. I picked up the oil lamp and helped Eli down the ladder only to find the doors and windows locked.

"I guess we'll have to spend the night here," I said.

"I don't mind," whispered Eli, "as long as we return to the attic."

*　*　*

It was chilly when I woke up. The lamp's tiny flame trembled. Eli was curled up like a kitten in a large armchair, her hair covering her face. I turned the shutter slats and looked out. The valley was bathed in moonlight. A jackal howled in the distance. A single light twinkled on top of Mount Tabor, perhaps a lamp in the cell of a homesick monk looking out on the beautiful but foreign landscape and wondering if he'd ever stop missing home. It'll never happen, dear monk. Trust me. Go back to bed.

Shouts and barks broke the silence. Men and dogs emerged from the dark looking for two missing children. I blew out the flame. As they got closer, I heard someone say, "That'll teach us to take in outside kids. Do we need this in the middle of cucumber season?" Satisfied that the doors and windows were locked, they walked up the path toward the dining hall.

* * *

When I woke up again, daylight was coming in through every crack and Eli was poking at my ribs. She put a finger to her lips and pointed across the room. A man was sitting at the desk writing by the flickering lamp. I brought my mouth close to Eli's ear.

"Who's that?"

The man spoke cheerfully without turning.

"Good morning, children. I tried not to wake you."

"Hello, Doctor Perlman," said Eli. "We were just…"

"You know, my dears," he interrupted, turning around and smiling, "everyone is looking for you. They haven't yet posted a reward, so maybe I should keep you here until they do." He was an elderly man with white hair and a rosy complexion that went well with his German accent.

"Dr. Perlman, this is Danny. He's my best friend. We were talking here yesterday afternoon, and suddenly it turned dark and we got locked in."

"Yes, when I saw you sleeping like two little angels, I thought something like that must have happened. I know it's hard to find peace and quiet around here. It took me years to discover this place. One day I looked at this building and decided there had to be an attic up here, and of course there was. I tell you kids, when I first found this room, I felt like an archaeologist entering a hidden tomb. I sorted out the mess and made this my secret study. My books on malaria and the poetry of the pioneers were written here. Have you read them?"

"Dr. Perlman," said Eli, "we're very hungry. Can we please go back to the children's house?"

"Of course. I'll take you back and have them call off the search. I enjoyed speaking with you. Please come and visit whenever you like."

Back at the children's house, the natives were eating breakfast. They welcomed us with whistles and probing questions such as "Did you play doctor?" and "Are you married yet?" We blushed but kept holding each other's soggy hands. Finally, they moved over and made room for us. We ate in silence and listened to Dr. Perlman tell Ofira and Freeda how he had hosted these two bright kids in his study the evening before and had finally decided, because of the late hour, to let them sleep there. It's true, he should have told someone. It was all his fault.

From that day on we sat next to each other in the dining hall, oblivious to everyone around us. Eli taught me how to make a salad and I peeled her oranges. I showed her my ramp in the field and she took me to her cluster of pines. On a thick, fragrant bed of needles we sat and ate pine nuts and promised never to lose each other, no matter what happened.

What happened was that Eli went to America, and I traveled an even greater distance, back to the small apartment in the city the buses came from.

* * *

From the top of Mt. Tabor, with the Church of the Transfiguration behind us, Josh and I will look at the valley below. It will be early in our road trip down the length of the country — my present to him on graduating from high school. I'll point out a couple of landmarks mentioned in the Bible, and he'll note that the pattern of fields, vineyards, and orchards makes the valley floor look like an Amish quilt. He will follow my stare to a distant group of buildings surrounding a water tower.

"It's that place, isn't it?" he'll say, and I'll just nod.

We'll drive down the mountain and across the valley.

"Let's go see it," Josh will say. I'll turn around reluctantly, drive up from the main road and park in a shady spot by the gate, hoping the guard won't let us in. No one will be minding the gate. In the barns, livestock will be chewing peacefully. Lunch will be served in the dining hall so we won't run into anyone. Shady paths will take us through a new residential area and toward the crescent of children's houses. I won't be able to identify mine.

I'll say something about how the trees have matured and obstructed the view to the Arab village but won't comment on the warm midday air laced with jasmine and distant smoke. We'll skirt the water tower and head back to the car, Josh's arm casually draped over my shoulder.

*　*　*

Years will pass, and one day Josh will say, "I'm immigrating to Israel." His eyes will warn, "If you object, I'll remind you that you left your country and your birthplace and your home and went to a land that God or whoever showed you." A Hebrew School education will again prove to be a double-edged sword.

I will say, "Just don't get too comfortable with the past. It isn't what it used to be, and it's not always your friend." Then again, maybe I won't say anything.

Unlike Josh, I will never be able to see my native land with fresh eyes, burdened as I am with old memories and expired recollections. Starting out is easy — climbing verdant mountains, looking at distant views, heading for blue skies. Starting over is hard — struggling up rocky slopes, looking for a foothold, turning old stones.

Day Ten *Postal Images*

— *Chapter Thirty-Seven* —

With Tom safely at the hospice and the decision to extend my visit supported by Lori, I sleep soundly and wake up early to call the airline. The agent tells me that this is peak season so any changes to my ticket will be expensive and will have to be done at the Tel Aviv office.

I take a bus to the train station, buy a ticket to Tel Aviv, and stroll through the shops and eateries in search of local color. The platform, lined with benches and billboards, is disheartening. There's no trace of the old chiseled stone station or resin-scented telegraph poles promising journeys on which anything could, and probably would, happen.

I watch my train — new, color-coordinated, and devoid of charm — pull into the station. Not even the familiar clickety-clack of the wheels can move me to like it. Its shadow, however, is another matter. I feel for this fellow traveler being dragged over gravel, assuming the curvature of every rock, and brushing past poles and switch levers.

The airline agent is pleasant and efficient, and soon I'm

back on Tel Aviv's bustling streets. I follow a salty breeze to the beachfront promenade. Seated under a colorful umbrella, I order an iced coffee and leaf through yesterday's *New York Times* which the waitress handed me, perhaps thinking I am on the staff of the nearby American embassy. Broadway is having a good season; election races are heating up; the stock market is volatile; our war up north is dragging on — all the news that would have been fit to print a year or five ago, as it will be a decade hence.

I hear quick steps, and the world abruptly goes dark. Warm hands cover my eyes. A familiar laugh fills my ears and Chanel No. 5 permeates my nostrils. These are all the clues I need. I take Shira's hands in mine. Her laughter stops as she sits down across from me.

"What are you doing here?" she asks, her voice betraying tears behind her sunglasses.

"Never mind that. How have you been?" I ask urgently.

Shira sips the last of my coffee. We weigh our words judiciously and dole them out sparingly, careful not to trip over unraveling heartstrings.

I look across the table at Shira, an unknown woman I once knew intimately. The face I kissed, the hands I held, the breasts that were mine, the thighs that welcomed me: all present and accounted for, but with our covenant broken, I feel like a trespasser for merely looking in her eyes.

"You're so quiet," she says.

We were always good at being silent together, which is not to say that we knew each other so well that little needed to be said. In fact, we were quite content not to know each other's thoughts. Even after all these years, it seems so much simpler and safer to keep quiet and look out to the sea. A distant sailboat is suspended above the curve from her neck to her shoulder, a site to which we had both been partial.

I look at her earlobes and think, have we ever shared a bed? I try to imagine it but feel embarrassed, as if peeping into a stranger's bedroom. Her hair is lighter than I remember, her jewelry richer, and I feel excluded, like a student returning to school after a long absence.

Shira looks out to the sea. I look at her manicured nails and say, "What I remember best is how we met."

* * *

On my first day in the army, I stood in line for vaccinations, uniforms, boots, and dog tags. Over the next few days, I learned to salute, whitewash tree trunks, peel potatoes, and stop asking questions. Fewer than forty-eight hours had passed before I was injured in action, punched for staring in disgust at a brawny recruit chewing with his mouth open while discussing novel masturbation techniques.

Having been issued antiquated unloaded Czech rifles, we were usually posted to nighttime guard duty near high security spots such as the kitchen and latrines. That night I found myself stationed at a gate in the perimeter fence, near a lamppost with a burned-out bulb. To pass the time, I listened to the hum of traffic from the nearby highway and watched the bright Tel Aviv sky to the west.

A Dodge coupe, the standard-issue model for colonels, approached from inside the base and stopped in front of the gate.

I couldn't remember what I was supposed to do first: salute, lift the gate, or check ID's. After a long moment of indecision, I walked up to the driver's side, bent down and looked in. By the dashboard light I could see a colonel in the passenger seat and a female sergeant in the back.

"Good evening," I mumbled. The driver tapped his fingers impatiently on the steering wheel, the sergeant smiled at me the way one smiles at a child with a toy gun, the radio played "The Great Pretender," and the colonel said quietly, "Open the gate, soldier."

"Yes, Your Honor... I mean, Sir! I'm sorry. I'm new at this," I said, and everyone laughed heartily.

"That's all right. You have three years to learn," said the officer. "Now, if you have no objection, we'd like to go home."

Who wouldn't, I thought. I saluted and walked over to the gate. I untied the rope, and the long steel pipe, a concrete block attached to one end, rose slowly. The driver accelerated and drove off into the dark. A moment later, breaks screeched and metal clanged. Paralyzed, my heart pounding, I saw by the glow of the headlights that the road ended at the rim of a ditch some ten yards beyond the gate. Like me, the colonel and his driver didn't realize this gate was used solely for training new recruits.

While I was looking at the perilously angled car, I saw the woman sergeant turning to look at me through the rear window. It was too dark to tell if she was still smiling.

I heard the colonel clear his throat and say politely, "Pardon me, soldier. If it's not too much trouble, would you kindly call for help? We would be ever so grateful."

"Sir, I think I'm not supposed to desert my post."

"Just tell your sergeant that a colonel volunteered to take your place. Don't worry. No tank in the Arab arsenal is going to cross this blasted ditch."

I went to get help, and a tow truck soon arrived to rescue the marooned party. The sergeant stuck her head out the window and said, "Don't worry, soldier, it wasn't your fault. I'm sure you'll protect our country just fine."

I saw her again a few days later. I was standing on the hot asphalt of the parade grounds waiting to board a bus that would take me north for three months of basic training. She was handing out wool caps knitted by volunteers.

"It can get pretty cold up there in winter," I heard her tell the soldier ahead of me.

It took her a moment to recognize me, but then she smiled and said, "I knew I'd see you again. What's your favorite color?"

"Beige," I said.

She rummaged through the boxes and pulled out a light brown ski mask. "Close enough," she said and pointed to a card tucked inside. "Don't forget to write a thank-you note to the granny who made it. If you get lonely in the Galilee you can drop me a line too. It can be a pretty melancholy place, especially at sunset." She jotted down her address on a piece of paper. "By the way, I'm Shira."

"Danny. Pleased to meet you." I decided not to shake her hand because mine was damp with sweat.

When I first wrote to Shira, the setting sun was spreading sadness over the bare hills and valleys. As lights began to bud in the gathering darkness, forming shimmering clusters in the distance, I felt removed from the rest of my small country and from the rest of the world.

* * *

"You didn't answer my first few letters."

"I know," she says. "I never expected you to keep writing. You were persistent, though, and your letters were so legible."

"I can't imagine how I found the time to write during basic training."

"I looked forward to getting them and kept them in a shoe box marked 'Armed Forces.' My mother encouraged me to get rid of them, probably because she had left Europe with only a few family photos. She said it was better to live without promises and false hopes. I told her that, in a country thousands of years old, you needed something in writing to substantiate claims. When we got married, I was glad I had kept your words and declarations. Your letters were more real than you ever were, and they were all mine. Now, of course, I'm sorry I held on to them, but I wouldn't dream of throwing them away. How about you Danny, would you ever get rid of mine?"

I remember how I used to save every scrap of paper, and not just love letters full of words I wished were true. I archived kindergarten paintings, grade school drawings, high school work sheets, ticket stubs, and a list of all the movies I had ever seen. I don't intend to read her letters again, but would I have the heart to discard them?

"Probably not," I reply after a long pause. Her expression tells me she has forgotten her question.

— *Chapter Thirty-Eight* —

I got to America by truck. The trip began toward the end of my three-year army service. I got off duty at midnight and tossed and turned in a fruitless effort to sleep. All I had to do to begin the transition from exhausted, stubble-faced soldier to college student was arrive in Tel Aviv before 9:00 a.m. and do well on the SAT. With little sleep, my dream to start the fall semester in New England seemed as elusive as the fog that swirled around the barracks.

I left the base before dawn and walked to the nearby intersection to hitch a ride. In my backpack I carried a change of underwear and socks, my shaving kit, and several pitas with scrambled eggs, vegetables, and hummus the cook had made for me. On the windy Galilee hilltop, I kept moving to stay warm while listening for cars and devouring one pita after another. I was feeling increasingly anxious about reaching Tel Aviv on time when a semi-trailer screeched to a halt in the middle of the road. The driver got out, relieved himself behind a tree and motioned for me to get in. A minute later we were heading south.

In my exhaustion, I kept dozing off. I woke up thinking of Shira. Our correspondence had slowed, but whenever we were on leave, we'd see a movie, browse in bookstores, or just meet for coffee. We even kissed awkwardly once or twice. Occasionally, she would mail me a poem clipped from the Friday literary supplement. At times, I'd take her mother up on her standing invitation for a home-cooked meal.

The next time I woke up, the driver was stopping for coffee at a service station outside the city. Drinking the muddy brew in the company of rowdy truckers, I decided I'd call Shira after the exam and suggest we meet. Maybe I'd even try to kiss her again. I very much needed a kiss.

As I entered the crowded exam hall, my adrenaline surged. Riding its crest, I finished early. Sweet fatigue washed over me as soon as I put down my No. 2 pencil and turned in my answer sheet. I walked out into the warm, salty air, bought an ice cream cone and sat under a beach umbrella. As I looked westward over the gentle blue-green Mediterranean, I felt certain I could almost make out the New York skyline on the horizon.

*   *   *

"The time I missed you most was the day I took the SAT. I called you later that afternoon. When there was no answer, I called your mother's lab. She told me you were studying in England, invited me to her office for tea and to her apartment for supper. We ate on the balcony. She told me you were a poor eater as a child and would throw your food over the railing when you thought no one was looking. Although your father was very ill, he would summon all his strength to sit with you while you had your supper. Later he'd entertain you with merry tunes on the piano. Music would spill out onto nearby balconies, and neighbors would applaud. After dinner, your mother said I looked exhausted and insisted I stay over. I helped her spread a starched sheet on your bed and was asleep in minutes. Over breakfast, I promised her I'd write to you. On the train back to base, I started a letter but never finished it. I can't remember why."

Shira says, "I spent a year in London studying, eating nothing but Indian food, and feeding coins into the antiquated heater in my room to keep warm. When I returned home, I learned you had gone to America a few months earlier. I found it hard to get used to the hot weather, but at least it drained the energy I might otherwise have spent feeling sorry for myself, watching friends get married, and wondering if my phantom boyfriend would write to me again."

We've rarely talked for so long. I once heard "monologue" defined as one person talking to himself and "dialogue" as two people talking to themselves. Is that what we are doing? Making statements for the record?

* * *

I recall the excitement of my first college year in America, marred only by a vague longing for home. I sometimes thought how wonderful it would be to have an Israeli girlfriend in New England. Thankfully, the novelty of autumn foliage and snow provided a welcome distraction.

After my second year, I returned home for summer vacation and reconnected with old friends. In July I received a telegram from my college admissions officer asking if I would interview Naomi Cohen, a prospective Tel Aviv student who was a late applicant. I said I'd be happy to.

On the day of the interview, I found myself with a few hours to kill, so I thought I might as well call Shira, my only friend in Tel Aviv. It had been three years since we last spoke, and I wondered what we would say to each other.

"Hello," said Shira.

I cleared my throat.

"Danny? Is it really you? It's wonderful to hear your voice. I never thought I'd hear from you again. Where are you?"

"I came home for a visit, but I'm in Tel Aviv for the day. Are you busy now?"

"Are you kidding? Come right over. I can't wait to see you."

A short time later we were sitting on her balcony, sipping cold juice.

I told her about my roommate from Hawaii who never wore matching socks, thought Israel was somewhere below the Sahara, and loved classical music as much as I did.

She told me about her English landlady who had taught her to bake scones and always spoke of her husband who had liberated the Holy Land from the Turks only to die of food poisoning in Jerusalem.

I described snowstorms and freezing rain and trees coated in ice, ablaze in frosty sunshine. She described rain and fog and disembodied spires afloat in a stormy sky.

I told her that I had bought a short-wave radio so I could listen to newscasts from Jerusalem. She told me she used to ride the tube for an hour just to buy skinny international editions of Israeli papers.

While Shira made coffee, I looked at her through the kitchen door and thought how much I liked her, how serene and peaceful she made me feel, but how little physical attraction I felt toward her. After a slice of her mother's walnut cake, it was time to leave.

We promised to keep in touch, and I kissed her lightly on the cheek before descending the slick terrazzo stairs, slipping only once.

"Be careful," she called after me, her voice reverberating in the stairwell.

* * *

I returned to my idyllic college and immersed myself in my third-year studies and in photographing the wonders of a New England autumn. Fall colors, like laundromats, still felt new to me. I never tired of watching leaves turn and laundry spin.

My dream of capturing an Israeli girlfriend in North America had not been realized. Although Naomi was eminently qualified both as a college applicant and prospective girlfriend, she withdrew her application, saying I had convinced her that Israelis belonged at home. I had no recollection of saying any such thing, but I might have in a moment of ambivalence.

The foliage distracted me until wind and rain put out its flame. Shira's first letter arrived about that time. I was going to answer it, put it off, got three more in quick succession but didn't find time for the long reply I thought she deserved. She eventually sent a card with a pencil inside which seemed to say, "No more excuses." I answered and she replied.

She wrote about unseasonable desert winds blowing dust into houses and offices. I wrote about a Thanksgiving blizzard. She craved anonymity in foreign cities. I yearned for a place where everyone had similar worries and hopes. She thought herself too cosmopolitan for local boyfriends. I felt too provincial for the bohemian student body. She imagined hitchhiking through Europe with me. I dreamed of taking her to a secluded New England Inn. She confided what her heart was telling her. I declared I must have been blind all those years.

"I wish we could have seen each other this past year…" I wrote, and she completed my sentence with "…but distance and expenses and school stood in the way."

I suggested, "Maybe we should talk about getting married."

She responded, "I see us spending the rest of our life together."

I proposed, "Let's get married this summer."

And so we did.

* * *

It was some months later, somewhere upstate off the thruway, that I first coaxed a shiver out of Shira's body. I can't remember why we stopped at the little motel, but it was quite pleasant, the lighting was adequate for reading, and the color TV worked fine.

I always felt comfortable with Shira. After all, we had similar backgrounds, grew up in the same country, knew the same songs, and wore our uniforms proudly. We liked the same foods, movies, and music. Passion and surprise were missing, but that seemed a small price to pay for contentment. It was safe to read in bed, hold hands briefly while recalling something from our past, and go back to reading. We could even risk sleeping in the nude. What could possibly happen?

Of course, there was always a chance that something could happen deep inside our heads, in a corner so remote that it might never happen again. On occasion, when our bodies intertwined,

I'd resurrect the image I had formed of her from her letters. The written evidence hinted at a romantic tease, an adventurous temptress who, taking me by the hand, would lead me to realms I could only imagine. What else did I need?

The waitress comes to our table with the check and takes my credit card. I turn back to Shira.

"Each of your letters was written on different color paper," I say, "but all were scented with the same perfume. I read them over and over, kissed the envelopes, licked the flaps your tongue had moistened, closed my eyes and imagined so hard it hurt."

"God, Danny, I don't know what I wrote in those letters, but I couldn't have lived up to your fantasies any more than you could have matched what I read between your lines."

But something happened that night which had not happened before, perhaps because we were together in an unfamiliar place, marooned in a tacky room outside any context we'd ever known, so isolated that even *The Tonight Show* appeared to have been beamed in from a distant planet. That may explain why we put away our books, turned off the TV and embraced in the dark for a long time. The sound of the ice machine and the hum of an occasional car were the only clues to the world outside our door. That night I felt I had gathered her essence as fully as I ever would, parting her lines, fingering each word, fondling the myriad connotations and arousing suggestive paragraphs. We never did go back to reading and were still in each other's arms at dawn. We couldn't stop smiling, even at breakfast in the nearby diner, surrounded by truck drivers on a first-name basis with the waitresses.

* * *

The waitress returns with my card. Shira seems content and says, "I suppose there's not much left to say."

I very much want to say that we didn't fall in love with each other so much as with writing and dreaming. We never communicated as well as we did via airmail. Distance made us more attractive, and we were infatuated with each other's postal images. I needed an anchor, she sought passage, both of us stowaways in trunks filled with excellent words. I say nothing.

Shira is staring at me as if surprised I'm still here. Would she prefer that I leave first with just a kiss on her cheek?

"I have to go," she says. I feel grief being unleashed deep inside me, so far down any rescue attempt would be futile. I offer to walk her to the curb. She hails a taxi. The door closes, and she is gone.

— *Chapter Thirty-Nine* —

I return to Haifa late in the afternoon with a more expensive open ticket, still bothered by the airline agent's words, "It seems you're not so sure you want to go back."

I pull out a crumpled piece of paper from my wallet and dial Tom's hospice. A woman with a Scottish accent answers. I ask her if I can speak with Tom, or at least find out how he's doing.

"Who's calling?" she asks.

"This is Tom's friend, Dan Holzman. I drove him there yesterday."

"This is Sister Marianne. It's good you called. Frankly, we're worried. Mr. Lev left this morning with one suitcase and refused to say where he was going or when he would return. As you know, he's very ill, but we can't keep him here against his will. Since he's paid up through the end of the month, his room will be waiting for him. Before I forget, Mr. Lev left a letter for you."

"A letter? Can you read it to me?"

"This is highly irregular, but... very well," she says, opening the envelope. "I'm so sorry, Mr. Holzman, but it's written in Hebrew. After thirty years in the Holy Land, I still can't read the language. I'm afraid you'll have to come and get it, or I could mail it to you."

I have an overwhelming urge to kick the wall. "No, there's no time for that. Is there anyone there who can read it to me?"

"Let me think," she says. "I'll get the nice man from the

watermelon stand across the road and call you back. What number should I call?"

I give her Esti's number and sink into the recliner. What have I gotten myself into? I'll have to come up with one heck of an excuse for Lori and my boss if I extend my trip yet again. "Cancer patient at death's door missing from Scottish hospice above spot where Jesus walked on water" won't fly, although it might win Best Tabloid Headline.

The phone rings. "Mr. Holzman? This is Sister Marianne again. Mr. Abutbool is standing next to me and will read the letter to you."

"Hallo! Abutbool here," roars a man as if to make sure I can hear him in case the telephone fails.

"Mr. Abutbool," I say, "thank you for your help. What does the letter say?"

He clears his throat importantly and reads in a monotone:

> *"Danny, I can't stay here. Not yet. Not as long as I can see the cross over my bed and care that I do. Maybe I'll come back when I'm closer to death. If you want to find me, think of the old radio show Treasure Hunt. I know I'm no treasure, but here's the clue: the name of this village has in it the letters for the words garden and color yet it means grief and agony. It's an easy one. Once you figure it out, come and visit, if you're not tired of me yet. I'm at the foot of the hill with a fig tree on top."*

Mr. Abutbool gives a little cough. "OK, that's it. Sounds a little crazy to me, but..."

"Thank you, Mr. Abutbool," I say and hang up.

I find a dictionary in my cousin's bookcase and quickly solve the riddle: *"Yagon."* Grief and agony indeed. Who would give a village such a morbid name? I walk to the corner and take the bus downtown. As I hoped, I find a large-scale map of the Galilee at the tourism office and on it the place where Tom sought refuge. It is located a few kilometers north of the road to Safed and, if the colorful map populated with sunglass-wearing deer and smiling cars is to be believed, it is in the middle of a forest. I check the schedule and buy a ticket for an early morning bus to Yagon, hoping Tom is still there when I arrive.

Day Eleven Treasure Hunt

— *Chapter Forty* —

The sun has barely cleared the mountains to the east when I get off the bus at a sign reading "Yagon 2 km." I cross the highway and start walking up the gently sloping road to the village. The chilly morning air is filled with the smells of wet soil and distant smoke. I close my eyes for a moment, but an unseen fighter jet breaks the sound barrier with a startling boom, jolting me out of my reverie. My shadow stretches to the left past the edge of the scarred road and into tangles of thorns but keeps pace with my steps. I tread carefully on the crumbling asphalt so as not to lose my footing.

The piercing sound of a lifeguard's whistle startles me. I look up and see two boys waving from the top of a nearby hill. I wave back, wondering what danger may lie ahead.

As the road descends into a valley, the forest shown on the tourist map cannot be seen for its trees: virgin green saplings that, with luck, will mature some decades hence. Yagon is true to its name, evoking a sadness that lingers as long as its wretched little houses remain in my field of vision: blank dice unfit for a game of chance.

I enter Yagon, a painful spot in the upper chest of my homeland, with dozens of small concrete houses scattered about, lacking any streets or commercial establishments. Not a tree or a shrub. No sound or color. I now understand why Tom chose this ghost town for his last days.

On the far end of the village, I see the hill with the solitary tree Tom mentioned in his letter. I proceed to the house at the foot of the hill and knock on the door. A skinny cat sidles over and, with a weak meow, rubs against my leg. The door opens and there stands Tom, wearing a light robe, smiling listlessly and looking years older than when I saw him two days ago.

"Congratulations," he says. "You found the treasure."

I follow Tom through the living room into the kitchen. He takes a pitcher from the fridge, pours me a glass of water, and tells me he's too weak to return to the living room. We sit at the kitchen table.

"I've been worried about you," I say. "What made you come here of all places?"

"I was here once before, during my army service. We were a week into field maneuvers and arrived at this hill on a Friday afternoon. The sergeant ordered us to get ready for Shabbat. We set up camp and tried to shave and wash up with water from jerricans delivered by a supply truck. We had an hour to rest before supper. After a week without a shower, we smelled so bad we stayed away from one another. When guys started taking off their boots, I almost gagged. Then I noticed this house. I waited for the right moment and literally rolled down the hill to the front door. I knocked and asked the owners if I could take a quick shower. I offered to pay, but they laughed and said that a shower before Shabbat was the least they could do for an exhausted soldier."

Tom pauses, his breathing labored.

"They gave me a new bar of soap and a fresh towel. Their little girl kept looking at me with huge blue eyes. It was the best shower I'd ever had. After leaving a few bills on the bathroom sink, I thanked them profusely and sneaked back up the hill. Fifteen minutes later, while we were sitting around the tree eating supper, I saw the man and his daughter approaching. I knew why they were coming and ran to meet them before the others could overhear us. The man insisted I take back the money I had left and wished me a restful Shabbat. His little girl smiled and hugged my leg. I thanked them again, and they walked hand in hand back to their house. It was one of the high points of my military service."

Tom picks up my glass and takes a few sips of water.

"When I escaped from that damn hospice, I knew there wasn't any place I'd rather be than with the Zerbibs, even though I didn't see them often. I got here by cab and knocked on their door. I asked them plainly, as only old or sick people can, if I could stay with them for a while. They immediately agreed and said they were glad for the company because all of their children were married and on their own. I told them I would stay only if I could help with expenses. Again, they refused payment, but this time I insisted. They treat me like a son. Mrs. Zerbib will be back around noon to prepare lunch. I told her you'd probably be here."

Mrs. Zerbib arrives and serves a delicious lunch which I devour. Tom runs his fork through his food but eats little.

"Yesterday I had a pretty good day," he says. "I took a short walk to a nearby hill, stopping often to catch my breath. There was a nice breeze up there. I looked north, away from Yagon. I know this area is usually brown and dry this time of year and looks pretty depressing, but what I saw was a blue river in a green valley, a little town with red roofs and a church with a bell tower. I'd like you to see it, Danny."

Cutting carefully around the brown spots on a peach helps conceal my disbelief. A river and a picturesque little town in the parched late-summer Galilee? A mirage is one thing, a delusion another.

We finish our meal in silence. Tom puts on a worn pair of sneakers and says, "Let's go." He takes my arm and we walk slowly, stopping to rest along the way. I think of Abraham and Isaac walking together, and I wonder what will be sacrificed today: reality or fantasy.

We stand in the shadow of a water tower, our backs to Yagon, and look down into the valley. Tom raises his hand and says, "Good, it's still there."

All I see is a desolate landscape strewn with rocks and dry brush. "I can't see a thing," I say haltingly. "Must be the haze, or maybe I need new glasses." I wipe them on my shirt with exaggerated gestures.

"You really don't see the river?" asks Tom incredulously. "What about the red roofs? Or the bell tower?"

I make a big production of taking off my glasses again, bending the temples slightly and putting them back on. How can I deny him this simple wish? After all, don't I occasionally visualize a water tower that is but a memory borrowed from Mother?

"Wait a minute," I say. "I do see something — cute little stone houses. They remind me of the German Colony in Haifa. And the river. I never imagined we had one here."

There's nothing like an imminent death to inspire crystal clear illusions. Tom seems pleased.

Back at the house, he sinks into an armchair in the living room and asks if I'd make him a cup of coffee since Mrs. Zerbib had gone out. While the water is boiling, I take out a few bills and leave them on the kitchen counter.

On my way back to the bus stop, blushing clouds, mirrored in puddles by the side of the road, keep pace with my steps. As their glow fades, I walk faster. A solitary crop duster buzzes in the distance, capturing the dying light in its spray. I feel a vague sadness descend as its fiery tail turns ashen.

Day Twelve *Magic Lantern*

— *Chapter Forty-One* —

Mother can't stop thanking me for arriving with a large bag of prepared foods. She tells me she can't imagine cooking for one just yet. Even making a cup of instant coffee and toast in the morning feels overwhelming, and having breakfast alone at the kitchen table is so sad she's been skipping it altogether. She doesn't protest when I take out the good china. We enjoy a relaxed lunch at the dining table, not taking our eyes off each other, if only to avoid seeing Grandma's empty chair.

When I return from the kitchen with two cups of tea and Mother's favorite apple cake, I find her leafing through my childhood photo album with a sad smile.

"Come, Dannika, sit by me. Who knows when we'll have another chance to look at this together?"

By the time she turns to the page with my high school picture, the tea is cold, which gives me an excuse to make a fresh pot and avoid seeing Mother cry. As the water comes to a boil, I go back and kiss her forehead which makes her smile but doesn't stop her tears.

* * *

Before this trip, I rarely spent time with my younger self, but now I feel a growing affection for him. Mother seems to know him better than she knows me. There's evidence that from an early age he showed imagination and initiative, mapped out his own course with minimal supervision, and compartmentalized pain, disappointments, and memories.

It pleases me that he always looked up to the future self he aspired to be. He learned early on to divine the path his future self might take and followed it. I now wonder what either self might think if, at this late stage, I made other choices. What if I abandoned architecture for writing, deserted my new homeland for the old, or left one love for another?

* * *

Toward the end of sixth grade, when leaving school one day, I noticed a black case with silver corner guards near a row of trash cans by the curb. Intrigued, I undid its two latches and opened it. Inside was a rusty magic lantern like the one our science teacher used to project slides of great forests, wide rivers, snow-capped mountains, and other sights I knew only from fairy tale illustrations. I had no idea what I'd do with it, but the thought of having my own projector was irresistible. Although it wouldn't be the same as a film projector, its still images would remain reassuringly unchanged, unlike the fleeting ones on a movie screen.

I picked up the heavy case and carried it the three blocks home. I set it on the living room rug and carefully removed its contents, including a single glass slide with a sepia image of three pyramids. I plugged in the magic lantern and watched with awe as the pyramids appeared on our living room wall. Mother, Grandma, and I enjoyed the view so much that we kept the magic lantern on until the bulb burned out. Sadly, I was never able to find a replacement. Ten years after it had gone dark and just before I went to America, I left the projector by the curb, adding yet another casualty to my to-mourn list.

I now imagine turning it on again. At first the pictures are familiar, the colors rich, the images sharp. I try changing their order, softening their focus, adjusting their brightness. I superimpose random slides, blending them into what could or should have been. Or perhaps actually was.

*   *   *

"Mother's Day is almost here!" bellowed Mr. Stein, looking at us gravely from under his bristly eyebrows. "You don't have much time, so get busy!"

My sixth-grade art teacher never cracked a smile and rarely adjusted the volume of his voice to the ears of his 12-year-old students. Severe, swarthy, and silver-haired, he had the countenance of a crotchety sphinx and acted as if sixth graders were the eleventh plague. Times being what they were, he suggested we use matches — used ones, of course — for our projects.

That afternoon I asked Grandma to start saving her used kitchen matches, expecting that, after a week or two, I'd have the raw materials for a nice little something. Three days later,

Grandma surprised me with a large Quaker Oats tin filled with matches she'd collected from neighbors, friends and family. Judging by the weight of the tin, I was now in the lumber business.

At four o'clock that afternoon, when Mr. Shaul reopened his stationary store, I was waiting, allowance in hand, to buy a small bottle of white glue. I ran home and took all my supplies to the weathered desk in front of the large window in Grandma's room. I emptied the tin onto a newspaper, stared at the pile of matches, and waited for inspiration.

The light softened outside. A few boys were kicking a ball in the yard. A bang on her piano keys told me Miss Rosenzweig was quickly losing patience with one of her students. I was choosing the best matches and shaving off their crumbly heads with the small pocketknife Father had given me for my tenth birthday.

Although I have no documented proof, this is what I believe happened that afternoon. If it did indeed happen, it would go a long way toward explaining my decisions about those matches and the rest of my life.

I looked for ideas in my picture postcard collection and chose Big Ben — tall, pointy, and textured. A showpiece. I finished the cardboard shell that same day and sheathed it in matches the next. After installing a battery in its shaft and a small light bulb behind the wax paper clock faces, I took it to school and learned an important lesson — playing with matches can be dangerous.

Mr. Stein cocked his head, cracked his knuckles, joined his eyebrows, circled Big Ben like a restless tiger, and bared his teeth in a smile that must have been as hard on his lips as it was on my eyes.

"Very impressive, Mr. Holzman," he declared. "Very bold. Now let's talk about where we go from here."

He took out of his desk drawer a guidebook to architectural landmarks. "I'm sure you'll find something here worthy of your talents."

Motivated by his words of encouragement, I spent the afternoon looking through the book and began construction of the Tower Bridge that evening: two towers this time, and a drawbridge with moving parts over a river of blue cellophane.

Mother was beside herself with joy when I transferred ownership of Big Ben to her. I next presented the Tower Bridge to Grandma who immediately began counting the matches I used to build it, stopping only when it was time to start supper.

My next project, a Wild West town, was from its inception a ghost town I inhabited with dreams in which anything could, and probably would, happen. The empty Quaker tin was never refilled after the saloon with its swinging doors opened for business. The only thing left standing after the inevitable shootout was my hasty decision to become an architect.

Was that how it really happened? It's been said that history is not what happened but what was recorded. Now it has been.

— *Chapter Forty-Two* —

Father and I made the trip every summer after I turned seven and he and Mother divorced. He took his two-week vacation, and we went to Jerusalem: Zion, City of David, City of Peace. The city where his brother Isidore lived and where Mother, therefore, never set foot.

I enjoyed those times alone with Father, close to him and far from home. In our tiny country, the two-hour train ride felt like a voyage to another world.

The train from Haifa traveled down the coast on a section of a dismembered railroad that had once linked Istanbul, Damascus, Beirut, Amman, Jerusalem, and Cairo. Old maps show its sinuous lines weaving through this cradle of history like the handiwork of a drunken tailor, stitching together Europe, Asia and Africa. This shoddy patchwork was nonetheless the pride of empires. Trains were as important to them as they were to me, providing us all with a means of escape. In dreams they transported me to faraway places, carrying me through great forests, over wide blue rivers, and across mountains with snowy peaks that kept watch over my solitary journeying.

While Father read the paper, I waited for the short man with the white apron to come by carrying two buckets of bottles in crushed ice. "Seltzer! Orange juice! Grapefruit juice!" he would call out in a gritty voice, a cigarette hanging from the corner of his mouth. As he made his way down the aisle with his legs far apart to steady himself, he searched the faces of the passengers for a gesture or a nod. Most of them slouched limply in their seats, facing the open windows and the breeze perfumed with orange blossoms, hay, and manure.

Father gave me a few coins for a bottle of juice. I pointed to the orange. The man removed the cap, stuck in a paper straw, and handed me the bottle. It was just a routine to break up the trip because the drink was always a disappointment. In a country famous for its oranges, the juice was a watered down, artificially flavored liquid with a vile aftertaste.

An hour later, the train turned east and started its climb into the Judean Hills. Hugging steep slopes, it slithered along narrow canyons, its engine clatter reverberating off ancient cliffs. In the shadows below, narrow channels fed sewage water to small vegetable patches. The smell wafting into the train was quite foul, but in this arid region the terraces and valley floor were a lush, deep green, abounding in enticing tomatoes and cucumbers.

Without diverting my eyes from the passing produce, I asked very quietly, so no one except Father would hear, "So, why did you and Mother get divorced?" Father exhaled an interminable breath likely pent up in his lungs since the train left Haifa, when he knew it would be only a matter of time before I asked. He was always ready with a story at the end of that sigh. The stories were always good, always long, and always tied to World War II but had nothing to do with my question.

Father opened his bag and took out hard-boiled eggs, rolls, olives and oranges. By the time we had finished eating, the train was entering the outskirts of Jerusalem, blowing its mighty whistle at some skinny goats grazing on the railroad bed.

I always felt relieved when the train stopped and its doors opened. Had it gone another few hundred meters, it would have plummeted to the bottom of Gay-Ben-Hinom, a deep gorge separating the new city from the old.

We stayed with Uncle Isidore and his family who lived on Wyndham Deeds Lane in the German Colony. In that neighborhood, houses had deep-set windows, ornate parapets, and Biblical inscriptions in German on the front-door lintels. The one over Uncle Isidore's counseled, *"Fear not sudden terror."*

The thick stone walls kept the apartment at a comfortable temperature year-round. Louvered shutters let in only thin ribbons of light. There was always a jar of apricot jam in the refrigerator, imported Palmolive soap in the bathroom, and the latest issue of LIFE magazine on the coffee table.

During these visits, Father became a different person. Relaxed and visibly content, he would spend hours conversing with his brother and engaging my cousin and me with humorous stories. Around the dinner table he was surprisingly talkative, sharing tidbits of his wide-ranging knowledge of history and politics, and, occasionally, even bursting out with an unfamiliar peal of laughter. However, when our vacation was over, he would leave his Jerusalem persona on Wyndham Deeds Lane where it awaited our next visit.

For me, the highlight of the visit was sitting in front of the ivory-colored record player built into a mahogany cabinet. I was fascinated by the tone arm, shaped like an aerodynamic locomotive, racing along shiny tracks across the black steppes of Red Army Choir records. Father would often join me, humming along and fitting in a war story between sides one and two. The

Russian tunes kept me transfixed until my cousin burst into the room spoiling for a fight or offering to share a cookie.

In my early teens, when fights began to outnumber cookies, Father decided we would stay elsewhere on our next visit. On a warm afternoon the following July, we walked down a quiet side street not far from Uncle Isidore's and stopped in front of a heavy wooden door set in a stone wall. Father asked me to pull on a rusty chain, and the muffled peal of a bell was heard from within.

A lion's head of cast iron in the center of the door opened its maw and a pair of friendly blue eyes peered out.

"Good afternoon," said Father in German. "We'd like a room for two, please."

The peephole closed, the door creaked open, and we entered the Garden of Eden. In front of us stood a Gothic edifice surrounded by flowerbeds and shady arbors. Centered in a square lawn stood a white gazebo encircled by cypresses. Fruit trees swayed in the light breeze, their soft rustle accentuating the peace of the hour when the Middle East napped.

"Welcome to the Convent of the Sisters of St. Anne," said a petite nun. "I am Sister Angelica."

Father told her we needed a room for two weeks. She said she could accommodate us since the stream of pilgrims had slowed that summer. While Father was completing a registration card in his impeccable handwriting, a young nun stepped out of the shadows. Sister Angelica handed her a large brass key and asked her to show us to our room.

We followed her along a colonnade, around a cloistered courtyard, up a circular stair tower, and down a dark corridor to an oak door. She unlocked it, handed Father the key, and glided away.

Our room was large and gloomy. Faint daylight came in through the wooden shutters of two arched windows. A ceiling fan turned slowly, promising peaceful slumber. Father surrendered. Saying a little nap wouldn't hurt, he took off his shoes and stretched out on one of the two canopy beds. Soon, his light snoring was the only sound disturbing the peace.

I tiptoed around the room and examined the dark furniture. A few pictures in gilded frames hung on the walls, depicting smoky Biblical scenes. I was trying to identify them in the dim light when I noticed an odd-looking object above the door. Standing on a chair, I got close enough to discern a man's figure with outstretched arms, his head slumped on his chest. I would have to ask Father about it.

Outside the windows, almost within reach, were the white gazebo and the circle of cypresses. The shadows were lengthening. A train whistle signaled an arrival or departure. A radio came alive somewhere with the five o'clock news. Father woke up from his nap with a series of yawns and contented sighs. The world was preparing for one last burst of activity, and we went out for a stroll around the neighborhood before supper.

* * *

A soft tap on the door woke us the next morning. Father said, "What?" and put his arm across his eyes. I jumped out of bed and opened the door. On the floor stood a ceramic pitcher full of hot water. I picked it up and put it on the basin stand. While Father shaved, I opened the shutters and peered into nothingness — thick fog swirling about, hiding the gazebo, the trees, the entire domain in its folds. As always upon seeing fog, I felt a surge of joy: fog meant no hot sun; it meant anything at all could be hiding behind the untouchable veil billowing with mystery and promise; it meant I too could hide and become invisible.

After breakfast, Father and I ventured out to what we thought was the lawn bordered by fruit trees. Father held my hand tightly and didn't let go. I stretched out my arm but couldn't see my fingers.

"Let's go in and explore the library," suggested Father.

"First let's play," I said, shaking myself free and running into the unknown.

"Come back, Danny, come back," he called anxiously.

"Just a quick game of hide-and-seek."

"All right, but don't go too far," sighed Father, resigned. A moment later he called out, "Where are you, Danny?"

"Here," I said, colliding with the corner of the gazebo. I felt my way up the steps and leaned on the railing.

Father's calls arrived erratically from all directions. As the fog began to lift, it revealed an empty garden with a solitary Father figure resting on a bench, his face shiny with perspiration.

When he saw me approach, he straightened his back and wiped his face with a handkerchief.

"So, are you having a good time, Danny?"

"I am," I said, sitting down next to him. "It's quiet here."

"We could also explore the city sometime."

"That would be fun."

"And maybe go a museum."

"Museums are quiet too."

"That's what's nice about them."

He opened his newspaper and moved closer to me.

"Let's see what's new in the world. Oh, look! A rare archaeological find in the desert not far from here."

Just then, an elderly nun carrying two watering cans walked slowly toward us, heading for the flower beds.

"Let's help her," said Father, putting down the newspaper. She smiled gratefully and handed the larger one to Father and the smaller one to me. She sat down on a nearby bench while we watered the flowers.

"Bless you," she said when we handed her the empty cans.

Walking back to our room, Father put his hand on my shoulder.

"I'm glad we were able to help," I said.

*　*　*

Pale moonlight was trickling in through the partially open shutters, brushing the tips of the fan blades silver. The mosquito net around my bed imparted a misty haze to the room. A cool breeze rattled the shutters, and I got up to close them. All I saw in the darkness were shards of moonlight in the dew.

Back in my bed, looking up at the slowly turning ceiling fan, I thought of how much I enjoyed having Father to myself, away from relatives pestering me with questions I didn't want to answer. Our days and nights were peaceful. Somehow I even found his snoring reassuring. Our visits to Uncle Isidore's were now quite pleasant but, on occasion, when my cousin became too annoying, I'd walk the few blocks to the convent, leaving Father and Uncle Isidore to do whatever loving brothers do which I, as an only child, knew nothing about.

* * *

The following day we ate lunch at the convent's refectory. The wrought iron chandeliers were stingy with their light, but circular windows high above funneled sunlight in diagonal shafts that pierced the gloom and collected in bright pools on the stone floor. Friendly nuns glided silently about, smiling at the guests who spoke in whispers for no apparent reason. We were served rectangles of meatloaf with embedded hardboiled eggs resembling petrified eyes. A beam of light from on high gave the food on my plate a ghastly pallor. I nibbled on a piece of rye bread, sucked on a few grapes, and told Father I was full.

I took my book to a remote corner of the garden and sat on a stone bench flanked by marble urns overflowing with red geraniums. A white dove looked for a foothold in the flowers but, finding none, took off with a rapid flutter of wings. It alighted atop a bronze statue of a saint whose entire back section was missing. On impulse, I put down my book and squeezed into the hollow saint. I pushed my feet into his, raised a finger into his to make a point, stuck my nose into his, and looked out through his hollow eyes. Two nuns were tending a vegetable patch. Father was walking toward the gazebo with a newspaper tucked under his arm. Water was trickling softly in the nearby fountain.

Extricating myself from the statue, I returned to my bench. Two pigeons were patrolling its length and a third was perched on my book. I didn't want to disturb them, so I lay down on the grass and closed my eyes.

A train whistle sounded, hinting at great distances and endless possibilities. From its window I saw green forests and blue rivers, villages with red tile roofs, cows grazing in peaceful meadows, and families picnicking under old oak trees. High above, snowy peaks bared their glistening teeth at the blue sky, keeping watch over my solitary journeying.

— *Chapter Forty-Three* —

Like an ambivalent student, my school seemed unsure whether to stay or leave. Half rising from the mountainside, it was clearly uncomfortable, hiding behind tall trees and turning its back on the view. It was never dressed for the weather, its thin walls letting in heat or cold, depending on the season.

Each morning we would line up in the paved schoolyard for announcements, holiday ceremonies, or admonitions from the principal. Afterwards, we would march off to our classrooms to the sound of martial music. Some days, the wind would turn the loudspeaker and direct it at neighboring apartment buildings, but there were no complaints because almost no one paid attention to marches or speeches anymore.

We spent recess among trees, bushes, and boulders in the wilderness just beyond the schoolyard. After school we would meet at the foot of the giant eucalyptus for a few rounds of a game we called Long Horse.

One day, as we were getting ready to play, Gideon came running, waving a newspaper. The boys were already lined up, bent over, each head butting the rear of the boy in front. The first in line was protected from the eucalyptus trunk by big Avi's shock-absorbing bulk. The girls were standing to one side waiting their turns to jump. Rikki had already begun her sprint toward the long row of backs with the goal of jumping over them and landing as close to the tree as possible.

Gideon suddenly called out, "Hey, guys, it says in the paper that the world is going to end today."

We all knew newspapers never lied. Their weather forecasts and war predictions were always reliable, self-fulfilling prophecies, so that when we heard the fatal words, we straightened up and looked at Gideon sitting on a boulder with the paper in his lap. Rikki, already airborne, landed with a shriek on the hard ground. As we congregated around the boulder, Gideon looked pleased with his newfound status as intermediary between us and fate.

"Tell us already!" whined Rikki, licking her scraped knees.

"Well," said Gideon, relishing his moment, "it says here that at 2:37 this afternoon the world will come to an end. It doesn't say how, but someone in America said it will definitely happen today." We all knew America never lied either.

We fell silent, contemplating our short lives. I realized I had never told Ruthy I loved her, and now time was running out. Ruthy must have noticed that I was slowly moving closer to her, because she suddenly turned to me and asked, "So, do you think we'll have school tomorrow?"

I shrugged eloquently and vowed silently that, if we survived, I would tell her how I felt sometime soon, definitely before the next calamity.

"They should have made an announcement on the loudspeaker," said Ami.

"That's it! I'm not doing homework," said Yossi.

Avi glanced at his watch and said, "We have time for a few more rounds of Long Horse," and walked over to the tree. No one followed him. We sat down in a circle around the pile of school bags. Gideon slid off his rock and joined us.

Avi came over and broke the silence. "Nonsense! No world is coming to no end. Look, there's a bus, and I just heard a police siren. I'm going home for lunch. It's already 2:30."

"It's hard to say for sure," said Sari, apparently feeling that, as the best student in the class, she had to weigh in. "It seems improbable, but, then again, anything's possible."

Aaron piped up. "Sometimes even newspapers are wrong. I read somewhere they invented glasses that let you see people's naked bodies through their clothes. Obviously, that's impossible."

Yossi and I had believed it was quite possible and had pooled our savings to mail order those very glasses from Germany. After we got them, they turned out to be just a pair of dark sunglasses that blocked out everything except the livelier figments of our imagination.

Everyone seemed to relax. Quiet chatting and even a giggle or two could be heard. Avi said, "I don't want to scare anyone, but it's 2:35."

Moish, who had built his own radio and subscribed to an adult science magazine, asked to see Avi's watch. After another minute, he began counting down, "Sixty, fifty-nine, fifty-eight, fifty-seven..." All eyes were now on Moish, our last best hope for survival. "... Twenty-four, twenty-three, twenty-two..."

"Wait, what about our parents?" asked Shuli. "Who's going to tell them?"

Moish looked around, still counting, "... four, three, two, one!"

"Boom!" roared Yossi, jumping up and waving his arms. My heart skipped a beat. We remained seated, looking at each other, waiting for either annihilation or a cosmic all-clear.

"So, where's your end of the world?" asked Rikki, looking at Gideon with contempt.

"It's not my fault it didn't happen," he said.

Avi walked up to Gideon, grabbed his newspaper and tore it to shreds. "Enough already with this craziness!"

In twos and threes, we turned and walked off to our streets, our homes, our lunches. I lived to tell Ruthy that I loved her but never did.

*　*　*

The houses of my friends and classmates lined the route I took to and from school. It was the route of choice for seeing and being seen. When Benny's father gave him a small transistor radio the size of a matchbox, Benny held it to his ear and walked up and down the street a dozen times to make sure people saw him and coveted the tiniest radio ever seen around here.

When I turned twelve, Uncle Meir gave me my first watch. I immediately strapped it to my wrist and took it for a walk, checking the time every few seconds. I was pretty sure many jealous eyes were following me.

When sweat started collecting under the leather strap, I returned home to tell Grandma about the most wonderful hour I'd just spent.

"Good, good," she said. "Be sure you put it in a safe place."

"I will," I promised, but when I looked down at my wrist the watch wasn't there. Panic ensued. Grandma and I searched the front hall and staircase. Nothing. We retraced my route, walking up one side of the street and down the other. Nothing. I felt terrible. Learning that Uncle Meir had put aside money for many months to buy the watch made me feel even worse.

The next morning, Grandma went to a jewelry store and purchased a less expensive watch that closely resembled the one I had lost. Grandma and I made a pact to keep it a secret. Whenever he saw me, Uncle Meir would smile and ask me for the time. I don't know if he ever noticed that the watch was different but, even if he did, he never said a word about it.

* * *

Each Wednesday afternoon during the year before I became a man, I would walk down the street to the apartment of Rabbi Klein, my bar mitzvah tutor. As soon as he opened the door, he would start humming my Torah portion, waving his right hand vigorously like a field commander gesturing "Follow me!" I hummed along then added the words from a tattered Pentateuch and eventually managed to cross the Deuteronomic minefield in one piece. From his post at the head of the table, Rabbi Klein would strategize a cautious advance into a group of seemingly uncomplicated verses, signal a retreat for review, then attack the next target. I followed Rabbi Klein as best I could, all the while counting the moles on his arms and the days to my bar mitzvah.

Today, twenty-seven years later, I walk to the synagogue where I was bar mitzvah'ed and join the sparse congregation for morning services in the timeworn sanctuary. Back then, the building was less than a year old, the men's section and the women's balcony were filled to capacity, and the toilets worked.

On my special day, Father came to Haifa and walked with us

to the synagogue. When I finished my chanting, Father smiled at me approvingly as our hands met on the Torah scroll. With tears in their eyes, Mother and Grandma tossed candy from the balcony. After the service, we walked home for a festive lunch with relatives. I tried keeping up with the other men, but my steps weren't any longer than they had been the day before, when I was still a boy.

Of course, I have no way of proving any of this. No one in my family owned a camera, so a rare opportunity was missed to catch Father, Mother, Grandma, and me in the act of impersonating a normal family.

After lunch, my first manly act was to unwrap my presents, mostly books, doubling the size of my library. At Mother's the other day, I found a favorite book that had survived the intervening years: the unabridged Hebrew translation of *The Count of Monte Cristo*. Thumbing through it, I found a dog-eared page with this passage:

> *What is the sense in recriminations about things over which the will of God itself is powerless?*
> *God can change the future; He cannot alter even an instant of the past.*

After leaving Mother's with the book and returning to Esti's apartment, I stayed up late rereading the passage. Unlike God, humans can and do change the past: rewriting, recasting, and restaging it for new tastes and preferences. While God busies Himself with the future, we play with our history blocks. We may remember what happened, or what we believe happened, but what about what we wish had happened, or what others say happened? Not to worry, because we can always forget selectively, remember judiciously, and revise creatively. If sufficiently inspired or cunning, we can even borrow the pre-owned memories of others.

— *Chapter Forty-Four* —

News travels fast in a small apartment, and after a while, there was no reason to hide anything, even from me. Mother and Grandma began to speak openly about the new man in Mother's life, confirming my classmates' breathless reports of sightings around town.

Judging from the increasing flow of information, this was no ordinary acquaintance. One evening, while I was doing homework, Mother sat down next to me and told me how she had met Oscar who was seated next to her at a wedding reception. There was something about the band, the sweet little breeze on the terrace, the garden in the moonlight. She had reached the requisite ripeness, Mother said poetically. How would I feel, she asked, if she got married again?

"Absolutely," I said with an encouraging smile.

That Oscar was a prize was clear from Grandma's referring to him as a *Balboos*, a Yiddish word for a man who takes good care of his house, cooks, cleans, and entertains guests. He also shared Grandma's views on the importance of furniture, fixtures, and equipment. Not only did this Balboos exceed Grandma's expectations, he also — and this she whispered — had money and a car.

OK, so it was a pickup truck, but it had the same number of wheels as a Rolls Royce. With a little effort, we all squeezed into it on the Saturday he drove us to his house for lunch.

Grandma's eyebrows rose higher and her smile grew wider

with each course he served. At one point, I excused myself and went to the bathroom, which was spotless and deodorized. I also know for a fact that it didn't have curly little hairs in the corners because I checked. On the way back to the dining room, I took a wrong turn, ending up in a spacious bedroom, discovering that this was not Mother's first visit there: her suitcase stood at the foot of the biggest bed I had ever seen.

After dessert, Grandma insisted on doing the dishes, and Mother, with less enthusiasm, offered to dry them. Oscar must have had Grandma pegged by then, for he did not object a second longer than etiquette required. He led me to the back of the house to show me his study, as he called it. I never learned what kind of work he did there, or anywhere else for that matter, because there were no clues in that perfectly neat room with its cleared desk, empty bookcase, and two armchairs symmetrically positioned on either side of a floor lamp.

Oscar directed me to a tall cabinet in the far corner of the room. Glass shelves mounted against a mirrored back held a display of woodworking tools: saws, planes, augers, hand and power drills, hammers, chisels, screwdrivers, and other implements I had never seen before. I noticed that all the tools were new and dust-free, protected behind glass doors secured by a brass combination lock.

I wanted to know more but didn't ask. As we were leaving the room Oscar said, "Someday, all of this could be yours." It sounded to me then, or perhaps just now, as if he were delivering a well-rehearsed line.

When Grandma and Mother had finished the dishes, Oscar gave his kitchen a quick inspection, hung the dish towels on the oven door handle, nudged the toaster a bit closer to the backsplash, rubbed his hands together and said, "How about a nice walk on the beach?"

I was about to accept when Grandma grabbed my hand and quickly said, "No, you two should go. Danny and I will stay here and rest." Additional pressure on my hand made me accept her decision without protest. Oscar brought us two fluffy pillows in lightly starched and pressed pillowcases before leaving on his walk with Mother. As soon as the door closed, Grandma said, "They should be by themselves now. Come, let's take a nice nap." She made herself comfortable on the sofa and fell asleep. I tiptoed out of the room and began exploring the house.

Things I expected were there: new furniture, lamps, and knickknacks; things I hoped for: a vacuum cleaner, a telephone, a mixer; and something I only dreamed of: a deluxe model train in its sealed box.

I returned to the living room, moving about quietly, opening and closing cabinet doors, looking for signs of life. As I opened one of the cabinets, a record player silently slid out. I found records on a nearby shelf, but all were sealed. I ran my fingernail along the cellophane wrapping of a Red Army Choir record and placed it on the turntable. I pushed a button and watched the tone arm swing out and the needle find its track. I lowered the volume until the music was barely audible, but Grandma woke up anyway and began humming along with the patriotic Russian songs.

"What a Balboos!" she sighed at the end of side one.

The wedding took place a couple of months later. It was a low-key event. Not even Grandma and I were invited. In fact,

I didn't know about it until Mother and Father returned from their second honeymoon in Cyprus and simply said, "We believe this is best for everyone." I gave a huge smile — I know, because I saw it reflected in Mother's new sunglasses — and a little cheer. Even the pressure from Grandma's hand failed to stop me from jumping up and hugging both my parents at the same time. "Unbelievable," I mumbled.

They contacted a real estate agent the very next day. A week later movers loaded our belongings onto a truck and moved us three blocks to a larger apartment, slightly higher up the mountain. It had a floor-to-ceiling built-in closet, a telephone, and an olive tree within reach of the balcony. Best of all, at age fourteen, I finally had a room of my own.

I was ecstatic. Father was happy. Mother seemed pleased, and Grandma didn't complain.

— *Chapter Forty-Five* —

It took the Israelites forty years to get from Egypt to the Promised Land. It took us less than an hour to get through stories about Pharaoh, Moses and Charlton Heston and arrive at the sumptuous Passover feast.

In early April, a few years before Grandma passed away, Lori and I left frigid Boston for balmy Haifa. It was to be my first Passover back home in ten years, Lori's first trip to Israel, and her first chance to meet my family. On the plane, over peanuts and soft drinks, I told Lori about the special holiday foods awaiting us at the end of our long flight. When our dinner trays were placed in front of us, she said that one thing our forefathers undoubtedly enjoyed in the desert was plenty of legroom and probably better food.

We arrived the day before Passover. After hugs and kisses from Mother and Grandma, we toasted *l'chaim* with brandy from a bottle that had been half-full since I was seven. I wished father had been able to be there too, but he hadn't lived in Haifa since he and Mother separated again when I left for college in America. I was happy to hear he was going to join us for the Seder.

The smells of my childhood woke me early the next morning. On my way back from the bathroom, I stopped outside the closed kitchen door to listen to comforting sounds of cooking and frying. I heard Grandma say, "So, what do you think of Lori?"

"Very pretty," was Mother's flat reply from the other end of the kitchen. "Dannika is looking a little skinny though," she added.

"What *pretty?* She's *beautiful! This* thin." Grandma, I was quite sure, was holding up her pinky to show Mother just how thin she thought Lori was. "Did you notice how she looks at Danny?"

"Of course," said Mother indignantly. "Why shouldn't she? She was lucky to find someone like him at her age."

"What *age?* She's only 26!"

Nothing else was said, but judging from the banging in the sink, I knew cooking utensils were being dropped with great force.

I went into the kitchen where Mother and Grandma greeted me with broad smiles and a sampling of Seder foods: gefilte fish, charoset, potato kugel, and brisket. Washing it down with chicken soup made me feel even more at home.

Grandma kept me company at the table, breaking a matzo into a mug of steaming coffee. I must have looked on with wonder at that long-forgotten annual custom, because she smiled and said, "I'm not just eating matzo in coffee, I'm eating memories, and they need to be softened for my dentures."

Lori shuffled in and got a big hug from Grandma. After a few sips of coffee, she dozed off with her head on my shoulder.

"Poor baby," said Grandma. "She hasn't slept enough. Put her in my room, Dannika, so we can set the table in the living room."

Jet lag caught up with me after lunch. I tiptoed into Grandma's room and joined Lori under the down comforter, a move that did not escape the watchful eyes of a dozen sepia ancestors chaperoning from inside dark frames. They needn't have worried because Lori didn't stir or alter her rhythmic breathing. I put my head next to hers on the enormous goose down pillow and fell asleep holding her hand.

Waking up later in the afternoon, I found my clothes on a chair by the bed. From the kitchen came the sounds of conversational German, Hebrew, Yiddish and English. Somehow the mix sounded right. I got dressed and peeked into the living room. The table looked beautiful with pillows on each chair. Father, already in his, was immersed in the story of the Exodus in his favorite Haggadah, as if eager to discover how it would turn out this time.

"Aba, it's so good to see you. Sorry I was asleep when you got here. This jet lag is a killer."

He jumped to his feet, and we hugged.

"I caught the last bus from Jerusalem," he said.

"Have you met Lori yet?"

"Of course. She's a sweet girl. She gave me a kiss and a cup of tea as soon as I got here."

Lori came over, wearing a fetching spring dress, holding her hand out, first to Father then to me, as if to accept the statuette for Best Costume at a Seder or Family Reunion.

Uncle Avrum arrived soon after and started rummaging through a pile of Haggadahs to choose the nicest ones.

When Alicia, representing Argentina, swept into the living room as if looking for a tango partner, it was time to light the candles and sit down for the Seder.

Although he no longer lived there, Father continued to hold the largely ceremonial post of head of the family. As such, he had the prerogative to lead the Seder but, deferring to age and experience, conferred the honor on Uncle Avrum who smiled gratefully and looked for approval from Grandma at the head of the table. She nodded, and he took his seat opposite hers. Grandma signaled to him, and he said, "Let's get started!"

Uncle Avrum raised his cup of wine and chanted the blessing, and we were off, racing to catch up with Grandma who had lost patience with her brother's dillydallying, nearly ran over the Four Sons, and was already within sight of the first plague. Uncle Avrum, rising to the challenge with a glint in his eye, barreled into the bloody frogs, sprinted through the crunchy locusts, caught up with her in the hailstorm, and left her behind in the darkness.

"What's the big rush?" she intoned in Yiddish, breaking his momentum. While he carelessly stopped to answer, she dashed down the page toward a rabbinical argument over precisely how many plagues were visited upon the Egyptians — 10, 50, or maybe even 250. Sensing this had to do with math, Lori gave me a glazed look.

Uncle Avrum, in a desperate bid to outpace his sister, gave chase and bolted past Grandma, briefly maintaining his lead before being stymied by fresh horseradish. She shrewdly bypassed that obstacle and made a final dash to the finish line, crossing it with a hard-boiled egg and salt water.

Father spent the entire race going through the motions. Mother turned the pages energetically, and Alicia, who spoke no Hebrew and used the illustrations as a roadmap, lost her way almost immediately, looking on helplessly from the sidelines.

"Well done!" called out Grandma to her worthy opponent at the other end of the table. "Let's eat!"

She and Mother went to the kitchen. Lori turned to Alicia

and spoke to her in halting Hebrew. Alicia attempted to respond in English, skipping syllables and whole words in her rush to communicate.

"What about your Spanish?" I asked Lori. Alicia's eyes brightened, and she launched into her native tongue with an even faster cadence. Lori joined in, cranking up her own words in an effort to keep up. Father and Uncle Avrum were debating current events and hazarding predictions on what would happen to our little country.

Every Haggadah can turn into actual recollections if repeated often enough. Grandma's stories are my own memories, the stories of the Exodus are my people's remembrances, and intermixed with both are hidden agendas, secret hopes, and a single-minded resolve to inspire, even inflame useful truths for generations to come. Pottery shards, scrolls, and broken vessels will never measure up to gossip and legends. The target audience clamors for bitter hardships in a cramped apartment, signs and wonders and a parted sea, blood and fire and billowing smoke. *Dayenu!*

The appetizer left the traditional traces of red horseradish on the white tablecloth. Grandma asked who wanted seconds. Father said he did, but she must not have heard him. Mother hesitated then served him another portion. The chicken soup that followed elicited an enthusiastic compliment from Father. Grandma didn't respond. He seemed content, though, and smiled whenever I glanced at him. That made me feel a little better but must have affected my appetite, judging by Grandma's asking why I was eating so little.

I pleaded temporary fullness and Grandma reluctantly granted a fifteen-minute recess before dessert. I stepped out onto the balcony, loosened my belt and breathed in the cool night air. Lori soon joined me and seemed to be on the verge of saying something. I kept silent.

"We'd better go in. They're waiting for us," I finally said

Back at the table I avoided eye contact. Mother poured the tea. Grandma cut the cake. I stared at my piece. Father said, "Best cake I've ever had!" Everyone heartily agreed. I took a small bite to see what all the fuss was about. It was the taste of my childhood, and I couldn't stomach it.

Day Thirteen Little Switzerland

— *Chapter Forty-Six* —

Oral arguments begin as soon as I tell Mother about my toothache. I try to defuse the situation by promising her I'll see my Boston dentist when I get home in a few days.

"No, no. You must see Ziggy today. I know I can get him to see you this morning." She hangs up quickly.

A few seconds later, the phone rings again. "As soon as you get *home?* What, you have another home now?" Again, she hangs up before I have a chance to protest.

Dr. Ziggy is qualified to be our family dentist primarily because he and Grandma had played together as children. Dr. Ziggy never worried about getting older and compensated by switching to ever-darker shades of hair dye. When I last saw him, his wrinkled face was framed by jet-black hair which clashed with his white five-o'clock shadow. This didn't seem to trouble him either.

But now, with the debris of my old silver filling twinkling in the sink, I realize I need immediate help. Even Dr. Ziggy can be trusted, I would think, to follow the recipe for a fresh batch of amalgam. Mother insists on going with me, and soon we enter the perpetual dusk of his waiting room. Dying plants in front of a cracked windowpane only increase my anxiety.

I notice a crack in Mother's voice as well.

"We weren't in a good situation. People gave us bad advice," she says, as if resuming a conversation she started without me.

"Advice about what?" I ask as she pulls a handkerchief from her purse.

"Can you ever forgive us for sending you to that awful place?"

This has been a taboo subject since I was ten, and I prefer we keep it that way.

"Only if we get out of here this very minute," I say too lightly, too late.

A door squeaks open, and Dr. Zigesmund Braun emerges from his inner sanctum, his eyes and dentures twinkling merrily. He takes my elbow and leads me into a back room where, with a blinding light shining in my face, he extracts a confession that my toothache has been getting steadily worse since I arrived.

"Now we know why. It's not a cavity anymore; it's a cave," he says in halting English, apparently for my benefit. Getting no reaction from me to his toothless sound bite, he numbs my mouth and reaches for the drill. I notice his trembling hands, but it's too late to retreat.

"So, we go spelunking, yah?" says Dr. Ziggy, gleefully grinding away, humming a little tune.

"Danny was a good boy today," he tells Mother. "Make sure he doesn't eat for the next two hours. The pills are for pain. This is for later," he adds, dropping a lollipop into her handbag and winking at me.

* * *

Tamar emerges from the closet like Venus from the sea and almost as gloriously nude. Judging from my reaction, or lack of it, Dr. Ziggy's painkiller is extremely potent, leaving me with nothing more than a desire to sleep.

"Hi, Danny. We just got back from the beach," Tamar says, struggling to restrain various body parts from breaking free of her skimpy bikini, while holding a red beach towel as if trying to arouse an exceedingly shy bull or a comatose matador. I almost doze off.

"I just wanted to tell you that Tom left a message on my answering machine."

I try to sit up. "What did he say?"

"That he's in the saddest place in all of Israel and, if I figure out where that is, I should come and visit. I don't understand his riddles."

I sink back into the recliner, the room spinning around me. "You are so..."

"Pardon?" She moves in closer, the better to hear me.

"Dr. Ziggy's pills," I mumble.

I can't keep my eyes open. Amorphous or amorous shapes dance before my eyes. Something soft seems to touch my lips, and I think or dream Tamar is kissing me.

When I wake up, two pairs of eyes are staring at me warily as if I were an exotic specimen who might make a sudden move, hurting himself or others.

"Hi there," I say. "What time is it?"

"Time to get up," says Dorit. "It's almost two o'clock."

"I'm tired of babysitting," sighs Eitan.

"Danny isn't a baby."

I yawn and stretch my body into wakefulness. "What's this about babysitting?"

"Mommy was worried about you," says Dorit. "She told us you were woozy. She had to go out and asked us to stay with you. Would you like a cup of coffee? Instant is my specialty!"

I hope I have a daughter some day. "I'd love one, thanks. When is Mommy coming back?"

"Later." She whisks the coffee, sugar and a spoonful of cold water into a thick paste and waits for the kettle to whistle.

"I have a great idea," I say. "I'm feeling better, and it's still early. Why don't we go on a little hike? There's a part of the Carmel that's special to me. I'd like to show it to you. I'll even buy you ice cream."

"Let's go!" says Eitan, sitting down to put on his sneakers.

Dorit carefully places the steaming cup in front of me. "What part of the Carmel?"

"Little Switzerland. Ever heard of it?" They haven't.

I leave a note for Tamar, and we head out. We change buses, and I look for familiar sights but see none among the terraced neighborhoods cascading away from the road. The bus driver, who looks to be about my age, remembers Little Switzerland. He lets us off between stops and points to a side street sloping toward the sea.

This area was well outside the city limits of my youth. With enough squinting and wishful thinking, it looked like the lower foothills of the Swiss Alps but without the snow, scenic peaks, or charming villages. It had a couple of deep ravines, a few impressive cliffs, winding narrow paths, and thick vegetation that screened the non-Alpine sea below. One particular spot produced great echoes.

Now it's part of a noose of new neighborhoods choking old Haifa in styles ranging from faux LA to mock Bauhaus. Grandma would have dismissed it as a "necklace on a pig."

We enter an affluent subdivision of white houses with professional landscaping and late model cars in covered carports. We pass a small convenience store, and I ask the woman behind the counter how to get to Little Switzerland.

"No, no. Russia!" she answers with a thick accent. "I from Russia, no *Switzland*."

On the wall behind her is a colorful poster promising "Views to the sea! A magical development in our own Carmel kingdom! Spacious homes with exceptionally high standards of construction and finishes!"

I buy us cold drinks, and we sit on a bench to cool off. Frustrated, I get up and trespass through a nearby yard to look for anything recognizable, but all I see are more white terraced houses with domesticated vegetation on the next ridge.

As if reading my mind, a man calls down from a balcony. "Pretty crowded here, isn't it? Soon there won't be enough room to breathe." Of course he knows about Little Switzerland and regularly hiked there until it was paved over. "It's right under the asphalt you're standing on." He invites me to come up for a cold drink and a little reminiscing, but I have to get back to the kids. "Stop by any time," he calls after me.

My disappointment must be showing because Dorit puts her hand in mine and says, "We liked the hike, right Eitan?"

"I guess. Are we still getting ice cream?"

"Of course," I say and take them to an outdoor café overlooking the city and harbor. They devour their ice cream and give me a taste. Artificial flavor, just as I remember.

Across the bay, sand beaches and high-rise apartment blocks are turning pink. Growing up in a city facing north and east, I rarely saw a sunset, so how did I learn to become sad at day's end? A glass office building in the distance catches the last rays and shoots them back at us. The reflections are even sadder than the original.

*   *   *

She rang the doorbell one evening and introduced herself. Petite, with shiny brown hair and sparkling eyes, Amy said she was an exchange student from New York spending part of her junior year at the high school I had graduated from the year before. She was writing a paper about Israeli and American exchange students and wanted to ask about my experience in New York during my junior year. Of course I invited her in. We sat on the balcony where a breeze from the sea made the humidity bearable. Grandma brought out a tray with a sweaty bottle of seltzer, raspberry syrup, and two glasses.

I poured the seltzer, stirred in a bit of syrup and offered her a glass. She sipped slowly and looked around. A few pigeons were perched on the olive tree whose branches brushed against the balcony rail. Across the yard, on another balcony, two middle-aged couples were playing cards, laughing boisterously, and chain smoking. Through an open window came an aria from *Turandot*, the soprano competing with a bass-baritone delivering the evening news on a radio in the next apartment. In the kitchen, Mother and Grandma were doing the dishes while listening to the daily Yiddish broadcast on the transistor radio. Father, in the living room, was placing wrinkled stamps from his worldwide correspondence between the pages of a heavy anthology of Russian poetry, weighing it down with some Pushkin, some Goethe, and the latest volume of Encyclopaedia Hebraica.

I told Amy it was hard to believe two years had already passed since my semester in New York. After returning home, I graduated from high school and completed basic training, but in my mind I was still leaping across the seven time zones, using Eastern Daylight to buffer Middle Eastern time. At 10:00 p.m. Broadway time, I went on morning runs in the damp Galilee air, ignoring my comrades' cadence calls and humming show tunes instead. When tackling an obstacle course here, it was time for *The Today Show* there. Lying on my cot in a tent smelling of sweaty boots and cheap soap, I would recall the fumes of Manhattan's rush hour traffic and long for the hazy skyline and the chime of my host family's Park Avenue doorbell.

Amy made notes in a pink notebook, her hand moving quickly, producing an even stream of writing. A sudden thud in the dark, followed by a loud protest from a cat, caused her hand to jerk and mar the perfect page, but she kept on writing. I didn't interrupt to tell her it was our neighbor, Herr Ellenbogen, bombarding stray cats with stones he kept in a rusty pickle tin, cursing in High German and telling his wife that someone should solve the stray cat problem and make this miserable country habitable for cultured Europeans like themselves. The late Frau Ellenbogen kept her customary silence.

"When I came back from New York I discovered what it's like to be homesick for a place that's not your actual home."

She gave me a sad smile. "I love it here, but it's stupid little things I miss, like Hershey's syrup. I don't talk about it, certainly not with my hosts. How could I? They had lost their son in a border skirmish just a few months before I arrived, and here I am feeling sorry for myself because I have to go without chocolate syrup for six months." Dabbing her eyes, she stood up and gazed into the darkness.

The neighbors had finished their game and were now waiting for the eleven o'clock news. Someone played the violin. Someone else yelled "Quiet!" I looked down at the top of Amy's head, more than a foot below my eyes.

"Your country is so crowded," she whispered.

Walking her home along deserted streets, fragments of classical music drifted from open windows and the scents of jasmine and pine clashed with the foul odors from the refineries.

I tried to see the drab buildings, dusty trees, and cars parked on sidewalks through Amy's eyes and imagine what was going through her mind.

"I was told I'd feel at home here," she said, "but to tell the truth, I've never felt so lonely."

I put my arm around her, and she clung to me fiercely. I kissed the top of her head and she looked up at me tearfully. In the dark stairwell outside her apartment, I saw tiny reflections of a street lamp in her eyes. An unseen radio marked the end of the day with the national anthem.

When I got home, Grandma was still up having a cup of tea. I placed the empty milk bottles outside the front door and joined her at the kitchen table. "I could marry her right now," I said. She sighed and offered me two chocolate squares.

Amy and I would get together whenever I was home on leave. One day I took Amy to Little Switzerland. We ran down a slope to a clearing carpeted with wild flowers. We spread a blanket on the grass and ate the sandwiches, oranges, and cookies Grandma had packed for us.

Amy sighed contentedly and fell back on the grass, pulling me on top of her. With shaky hands and fingers smelling of oranges, I unbuttoned the top of her blouse, wondering how I summoned the courage. She laughed, pressed my face to her bosom then gasped. Feeling her body tense up, I looked up and saw a troop of wide-eyed cub scouts staring at us.

I grabbed my backpack and helped Amy up. Some distance away, we looked back and saw the cubs still standing in formation, as if afraid to break the spell.

"It's a small country," I said.

I took her home. She said goodbye, touched my cheek and started to close the door. I love you, I thought.

"There's no room to breathe here," she said.

I had the last thought. Amy had the last word.

* * *

By the time I get Dorit and Eitan back, Tamar is already home. I go out again. Sidewalks and shops are crowded with strangers.

I stop at a bookstore to browse recently published Hebrew

novels. I'm tempted to buy a few before I remember that the ones I bought on a previous visit are stacked on my nightstand, still unread. On my way out, I see a rack of postcards and stop to get one for Lori.

Someone behind me exclaims, "Danny! Imagine, I still remember your back side."

I don't even recognize her from the front, with her unnaturally red curls, huge glasses, and strong tobacco smell.

"Ilana," she says. "Have you forgotten me?" She touches my arm just like the skinny girl with that name used to do in 9th grade. She takes off her glasses and gives me a wistful look that clashes with her smile. Now I remember her.

Ilana was the first girl I'd had the courage to invite to a movie and later to a dance at a club above the bank where I had opened my first account when I was eight. Paul Anka sang, "Put your head on my shoulder," and we slow danced one floor above the tellers' windows where I had joined the junior savings plan whose mascot was a neatly dressed schoolboy named Dan the Saver. As we danced, I wondered about my current balance.

Other memories I once had of her had gone the way of the demolished movie theaters of our youth and the grainy black and white newsreels that, with tight editing and patriotic tunes, became interest-bearing deposits in our shared memory bank.

"Sure, I remember perfectly," I say, apologizing that I must get going since I'm here only for a short visit.

"Still good at leaving," she says walking out into the crowd.

* * *

I walk back to Esti's apartment in the hot humid night, thinking of my parents' story about the time they saw Marlene Dietrich at the Armon when they were young. Although the theater's roof had been retracted for ventilation, by intermission the audience looked as if they had been caught in a rainstorm. Throughout it all, Miss Dietrich only glowed.

I sit down, cool off, and write the postcard to Lori. Tamar knocks on the door and invites me to join her at a sing-along concert of old standards we grew up with.

"You'll love it," she assures me. "Nostalgia and familiar tunes are just what you need. Get ready, I'll be back in fifteen minutes."

I shower quickly and give my beard an overdue trim. Thinking it's going to be a casual event on a hot night, I put on a pair of jeans, a striped polo shirt, and a pair of running shoes betraying considerable mileage.

Tamar, on the other hand, is dazzling in a mini skirt, provocative top, and alluring smile.

"All this in fifteen minutes? Are you sure you want to be seen with me?"

She just smiles and, taking my hand, leads me to her car.

Most of the capacity audience is of my parents' generation, looking for a reprieve from the current music scene, but Tamar points out a group of teenagers as proof that secondhand nostalgia still exists.

A short, balding man in his eighties walks on stage and takes his place at the piano to thunderous applause. He is one of the country's most revered songwriters with countless hits over the past six decades. With the lyrics projected on several screens, he leads the audience into the first of dozens of his most popular songs which awaken memories and open tear ducts. It's good the house lights have dimmed, not that I'm the only one reaching for a tissue. I choke up when I try to join in and resort to humming until I catch my breath. How can silly ditties and love ballads possess such firepower? I'm tempted to reach for Tamar's hand but grasp the armrest instead.

"I know what you mean," she whispers, patting my hand in time to the beat of a lively song.

Day Fourteen *Deux Chevaux*

— *Chapter Forty-Seven* —

Now that my visit is coming to an end, I suggest to mother that we visit our first Haifa apartment. She enthusiastically agrees.

In my absence, the three-story Bauhaus style building has continued to decay with deepening cracks and shedding flecks of stucco. Scattered patches of moss are its only adornment.

We climb the stairs to the second floor. I ring the bell. Someone inside asks a question in Romanian, and Mother answers. The door opens a crack, and an old woman peers out suspiciously. Mother explains that we lived here about thirty years ago and, if possible, would like to see our home one last time.

"Please," says the woman, letting us in.

Mother's eyes overflow. A familiar pressure in my stomach reminds me of earlier times. We head for the kitchen where a dying plant by the window is the only sign of life. I avert my eyes from the peeling cabinets and rusty faucet.

"It used to be so beautiful," Mother whispers.

She turns and points toward the living room, now dark and

empty except for two narrow beds on opposite sides. I reach for Mother's hand and gesture toward the attic hatch in the hall, trying to distract her so she wouldn't see the mildew in the bathroom.

"Thank you," says Mother, hurrying down the stairs and out onto the sidewalk.

"Sorry I suggested we come here," I say. "Now we won't have our good memories anymore."

"We will, Danny, we will," says Mother, dabbing her eyes. "What's more important to remember, anyway? The seven years of our life here or the seven minutes of our visit today?"

We reach the corner of Masada and Balfour, and Mother says, "You have only one past, Danny. Don't lose it."

* * *

Our rules of engagement were clear: I pursued Ronit, she politely disregarded me; I invited her to a movie, she had already seen it; I suggested an exhibit, she didn't like the artist; I asked her to a concert, she had other plans. I persisted, yet I could only get her to agree to study together for final exams.

One afternoon, on my way to her house to study for an English exam, I took the shortcut behind the water tower. With its hand-hewn blocks, octagonal bulk, and eight turrets, the water tower looked like a dignified sentinel protecting memories of long-lost times against the onslaught of modernist stucco facades, metal shutters, and pipe railings. The salty sea air had wreaked havoc on those incongruous materials, causing them to peel, warp, and rust while adding character lines to the tower's handsome features.

The shortcut was a narrow lane bordered by what had become an open-air latrine for children in the nearby playground. Whenever I walked there, I would hold my breath and hurry along. On that day, however, I slowed my pace. I was leafing through my English anthology and saw a poem that looked simple enough for a speaker of English as a third language. I was drawn to its title, "Annabel Lee." Grandma's name was Anna.

I sat down on a nearby bench, caught my breath, and read the poem again and again. I had it memorized by supper.

When I learned more about Poe, I thought it fitting that I discovered his famous poem in a dark rank lane behind a tower, but all I cared about that day was the magic of his words:

> *It was many and many a year ago,*
> *In a kingdom by the sea...*

Four years later I arrived in Rhode Island to study architecture just blocks from the Providence house Poe visited, on a hill above a foul-smelling canal that was a shortcut to the ocean.

*   *   *

One day, Mrs. Pincus, my high school biology teacher, could no longer restrain herself and mounted a frontal assault on my dreams.

"Forget architecture! You should be a doctor," she said, capturing me with her blue-eyed stare. Her smile was warm but disconcerting in that she turned it on and off as needed. Off at the moment, she continued, "I just can't see you with a T-square and a pencil. It's fine as a hobby. Go ahead, draw, build models in your spare time, but medicine must be your career." Her smile came back on.

She was kind and quite persuasive but doomed to failure, poor woman. Little did she know the forces of architecture were already entrenched around me, ready to repulse any attempt to change my mind.

Mrs. Pincus did not concede defeat easily. With her New York accent and annoying habit of translating American expressions verbatim into nonsensical Hebrew, she finally wore me down, and I agreed to hear her out. We were to meet at her husband's store where she helped out after school. Mr. Pincus manufactured laboratory glassware. I knew the place quite well because it was near the water tower, and I peeked in occasionally to watch him blow glass and shape it into vials, beakers, and test tubes.

A few days later, a little after three o'clock, I entered the Pincus Glassworks ready to defend my dreams while hoping for a chance to sneak out unnoticed. The place seemed deserted. Perfect, I thought. As I tiptoed back toward the door, I heard gentle clinking from the rear of the store, glass touching glass. I stopped to listen.

"C'mon, honey, let's hurry, in case Danny comes by," said my biology teacher sweetly somewhere in the shadows behind shelves laden with glass treasures.

"He probably won't come, but I will," said her husband with a chuckle.

"That's good. Don't stop now!" Her appeal, accompanied by louder clinking, was delivered in the same emphatic, mildly threatening tone she used when telling her class to quiet down.

I turned my head. Sighs and moans were coming in loud

and clear. Moving toward the door, I knocked over a rack of test tubes which fell to the floor and shattered. I lost my balance and landed on the glittering shards.

Silence. I was amazed that Mr. Pincus had disobeyed my teacher's clear instructions and stopped doing whatever she was grading him so highly on. No one had ever gone against Mrs. Pincus' orders and gotten away with it.

"What was that?" whispered Mrs. Pincus sharply.

"Hi, Mrs. Pincus. It's me, Danny Holzman. I'm here to discuss my future."

"Oh, God!" said Mrs. Pincus. "I'll be there in a minute."

"I can wait," I said, removing shards of glass from my pants. A loud bump made me turn in time to observe my teacher moving toward the storage area.

A moment later, Mr. Pincus emerged from behind the shelves. Our eyes met and he gave me a friendly wink before realizing he wasn't wearing pants.

"Oh, crap," he muttered, turning quickly and causing his large frame to collide with a shelving unit that fell backwards, releasing a cascade of glass onto the floor.

I ran out of the store and raced home where I shared a piece of cake with Grandma. I brought up the subject of architecture and medicine.

"All doctors are charlatans unless they can prove to me they're not," she said, eliminating the final obstacle on my chosen career path.

*   *   *

Later that Spring, as I was putting away my biology books, Mrs. Pincus passed my desk and caught a glimpse of a British architectural magazine sticking out of my book bag. She stopped and looked at me sadly. I pushed the periodical out of sight.

"Sorry," I said. "I don't totally understand it myself."

As Mrs. Pincus turned to leave, I said, "Just out of curiosity, what would you have done if your teachers had tried to discourage you from studying biology and becoming a teacher?"

She spoke softly, as if trying to avoid hearing her own answer. "I'd have been miserable for a while but then ecstatic after realizing that what I really wanted to do was move to LA and write movie scripts, but because everyone was so supportive and encouraging, I ended up here. In the end, Danny, only you can decide what's right for you." She picked up her briefcase. "I hope your dreams come true."

All these many years later, so do I.

*   *   *

My old high school, although highly regarded academically and loved by the students for its homey atmosphere, left much to be desired architecturally. It had been cobbled together from a number of converted flats in an aging apartment building and featured narrow corridors and kitchen sinks in some of the cramped classrooms. Its diverse faculty included a number of repurposed teachers: a Texan who taught Hebrew, a German who taught Arabic, and an Iraqi who taught English. The latter, Mrs. Karadi, was a tiny, stooped lady who wore only black. Her

Hebrew sounded like Arabic, but her English sounded like that of a BBC announcer.

Mrs. Karadi loved all things British, especially the quaint expressions she frequently used.

"Danny, you are the caterpillar's boots!" she would say when returning a test or homework assignment. If she were here today, I would gallantly say, "And you, dear lady, are the lobster's dress shirt."

Many of my classmates did not appreciate English or English teachers. One of those was Tedescu, a new immigrant from Romania. Like most East European classmates I knew, Tedescu was an outstanding student, always shining when he opened his mouth, dazzling his listeners with brilliant answers and gold and silver teeth. English, however, set his fangs on edge.

One wintery morning in my junior year, I saw Tedescu in the boys' restroom. It seemed he had been waiting for me.

"I have something to show you," he said, pulling out a large black and white photograph from the envelope he was holding. I moved closer, but before I could get a good look, Tedescu stuck it back in the envelope.

"No, you're too young for this," he said.

"OK," I said and headed for the door. I didn't want to miss a minute of Mrs. Karadi's class and a chance to compare and contrast the deaths of several Shakespearean characters.

"Wait," called Tedescu after me. "I'll let you see them anyway. Here." He handed me the envelope and ran out. In it were photos of nude women in positions defying gravity and imagination. I thumbed through them twice before realizing I was late for class. I stuck the envelope in my book bag and ran to the classroom.

I opened the door softly, hoping to make it to my seat before Mrs. Karadi saw me. She was hunched over a newspaper on her desk, sobbing.

"Hi Danny!" shouted Tedescu.

Mrs. Karadi looked up and promptly fainted.

Tedescu ran over to me and held up her newspaper. In the middle of the page was a large obituary framed in black:

In Memoriam

DANIEL HOLZMAN

Of blessed memory

Mourned by his wife, children, and grandchildren

Clearly, Mrs. Karadi had not made it to the fourth line.

In the ensuing silence, only Tedescu spoke. "Sorry. I didn't think she'd take it so hard."

I pushed him aside and ran to the office for help, which, as it turned out, wasn't needed. Mrs. Karadi, as usual, kept calm and carried on.

*   *   *

It took weeks before talk of my alleged demise subsided, only to be replaced by a new incident. One rainy winter day, we spent recess indoors and heard a scuffle down the hall followed by a loud shriek. It turned out that Tedescu had either fallen or been pushed against the wall and suffered a severe concussion, forcing him to spend weeks in the hospital. When he was finally allowed visitors, I stopped by one afternoon to return all his photographs but one. He never missed it, or at least never asked for it, and

I filed it away with my James Bond movie stills and a tattered Buck Jones book jacket, archived in my bottom desk drawer to this day.

* * *

Remembering Mother's advice not to lose the one past I have, I realize that, with Grandma's Shiva, the onslaught of memories, and Tamar and Tom's saga, I haven't had time to contact any of my old friends. I got to thinking about my high school study partner Ronit, and called her. I asked if I could stop by for a quick visit, and she agreed.

I knock on her door at the appointed time. She doesn't answer.

Ronit's apartment building has a void in its center, like the one that opens inside me when I realize I've lost touch with almost everyone I knew and cared about. Thinking she probably was detained, I decide to wait. I sit down on the terrazzo stairs and gaze into the atrium. Withering plants, bedding, and bicycles hang from the railings surrounding it. An unseen radio plays a Russian song about a maiden strolling along a riverbank with apple trees in bloom. Swirling out of this void is a circle of teenagers clapping their hands in time to the music. Inside the circle, a girl skips and finds a partner. They go round and round, holding hands. I can't recall if any of the girls I secretly admired had chosen me for a dizzying romp. I imagine several did.

"Sorry I wasn't home" says Ronit when I call her later. "How about we meet at the new high school? I love that place. You really must see it. I'll be there around four. Please come."

On the way to meet her, I stop by our old high school. Overgrown weeds surround the building. Most of the classroom windows are boarded up, but through the smashed panes of others I see dark interiors. I peek into what was once Mrs. Karadi's classroom. Dusty desks and chairs are neatly lined up, but rowdy memories intrude and speak out of turn.

* * *

The new modern school shares only a name with my old homey one. The exterior, with its Brutalist elements, resembles an impregnable concrete fortress. Inside are wide corridors, color-coordinated classrooms, and shiny, brightly lit labs.

In this building devoid of charm, the principal would not have bumped into me in a narrow corridor and led me to a quiet corner to tell me that I'd been chosen to spend a semester of my junior year as an exchange student at a renowned New York school. Here, I probably wouldn't have found an old gramophone like the one my music teacher had discarded. After cleaning and oiling it, I tried it out with a 78 RPM record I borrowed from Lilly, a classmate who shared my love for music and classic films such as *Forbidden Games* and *Rules of the Game*, and who taught me that even the forbidden had rules.

I pass a display of student art and reach the requisite memorial corner at the far end of the lobby. An eternal light on the wall is flanked by photographs of students and teachers who gave their lives protecting the homeland. Some I knew personally. The photos, in identical black frames, are arranged by date of death. I soon reach the last one, dated just two weeks ago. Although I don't recognize the man in the blurry enlargement taken from a class photo, his name is painfully familiar. "Uri Oz, decorated reservist, killed in action on the northern front." He was my former commanding officer, five years my senior.

Tears don't come easy in this arid land. I think of those characters in *The Tin Drum* who had to resort to gathering at an exclusive club to cut onions before being able to cry and express their emotions.

It's just as well Ronit never came. Right now, I need to be alone. I'm craving an onion with crusty bread and hot tea. If I catch the next bus, I'll be back in Esti's kitchen in no time.

— *Chapter Forty-Eight* —

Uri was behind the wheel of the Deux Chevaux that afternoon, whistling along with a miniature transistor radio hanging from the rear-view mirror. At that time, his last name was still Ozhik. Over the years, his family shortened it to Oz: so concise and Biblical, hinting at its Hebrew meaning of strength and fortitude, and so easy to spell in whichever foreign countries they immigrated to.

The tiny radio was playing *"Those were the days my friend / We thought they'd never end…"* Ozhik was whistling, and I was tapping the beat on my knees, wishing the song would go on forever.

We were heading west into the late afternoon sun which was coaxing wavy currents from the road ahead. The Carmel range stretched across the horizon like a gauzy backdrop. Behind us, over the hills of Nazareth, the sky had already turned a deeper blue in anticipation of twilight.

The body of the Deux Chevaux, so thin one could dent it with a vigorous push of the thumb, performed remarkably well in trapping the heat. The rear windows were inoperable, the better to prevent cross ventilation. Even on the best of days, it was an odd little car. With its frog-like countenance and sloping hood, it promised a nimble aerodynamic performance, yet all it could deliver was moderate speed with just enough horse power to satisfy French farmers, its intended users.

It was also odd that Ozhik, only a second lieutenant, had exclusive use of a car that was standard issue to majors. No one besides Ozhik knew why, and he wasn't telling. I didn't really care, being much more curious about his many female conquests across the region.

I was nineteen when we met, with half of my three-year service still ahead of me. Ozhik, with his good looks, penetrating dark eyes, and gentle way of speaking, looked and acted older than his twenty-four years. In fact, I often thought of him as my younger father because of his uncanny resemblance to him in old photos. Unlike Father's, Ozhik's opinions were simplistic, his life experiences limited, and his advice sparing. I liked him.

Heading home on overnight leave, I kept my eyes just below the dashboard to avoid the intense glare. Ozhik was silent. His latest affair had just ended, and he seemed subdued. Abruptly, he stepped on the brakes and said, "So, what do you think?"

Through the quivering haze I could make out two female figures standing at the bus stop ahead.

"Got any plans for tonight?" asked Ozhik, and without waiting for an answer, pulled over and stopped the car in a cloud of dust.

The two young women looked at each other and started walking toward us slowly and deliberately, not concealing their disappointment with our cheap little car, yet grateful nonetheless. They looked to be in their early twenties, one a curvy blonde, the other a skinny brunette.

"How far are you going?" asked the blonde, her flushed face inches away from mine.

"Haifa," I said in a hoarse whisper, my mouth gone dry. Feeling I had done my part, I hoped Ozhik would take over and start the inevitable game.

"Hop in," he said. I got out and let the blonde sit next to Ozhik then joined the brunette in the back seat. As we drove off, he leaned ever so slightly to the right and said, "So where to?"

"Just down the road a bit," replied the blonde who reminded me of a young Brigitte Bardot. "We'll tell you where to stop."

"So, you're from Tivon," said Ozhik, referring to the small resort town straddling a group of low wooded hills already coming into view.

"How did you guess?" exclaimed Brigitte cheerfully. It was, I thought, the invitation to proceed which Ozhik had once told me to listen for. The banter, he insisted, had to be kept going at any cost. Quickly turning to the brunette, who reminded me of a young Audrey Hepburn without the smile and sparkling eyes, I said, "So you must know Esther," using the first name that came to mind. Ozhik's amused smile in the rear-view mirror told me I was on the right track.

"Esther who?" said the blonde turning around, her low-cut blouse shifting to reveal the top of her ample breasts. It occurred to me that, so far, the brunette hadn't said a word. What sort of breasts did she have? I must have hesitated too long, for Ozhik came to my rescue.

"Esther, you know... the secretary to the regional artillery commander. She lives in Tivon too. Anyway, what are your names?"

"I'm Mikki," said the blonde, "and this is my sister Sharon. She's the serious one. She speaks only on special occasions."

"Well, what a coincidence," said Ozhik. "This happens to be a very special occasion. It's our first leave in three months, and we almost forgot what girls look like in civvies."

I wished my uniform hadn't been so clean and neatly pressed, and some dust on my boots would have been a nice touch, but then we all knew it was just a game.

"How about we pick you up at eight? Sharon can deliver a speech," said Ozhik.

"Any questions, Sharon?" asked Mikki. "OK then, see you at eight."

We got to my parents' apartment half an hour later. Ozhik planned to go home to change and pick me up later for what we would tell our loved ones was an unscheduled nighttime exercise.

Serving so close to Haifa, I was permitted to go home almost every night and was greeted as if I had just returned from the front. Grandma's generous portions were more than I could face that evening, so I left early to wait outside.

As we pulled up to their house, Mikki and Sharon emerged from the shadows and stood at the curb. Ozhik turned the wheel sharply and caught them in the headlights. Mikki was wearing a short skirt and a low-cut blouse buttoned in front. Sharon had on a high-cut blouse and jeans with a black leather belt. She seemed as new to the game as I was.

I got out of the car and Mikki jumped into the front seat, causing the air shocks to hiss in protest. Sharon and I got in the back. Ozhik placed a casual hand on Mikki's left knee, turned the car around, and moved his hand up her leg, encountering no resistance.

"Where to?" he said.

"Let's go as far as this tin can will take us," said Sharon. Ozhik shifted into second and coaxed the Deux Chevaux into a gallop.

"We all need to get away sometimes," I said in the most mature tone I could muster and put my arm around Sharon's shoulders. She seized my hand, slapped it back into my lap, and turned away to gaze out the window. In the feeble dashboard light, I could see Ozhik's hand advance up Mikki's thigh and disappear under her skirt. I looked out the other window.

"OK, listen up," said Ozhik, navigating the car in a zigzagging course down the road out of town. "We're close to a base I know. I'm pretty sure I can get us in. We can find some privacy there."

A few minutes later we turned onto a dirt road and followed it to a eucalyptus grove. Ozhik halted at the gate and went to have a word with the guard. Mikki straightened her skirt. I put a hopeful hand on Sharon's knee. She didn't resist. With fresh confidence, I ran my hand over her rough jeans until she stopped me with a menacing, "What the hell do you think you're doing?" I retreated to the safety of her knee and waited for Ozhik to return.

"No luck," he said getting back in the car. "The base is on lockdown. Any other ideas?"

"Maybe a fragrant pile of hay in a barn somewhere," I said facetiously.

"Do you know such a place?" said a voice in the dark, urgent and tinged with longing. Sharon brought her face close to mine.

"I do. Nahallal. Really close by."

"Let's go," she said.

"Nahallal it is," said Ozhik and returned to the main road.

My arm went back around Sharon's shoulders, this time unopposed. I figured I no longer needed to impress her, so I didn't tell her that Father had taught there when I was three, had introduced me to my first tractor, and had someone take a picture of us sitting on a horse.

A road sign came into view: "Nahallal 1 km."

A cool breeze carried fragrances of fruit trees and freshly plowed soil from nearby farms. Ozhik parked the car near a cowshed, and we tiptoed in. A solitary light bulb dangling from the rafters barely illuminated a number of black and white cows. Sharon was the first to notice the pile of hay in the far corner. Ozhik and I helped the girls onto the prickly stack, whereupon he and Mikki dove into the golden stalks and set the mound quivering. As I reached for a roof beam to steady myself, Sharon grabbed me from behind, her small breasts touching my back.

We heard the grinding jaws, stomping hooves, and swatting tails and watched the miracle of the dancing bale before us. A second light bulb came on some distance away, and an elderly farmer made his way down the line, mumbling soothingly while gently patting the cows. As he was refilling the feed and water troughs, we heard him say, "Don't mind me, kids. There's always some action on that haystack, but I pretend not to notice and just do my work."

The quake next to us slowly subsided, and Ozhik and Mikki came out from under and brushed themselves off. Ozhik motioned to us, and we slipped out quietly as the man shuffled over to the next trough. Sharon put her hand in mine. After we got back in the car, she moved closer to me and put her head on my shoulder.

"I've had it with stupid cows," I blurted out. "Let's just go to the beach." I didn't bother to look for Ozhik's amused eyes in the mirror, but I was sure they were there.

"The kid has a point," he said, starting the motor.

"Don't call him kid," said Sharon.

Ozhik drove back to Haifa and onto a narrow beach at the foot of Mt. Carmel. Stepping onto the sand, he looked at the lighthouse above as if to make sure we'd found a safe haven. Its white beacon swept the wet sand as we stepped out of the car. Moonlight silvered the crests of shallow sand dunes. City lights kept a discreet distance. Gentle waves shed their foam at our feet. I reached for Sharon's hand. Ozhik removed the car seats and threw them on the sand. He spread a military blanket on the car floor and pulled Mikki in, locking the doors behind them.

Sharon smiled. I bent over to kiss her, but she turned and walked toward the water. We took off our shoes, rolled up our pants, and waded into the warm tide. I caught up with her and planted a quick kiss on her cheek. She playfully chased me, grabbing my belt and pulling me onto the sand. I covered her mouth with mine. She didn't object. I pulled her closer.

Suddenly she tickled me and ran off. I followed her into the water though I had no other uniform to change into. Sharon was now sprinting along the beach, pulling off her blouse and throwing it on the sand. I slowed down, feeling my knees go weak. Hopping on one foot then the other, she got out of her jeans and climbed up a dune. A moment later, I saw her silhouette against the shifting glow of the lighthouse. She waved her bra with one hand, her panties with the other, and I began scaling Olympus to claim my goddess.

Just when I was about to reach her, she turned and ran down the other side of the dune, dashing along the water's edge and picking up her clothes. I brushed the sand off my uniform and followed her footsteps which the waves were already washing away, destroying the only evidence of our presence.

I found Sharon, fully dressed, sitting in one of the car seats in the sand. The doors of the Deux Chevaux were still closed. I slumped into the other seat, facing the curling waves. We waited in silence. The car door finally creaked open and Ozhik and Mikki emerged. "Hi kids!" he said. Getting no response, he proceeded to put the seats back in place, and we all got in.

I must have dozed off. When Ozhik woke me, we were alone in the car in front of my parents' apartment. Dawn was breaking, and there was a chill in the air.

"Where's Sharon?" I asked drowsily.

"Home. We tried to wake you, but you were fast asleep. Sharon wanted you to know she kissed you goodnight."

"I liked her."

"Listen," said Ozhik softly. "Take a shower, ask your mother to press your uniform, and don't forget to eat a good breakfast. I'll see you on base." As I stepped out of the car, he gave me a pat on the back and said, "Don't worry. Everything will be fine."

I took a shower and made coffee. I turned on the transistor radio and listened to Tom Jones begging Delilah for the answer she kept to herself. I sipped my coffee, munched on a roll and watched the sky lighten in the kitchen window. When I could distinguish the silvery from the green side of the olive tree leaves, I ironed my uniform, left a note on the kitchen table, and walked downtown to catch a ride back to base.

— *Chapter Forty-Nine* —

With only one day before my flight, I take Mother to dinner at an upscale restaurant. Her face brightens when the server lights the candle and hands her a menu. Over her protest, I order an expensive bottle of wine.

"Who's going to finish it?" asks Mother, but by the time we get to dessert, she tells me how much she enjoyed it. We linger over coffee, and I find the right moment to tell her I booked my flight and will be leaving the day after tomorrow.

"Good. It's time you went back to your family, Dannika," she says. I'm relieved she doesn't reach for a tissue.

Waiting for a cab, we agree it was one of the best meals we've ever had.

"What a great restaurant!" she says, taking my arm. "The three of us should come here next time you visit."

Back at her apartment, she must be reading something in my eyes because she says, "Don't worry, Dannika. I'll be fine."

I kiss Mother and wait outside the door until the bolt clicks and her footsteps recede.

With my jet lag long gone, I expect to sleep well without having to summon up memories of old girlfriends to help me drift off. Good old girlfriends: Liora in kindergarten, who brought me cookies from home in her sticky little hands; Ruthie in grade school, whose hand was the first I'd ever held; Mia in the army, whose hand I almost asked for; and Sharon, who enforced a no-hands policy even while prancing nude on a moonlit dune. Strange that no American girlfriends made an appearance.

I've almost forgotten that I took a chocolate bar to bed for a late-night snack. Now it's too soft to eat, so I put it on the nightstand to harden.

I think back to my first year in Providence. The freshman class had gathered in Memorial Hall for a series of performance art pieces by fellow students. My closest friend at the time was an army veteran my own age who liked to wear a threadbare Confederate coat decorated with the medals he had earned in Vietnam. That evening, I wore a blue Union coat I had bought for the occasion at a vintage shop on Benefit Street. Side by side, we marched into the auditorium in a symbolic act of some significance, or so we thought. No one gave us a second look.

Spotlights converged on the raised platform in the center of the auditorium. Two young women, carrying buckets, stepped onto the stage. Putting them down, they turned and locked eyes as they leisurely undressed each other. Each picked up her bucket and slowly poured a thick brown liquid over the other's head. Coated in chocolate syrup, with heavy drops dangling from their noses, earlobes, and nipples, they walked into the aisles, handing out plastic spoons and inviting the audience to help themselves to dessert. When they had been scraped clean, they walked off to thunderous applause.

"Josh has a little cold," says Lori hoarsely when I call to say goodnight. "I think I have it too."

"Sorry," I say drowsily. We're both quiet for a long moment.

"Are you still there?"

"What? Oh, yeah. What if you got a babysitter to look after Josh and just rested for a couple of days?"

"I'll be OK," she says. "You must really be tired. Your Israeli accent is acting up. Get some sleep."

"I'll try. Goodnight."

What if I had a bite of that chocolate now and didn't brush my teeth?

What if I were able to hear those six beeps from a neighbor's radio without feeling compelled to listen to the news?

What if traveling back and forth more frequently were to bring my two homelands closer together, stitching them into one shore-to-shore carpet without mismatched colors, clashing patterns, or frayed borders?

I really should go to sleep now. Are there any thoughts I still need to have? Any doubts or regrets I should consider at this late hour before it gets even later, or too late?

Day Fifteen Return

— *Chapter Fifty* —

The day trip is Tamar's idea.

"Hi there," she says when we collide in the closet. "Looking for something?"

"You, actually."

"Be careful. It's dangerous in the dark."

"How dangerous can it be?"

"As dangerous as you'd like." She hugs my waist.

"That's plenty dangerous for me," I say.

"All right. I was just coming over to see if you'd like to have breakfast with us."

"Great, but first I have something to tell you."

"What?" She smiles expectantly.

"I'm going back to Boston tomorrow."

Her smile fades. "Already? That wasn't the plan."

"Whose plan?"

"Well, you can't just leave. You're needed here."

"There too," I say.

"Yes, I know. Widows-in-training can be so needy."

She turns, and I follow her to the kitchen where Dorit and Eitan are waiting for breakfast. Sitting with them at the table, I know I'm going to miss this little family.

"Feel like being spontaneous?" asks Tamar before the kids leave for camp. "I called my mother and she'd be happy to pick them up and stay with them until I get back."

"Sure," I say. "Let's be spontaneous."

"I'll just call her to confirm."

Tamar drives north along the coast and turns east toward the jagged horizon. We stop to have a snack in the shade of a sheik's tomb and refill the water bottle at the nearby shrine of a Jewish sage.

Tamar drives on. We leave the car at the foot of a hill and climb to the top to see the ruins of a Crusaders fort. I snap a photo of the interior courtyard, careful to leave Tamar out of the frame. After exploring crumbling walls, fallen arches, and decapitated columns, we sit and rest in the shade.

I close my eyes and remember what Tamar had said about making love among ancient ruins. There isn't another soul around. The war is far, Tamar is near, but I am determined to adhere to the code of chivalry. I open one eye and see her lying on a stone slab, a silky breeze ruffling her low-cut blouse. God in His wisdom stays my hand but gives me voice as He had done once before to a biblical ass: "We'd better get going."

Stopping in front of a battle marker by the side of the road, Tamar turns off the engine, takes a sip from the water bottle and offers it to me.

I take a long sip from the bottle her lips have just touched.

"Your turn to drive," she says.

Sitting behind the wheel, I see that the car has a stick shift which I haven't driven since high school. Finally remembering how to work the clutch, I shift into gear. We lurch forward and get back on the road.

Tamar turns on the radio and taps the beat on her knees. She points, and I turn and follow an unpaved road to a lookout on top of a bald hill. I'm hoping for a spectacular view but find only a barren valley rendered in muted browns and yellows.

"Once!" exclaims Tamar. "Just once I'd like to reach a summit in my own country and see a blue river and a green forest."

"What about red roofs and orange sunsets?"

She looks at me, not amused.

"I used to have the same wish," I say. "Trust me. It's pointless."

Tamar nods and looks so forlorn I feel it my duty to put my hand on her shoulder. She leans against me and we look out at the great emptiness.

I make up my mind. As long as we're feeling all this sadness, I might as well take her to the saddest spot of all: Tom's foldout deathbed in Yagon. There may still be time.

"It's getting late," I say.

Back in the car, I chase the declining sun and turn off the highway.

"What a name!" exclaims Tamar when we pass the sign to Yagon. "Grief! Agony! I feel better already. And why are we going there?"

"To say goodbye to a friend."

When the little houses appear in the distance, Tamar says, "I've never seen such a desolate place."

"Pretty grim," I say.

"So are you," she says. "Why are you so subdued all of a sudden?"

"I'm always like this at sunset."

I get as close to the Zerbibs' house as the road allows and ask Tamar to wait in the car. She gives me an encouraging smile. I force myself to smile back. I walk up to the house and find the door open.

"Thank God, thank God," says Mr. Zerbib when he sees me.

"I just happened to…"

"Thank God."

His wife explains. "Tom is close to death. He keeps calling your name. Today he started calling for Tamar too. His wife, yes? Of course, we'll take care of everything, but we've been praying that you or his wife would get here before it was too late."

How can Tom be almost dead? I just saw him a few days ago, and he was strong enough to go for a walk with me.

"Can I see him now?" I ask with a touch of panic.

"Of course. Go right in. I'll get you some cold water."

I enter the dark living room. Since the window is covered with a blanket, it takes me a moment to see Tom. Lying on the foldout bed, propped up against oversized pillows, Tom looks smaller than I remember. The medicines on the side table must be helping because he appears to be pain-free.

I pull up a chair next to the bed and take his hand.

"It's Danny. I'm here," I say.

His eyes are closed, his breathing irregular. He opens his eyes, and we look at each other for a long time. His lips move. I bring my ear close to his mouth but hear nothing. His eyes close again.

"Goodbye," one of us whispers, maybe both.

I gulp down the glass of water Mrs. Zerbib hands me and go into the cramped bathroom. I guess at the cost of a headstone and leave a pile of shekels and dollars on the sink.

A bearded man wearing a yarmulke and a black suit, probably the local rabbi, is huddling with the Zerbibs in the kitchen. I say goodbye and hurry back to the car so we can get away before Mr. Zerbib discovers my contribution and insists on returning it.

Tamar greets me with teary eyes. "I just solved Tom's riddle. This is the saddest place in the country, isn't it?"

I nod.

"How's he doing?" asks the soon-to-be widow.

"He passed away yesterday," I almost say but stop myself for reasons I hope to understand one day. "Go in. He's been asking for you."

Ten minutes later, Tamar returns and says, "Tom's gone. We got here just in time." She dabs her eyes. "The rabbi asked me what should be inscribed on the headstone. I have no idea. What do you think?"

"You know he loved you."

"Right. He loved me so much that he left me and the kids and disappeared from our lives without telling me he was dying."

I sink into my seat as a messenger does when trying not to get shot.

"Tom told me why he felt he had to leave. He wanted to spare you and the kids the prolonged suffering he and his family endured while his father was dying."

"So his story about hating this country and wanting to help starving people in Africa was just a charade. Why did he think he had to spare my feelings? I loved him and would have taken care of him."

Sobbing, she buries her head in her hands. I remain silent and offer her my handkerchief.

After a while I answer her question about the inscription.

"Tom Lev — loving son, husband, and father."

Tamar looks up and nods approvingly.

I step on the gas pedal as if it were a viper's head. Before long, the little boxes of Yagon are far behind us.

"I think it's all right to shift into second, Danny," says Tamar tenderly.

*   *   *

We return to Haifa. Before Tamar goes in to check on Dorit and Eitan, I tell her I'll be back soon.

I order a cab for 5:00 a.m. and call Mother. Father answers.

"Is everything all right?" I ask nervously.

"Everything's fine," says Father. "I'm doing the dishes. Here's Mother."

"The dishes?"

I never asked him about the witch in the hut or the picture that fell out of his Russian book. Some answers I've discovered on my own. The rest remain a mystery. I suppose this new surprise will eventually fall into one category or the other.

"So, Dannika, what do you think?" asks Mother.

"First, let me pinch myself."

"Listen, Danny, things change. It's going to be fine, you'll see. So, the dishes are a little greasy after he washes them. Who cares? What, am I so busy I can't wash them again?"

"I'll be right over to say goodbye," I say.

Before leaving, I knock on Tamar's door. Her mother lets me in, saying, "You must be Danny. Tamar told me about you and how much you helped her."

Tamar, Dorit, and Eitan are fast asleep on the sofa in front of the snowy TV.

"Danny?" says Tamar drowsily.

"Don't get up. I'm going over to see my parents, but I'll be back in a little while to say goodbye."

"I'll wait for you," she says, dozing off again.

Father opens the door, and we embrace. Mother comes over and hugs us both. The coffee table is set with three teacups and a tray of cookies. I sit down on the sofa between my parents. Words fail us. I stare at the cookies and sense that my parents are exchanging glances. I take Mother's left hand and Father's right and hold them in mine.

Mother goes to the kitchen to get the tea. Father moves the sugar bowl and cookies closer to me.

"I'm glad you're here," I say. "I never expected this."

"Life is full of surprises, Danny," says Father.

"Absolutely."

"It's late," says Mother. "You should go back to Esti's and try to get some sleep before your flight."

"Remember, twelve hours in the air is longer than on the ground," says Father cryptically.

We kiss goodbye, and I leave them to their new life together.

On the way back to Tamar's, I start wondering what a proper goodbye should look like.

"It's been a long day," I say. "You must be exhausted."

"I am. I could never have imagined such a day."

"I'm relieved you got to see Tom one last time. I'm just sorry I can't be with you for the funeral."

"Don't worry, Danny. I understand you have to get back to your family and your life in America. I know how much you've done for Tom and me, and I can't thank you enough. My mother's going to stay with us for a few weeks which will be a great comfort." She looks into my eyes. "I still don't know what I should tell Dorit and Eitan."

"You're a great mother, Tamar. I'm sure you'll find the right thing to say. A year ago, you told them their father had died a hero. Now, in a way, he has. When the time is right, you'll take them to see the headstone and help them remember their loving father."

Tamar nods. Finally she says, "It's very late, Danny. You have an early flight. You should get some sleep."

She walks me to the door.

"Thanks for everything," she whispers, hugging me hesitantly.

"I promise to stay in touch."

"I hope so," she says, closing the door.

I put my passports and ticket on top of my suitcase. I have a vague sense I'm leaving something undone, but what?

I turn off the lights but can't sleep. I step out onto the balcony. The humid air is laced with a hint of pollution that reminds me of home. Both homes. This much they share.

I imagine Father and Mother lying in the same bed for the first time in many years. Grandma, resting by the seashore, knows nothing. Across the ocean Josh is staring at the happy bunny family on his crib bumpers. Lori is watching late-night TV hosts who often seem to be our only extended family. And I'm about to return from one home to the other. There's no place like either.

The taxi will be here soon. The clouds overhead are stretched so taut that the sky looks almost clear. Somewhere above that opaque canopy, helicopter rotors chop and blend. I look up and see the flicker of a signal light winking at me through the gauzy air. I go in and lock the door. The thunder continues, rattling the windowpanes and causing the glasses in the kitchen cabinet to clink softly as if toasting my good fortune: I've survived another war.

Acknowledgments

I am forever grateful to Suzanne Frauenhoffer for her yearslong support and selfless labors as first reader and editor. Her vision and feedback helped hone the narrative and shape the novel.

Sincerest thanks to Jeffrey Duban, man of letters and lifelong friend, for reviewing the novel's many iterations and for providing invaluable input and suggestions.

Many thanks to Gary Rosenberg, whose knowledge and expertise were invaluable in guiding me through the production and publication of my first novel.

About the Author

Shlomo Shyovitz grew up in Haifa, Israel. During high school, he spent a semester in New York as an exchange student at the Horace Mann School. After completing his high school studies and army service, he returned to the United States and earned degrees in architecture and urban design from RISD and Harvard. Based in the U.S., he has worked with architectural firms on both domestic and international projects.

His passion for writing developed in his teens when he reported for a youth magazine. During his army service and professional career, he wrote short stories as well as a multigenerational history of his family. *Borne Back* is his first published novel. He is preparing a short story collection for publication and is working on a second novel. He lives in suburban Philadelphia.

www.ingramcontent.com/pod-product-compliance
Lightning Source LLC
Chambersburg PA
CBHW071244300726
48975CB00002B/548